I WAS CALLED BARABBAS

I Was Called Barabbas
Copyright © 2019 by M.D. House

Cover and Interior Design by Lance Buckley
www.lancebuckley.com

All rights reserved. No part of this book may be reproduced
or used in any manner without written permission of the author
except for the use of quotations in a book review.

ISBN: 978-1-6957-9028-5

I WAS CALLED BARABBAS

A NOVEL

M.D. HOUSE

CONTENTS

ACKNOWLEDGEMENTS | vii

PROLOGUE | 1

CHAPTER 1 | 15
CHAPTER 2 | 30
CHAPTER 3 | 44
CHAPTER 4 | 56
CHAPTER 5 | 73
CHAPTER 6 | 89
CHAPTER 7 | 108
CHAPTER 8 | 125
CHAPTER 9 | 150
CHAPTER 10 | 167
CHAPTER 11 | 176
CHAPTER 12 | 199
CHAPTER 13 | 213
CHAPTER 14 | 227

EPILOGUE | 239

ACKNOWLEDGEMENTS

This book has taken a long time to write and a lot of work to get right. I have a busy full-time day job, plus a family, plus church and civic responsibilities. The story of Barabbas came to me in small bursts over several years—usually as single scenes that I wanted to explore in my mind and write down. After completing a few of these, I started putting them together, and the project became interesting.

The first draft of the "completed" story had some powerful pieces, but overall it wasn't very good. The second draft had major additions and revisions, but it, too, was lacking cohesion and overarching focus. The third draft felt like it was getting close, and so I set a timeline for publishing and laid out the remaining steps.

One of those steps was to get a cover designed. I used a website called reedsy.com for the first time, where one can outline a project and request bids from various vetted publishing industry professionals.

Lance Buckley was the design professional I chose, and I gave him a fairly complex set of instructions for what I envisioned (probably too complex). Not having worked with him previously, and not being super-excited with a previous experience using a different designer I had found elsewhere, I wondered what I would end up getting.

Lance blew me away with his design. We only ended up making one minor change to it. It was awesome and inspiring and as near to perfect as I could have hoped. He had taken my ideas, simplified and focused them, and let his artistry do the rest. Thank you, Lance!

I also knew I needed to have some professional editing done, and again I turned to reedsy.

Robin Patchen was the editor I selected, and she warned me that she was a "heavy" editor. I suppose some people don't like that, but I wanted the best professional help I could get.

As with Lance, I probably gave Robin a bit more than she had bargained for. She was diligent and conscientious, though (and patient!), and the copy I received back from her was exactly what I needed. To wit:

There were tendencies in style that I needed to change, and I could see how the changes made the story read better.

There were some complex scenes that I needed help with. She helped me and taught me—and I could tell that sometimes it had been a slog for her.

There were thematic elements that either didn't fit or were distracting, so I was able to alter or remove them.

There were a few gaps in storyline and purpose that she pointed out, which I was able to address, including some refocusing on the primary theme of the book, which is personal progress and redemption.

A thousand thanks, Robin.

My nephew Haden was also willing to step into the fray. He is a smart, thoughtful young man (young compared to me, that is), and he offered some interesting ideas that led to a couple of key additions to the final copy. Thank you, Haden.

My brother Brent and sister Michelle both read the first draft, courageously, and both offered key suggestions. As an example, it was Brent's idea to take the scene now found in the Prologue and bring it to the front, as it is a more powerful way to introduce the story.

A good friend, Russ Dart, also read the first draft, and his unbridled enthusiasm for the project was contagious and motivating. He took copious notes and then sat down with me to go through various ideas on how to move Barabbas forward. That was very useful and much appreciated.

My wife and our grown children have provided encouragement in various ways over the years, and my wife agreed with the monetary investment it would take to make the final push. It is for them, primarily, that I wanted to make this book the best it could be.

I hope you enjoy reading this as much as I enjoyed writing it. More importantly, I hope you find it helpful. This book was never meant to be just entertainment—a mere distraction from the daily grind that life can sometimes be. It is meant to be educational, inspiring, and empowering.

May you find it so. A sequel is already underway.

M.D. House
Aurora, IL, USA
September 2019

PROLOGUE

Which none of the princes of this world knew: for had they known it, they would not have crucified the Lord of glory.

1 Corinthians 2:8, KJV

My given name was Jesus. I never liked that name, even as a boy. It didn't fit me somehow, and my later infamous connection to the son of Joseph the Carpenter made it unbearable. So, I chose another name. Not that it mattered, because after that fateful, momentous Day, everyone began to call me Barabbas—Son of Abbas in the Aramaic—some in scorn, some with indifference, and a few with feigned pity. Not in a thousand fevered dreams could I have predicted my life's eventual path, and it will be left to future generations—and to God—to judge me for who I truly am. I know I have been too hard on myself at times, and too lenient at other times, never fully understanding the great gifts of God to His children. But I leave here my story, unafraid to tell the bad with the good. Some say that my story is inspiring, but I hesitate to hope that it may be of great use, nor do I presume that it will be. What I write is true, however, and I believe that truth should be preserved as untainted as possible. Thus I write, thus have I lived, and thus am I judged.

Because my most vivid memories are of *that* Day, it seems fitting that I should tell that part of my story first. Relating it makes me feel differently than it used to, though it is hard to describe how. I still feel some of the confused and chaotic shame it heralded, but mostly I feel reverence and awe. I did not fit in that scene, much less did I comprehend it, and yet I had a hand in making it real.

Endless was the name of each new day in the prison after those agonizing first few weeks of torture and terror. But one particular day more justly earned the name. I was restless and didn't sleep well during the night. There seemed to be some kind of commotion among a few of the other prisoners, but I was used to ignoring that sort of thing. Gossip wasn't that interesting, and it certainly wasn't useful. My fate was sealed. In a few days I would die. I dreaded it, but at the same time I welcomed it. People died all the time. Why not me, and why not then? I certainly deserved it. If there really was a god or gods in the heavens, maybe it was time for me to ask them a few questions face to face. Assuming any would see me.

I came fully awake at the break of dawn. I lay in the dirty straw on the cold, stone floor, and the first thing that struck me was how quiet it was. A perfect stillness had seemingly enveloped the entire world, with my breathing the only sound. It was a disturbing thought. When my breathing stopped for good, the silence of that place would be complete.

I tried to go back to sleep, but my body refused, even though I felt exhausted. The pains from torture were always difficult to ignore, and achieving even a fitful sleep once in a day was hard enough. Then there was the guilt, as consistent as the dawn at each day's awakening. I had given up almost everything I knew about my brothers in the rebellion, desperate to stop the pain, my courage having fled under the expert ministrations of the final interrogator, an old former centurion with more scars on his face than I had on my back. More than once I had wondered if he knew torture so well because he had experienced it himself.

Perhaps hope had finally deserted me completely. Strangely, I didn't panic at that thought, as I might have expected. Hope was just…gone. Perhaps that had been inevitable all along. I had thought for a while after being arrested that there might be some way out of the prison, that my friends would be able to miraculously rescue me or secure my release, but hours turned into days, which bled into weeks, and I was broken.

Thinking about my brethren in the cause *did* invite panic. What would happen to them? How many others had already been caught? Were some of them in the same prison with me? There was no way to know. Oh, how I wished, in the midst of my dread, that there was something I could do, anything to help them. But there I was: trapped, weak, exhausted, and useless.

A loud rap of wood on wood at my door was immediately followed by a gruff, commanding voice. "Barabbas, on your feet, scum. We're taking a walk!"

I wasn't sure I recognized the voice, but between the Roman guards and the Sanhedrin officers, there were dozens who had taken pleasure in tormenting the 'pitiful Barabbas, impotent rebel.' I felt a brief pang of fright, then weary resignation. I couldn't even work up much anger anymore. Yes, they had broken me, and I didn't care.

With painful difficulty I slowly rose to my feet from the dirty floor, not even flinching when the door swung open. A gleaming Roman centurion loomed proudly in the doorway, gripping a tall spear he must have appropriated from the spearless legionnaire standing a pace behind him. I had never seen this centurion before, but I had seen plenty of vine rods like the one he held in his other hand, and I wore the bruises to prove it. His *lorica hamata* chain mail glinted like a cluster of stars. It was the finest armor I had ever seen. Across his torso marched a double-handful of *torques* and *phalerae*, marking him a highly-decorated veteran who probably had at least three names. His imperial Gallic helmet was liberally embossed with gold and crested with brilliant white horsehair, and the greaves covering his shins glistened like a calm sea at midday. He wore no cape, which seemed a little odd given the rest of his magnificence, but many centurions chose not to wear capes, at least some of the time. The thin, straight scar under his left eye was another bold battle decoration, and I felt the urge to salute the man, even though he was the enemy…and my assigned executioner, whose face and manner I won't ever be able to forget.

He must have noticed the stupid, starry admiration in my eyes, because he gave a slight smirk. That produced a wave of shame inside me, and I quickly looked to the floor, noticing as I did the rich new leather of his sandals. My eyes flicked to the side and behind him at another pair of sandals of even richer leather, obviously new, peeking from below the intricately-brocaded hem of a fine white linen robe. I dared not look up so see who belonged to the robe, but it had to be one of the leaders of the Sanhedrin. Why a member of the ruling council in Jerusalem was standing with a decorated centurion at my cell I had no idea, but they were both my enemies. A spark of anger ignited in my belly, but I doused it quickly. I had no way—or will—to fight.

"Well, you're…less than I was led to believe," said the centurion sardonically.

My cheeks burned in shame. I closed my eyes, then forced them open again, still aimed toward the floor. I didn't reply, of course. I didn't feel like getting beaten again.

"He is more than he seems," said the Sanhedrin official. His voice was high, reedy, and so full of self-importance I wondered if he had been born wearing those costly sandals.

"Humph." The centurion's voice dripped with scorn, betraying his disbelief that I was anything more than gutter trash. "Bring him," he barked at the legionnaire. He turned and started walking, and with alacrity the soldier stepped into my room, grabbed me firmly by the elbow, and dragged me along with him. The Sanhedrin official followed, the whisk-whisk of his stately steps in stark contrast to my uneven stumbling shuffle along the dim subterranean hallway. The smell was awful, as usual, but neither the centurion nor the Sanhedrin commented on it as everyone else from the outside did. They kept quiet, and so did I. My doom was upon me.

I heard the sound of a great and restless crowd as we emerged from the highest basement level onto the first floor, but given the thick walls it was muted to a low buzzing. We turned down an interior colonnade, then up a narrow set of stairs to the second floor, where we continued toward the slowly growing sound. It sounded like an execution crowd, where anxiety rode the edge of bloodlust. I had witnessed such a thing before, and I had felt it myself, to my disgrace. I swallowed hard, my heart nearly freezing upon realizing it was nearing its last beat.

Why should I be afraid, though? Why should I panic? I had known it was coming. I should be rejoicing that my torment was finally going to be over. I would at last pass from that prison to the prison on the other side. It couldn't be any worse, could it? At least I wouldn't be hungry, and I wouldn't hurt so much. Maybe I would finally get some decent sleep…if sleep was even necessary after death.

Suddenly I dreaded the thought that I might never be able to sleep again. It was a horrifying image.

I stumbled, earning a rough knee to the back of my left thigh to keep me focused on marching to my execution. The painful distraction helped, and when the dread returned, it wasn't as sharp. I was numbing to my fate.

I must have closed my eyes and drifted, because I was surprised when a gust of cool wind hit me and caused me to stumble again. I realized I was outside, shuffling along a raised wooden platform. Loud, disjointed chants rose from a teeming mass of people gathered in the large outer courtyard of Herod's fortress. I stopped and blinked, turning my head to determine where exactly I was, which earned me a slug in the back and a muttered Roman curse. I staggered forward again, following the gleaming centurion and his Sanhedrin accomplice. I gazed upward, noting the overcast gloom, the clouds streaked in odd colors and shapes. Despite the invigorating freshness of the air, the sights made me dizzy, so I looked back down. The wind was strong, punctuated occasionally by gusts that caused even the centurion to alter his footfalls to maintain his balance. He finally stopped and turned toward the crowd, scowling as his eyes settled upon them briefly. He glanced at the sky, his dark mien deepening, and then he looked at me.

"Step forward, traitor," he commanded.

I wasn't entirely sure which way was forward, but the legionnaire at my back let me know clearly. I was shoved toward the edge of the platform, stopping inches before I fell headlong off it. The people, their heads just an arm's length below the level of the platform, seemed to grow more frenzied, and I could see the spittle flying from some of their mouths as they shouted incoherently, some jumping up and down and raising their fists. There were no commoners among them that I could see, and it startled me that I had never seen the genteel class behave this way, at least not en masse. I wondered if hands would suddenly reach up to grab me and pull me into the crowd, where I would be torn apart like a lamb caught by a pack of wolves. Distressing as that thought was, I dared not step back because of the soldier behind me.

The surging shouts continued a few moments longer, and then the centurion blew a small horn and shouted for silence. The crowd quieted, and then in almost perfect unison snapped their heads toward the other side of the platform. My eyes and head followed. I saw a man being led by a rope around his neck—and not gently. His simple gray robes looked dusty and slept-in, though mine were worse. His gaze paused briefly on me as he calmly took stock of the situation, and in that instant I felt a shiver—not of fear, but of a strange, far-distant awe that I couldn't define. I bore him some resemblance physically, but that was the extent of our similarity.

He was led to a similar position near the crowd, about eight paces to my left, and then he straightened to his full height, fixing his eyes on a spot above the human maelstrom, seeming to see beyond the thick walls of Herod's fortress. The assembled scribes, elders, and nobles rustled and murmured anew, just as the wind gusted hard again, causing everyone to pause and look up at the sky momentarily. The other prisoner did not move. In fact, even his long, bedraggled hair was still. His face was the personification of both intense focus and tranquility, though I will never be able to adequately describe it. After a few more buffeting gusts that refused to touch him, the eyes of the fidgety crowd turned again, this time toward the large archway at the back of the platform. I dared not turn in that direction, so I gazed at my feet, noting with detached curiosity that they were cleaner than I remembered, and they didn't seem to hurt at the moment.

The centurion's voice rose again, this time to announce the Roman prefect, Pontius Pilate. In the eerie silence that followed I heard the soft, slippered footfalls of the august representative of Rome as he walked forward until he was between me and the serene prisoner. I wondered only briefly at why the proud but superstitious ruler had come there rather than having everyone go to him. Not that it mattered at that point. It appeared that the Romans were preparing for two executions.

The crowd remained hushed, as did the fickle winds.

"I have received the request made by your elders," Pilate began in a stentorian voice, addressing the crowd as he pointed toward the other prisoner, "and I have examined this man called Jesus of Nazareth to satisfy myself that your demands are just under Roman law." He paused as if looking for some reaction, but there was none. If anything, the crowd grew quieter, achieving a heightened sense of expectancy. He dropped his hand and turned his head to look directly at the smoky-haired member of the Sanhedrin standing with him on the platform. His voice lowered, though it could still be heard clearly. "I find that they are not, Master Amalek." Many in the crowd muttered angrily at that, and he turned again toward them and boomed, "He has broken no Roman laws and is worthy of no Roman punishment!"

The protests grew louder and angrier. Amalek seemed to gather their energy as he stepped up to Jesus of Nazareth and backhanded him viciously across the face in an insult to his manhood. Then Amalek raised his arms as if he were Moses with the tablets of God and declared, "He has blasphemed against the loyal Jewish subjects of Rome and caused sedition among us! He has energized mobs. He claims to be a king with no master but himself!" He gestured toward Pilate, both hands open and head slightly bowed, though his face was stern. "Esteemed governor, you have trusted us to help you maintain peace and prosperity in this region, and so have we done, rooting out the traitors and the spies among us. Trust us now that this man, this imposter who has even claimed to be a god, must be executed for his dangerous crimes against your loyal Jewish subjects, that peace may continue to progress and your tenure may be blessed and prosperous."

I was still processing how this could be *the* Jesus of Nazareth, the man whose growing legend of invincibility was oft whispered among the other prisoners. I had only seen him once, briefly, as he was teaching in what seemed a faraway place a very long time before, and he had seemed uncommonly powerful.

Pilate frowned. "He has committed no crime worthy of death."

Amalek seemed taken aback by the response, almost as if a script had been agreed upon and the prefect had departed from it. "We have judged him worthy of death, and in the past you have honored our judgments and traditions in your wisdom as prefect."

"I have indeed honored *sound* judgment and *worthy* tradition," responded Pilate coolly, "and I will continue to do so." He shifted his attention again to the crowd, his voice rising. "You ask for a noteworthy prisoner to be released at the celebration of your Passover feast, and I give you Jesus of Nazareth that you may show your great mercy and forbearance in sparing his life while you denounce his claims. This will raise your esteem among your people, and lessen his. Is that not fair? Is that not wise? At the same time, I heed the words of your High Priest, Caiaphas, that the blood of a man is required as a sacrifice for your people at this time, and since you cannot shed this blood, I do it for you. I shall execute the murderer Barabbas, also called Jesus, as an example to all those who fight against Rome, betray your people, and sin against your god. *This* is the true path forward."

The crowd appeared stunned, flummoxed like a goat hit between the eyes with a stone. Some appeared to be considering Pilate's words as they conversed in sharp whispers, while others began shaking their heads and stamping their feet like jilted toddlers, their faces going red. I looked to see Amalek's reaction. His brow was furrowed in frantic thought and apparent anger, which he attempted to keep in check in the presence of the Romans.

Pilate lifted his chin slightly and smiled at Amalek. Beyond them, I noted that Jesus remained as composed as before, his eyes tinged with sadness instead of fear.

Finally, Amalek spoke, again paying obeisance to Pilate. "Your proposal has merit, wise prefect, but our scribes and elders have been out among the people, finding out their minds, weighing their reactions to what we might do today. Many of those scribes and elders are here, and their counsel is much greater than mine, so we should ask them which choice is best…by your leave, of course." He said the last with a deep but brief bow, and Pilate stared at him a moment before giving a curt nod.

Amalek turned to address the crowd. "You have heard our wise governor's reasoning, and I ask you now to weigh it against the present mind and mood of the people that many of you have been diligently and privily finding out. Which prisoner should be executed, that goodwill may be maximized across the entire province, this peaceful land of the children of Abraham?"

In ragged but energetic unison the gathered elites yelled, "Jesus of Nazareth!"

"Are you sure?" asked Amalek theatrically.

"Crucify him!" they shouted again, even louder. "Crucify him!" They continued to chant that boisterously for nearly a full minute, until Amalek raised his hands again, quieting them. He turned to Pilate, gesturing at the crowd.

"We believe in the *Pax Romana*, most honored prefect. And the voice of the people believes that the blood of the false king Jesus of Nazareth is required for that peace to be maintained." I detected a threat in his tone, which was daring.

I had nearly turned my entire body toward the scene playing out between Pilate and Amalek, and the centurion was so focused on them as well that he either didn't notice or didn't care. Pilate stared at Amalek for several long moments, then at the crowd, full of men and women of great influence and wealth in what had always been a restless province. Finally, he turned and gestured to someone behind him. A young boy hurried forward carrying a small basin of water which he held in front of Pilate. The prefect thrust in his hands, then removed them and rubbed them together vigorously as if washing them. Then he raised them, palms outward as he faced the crowd.

"Rome will execute your chosen prisoner," he intoned solemnly, "but his blood is not on Rome, and it is not on me. His blood is your responsibility alone."

Amalek nodded gravely, though I could tell he was trying not to gloat in front of his audience. "We accept this responsibility, prefect. God requires his blood, so let it be upon us as a gift for our obedience."

A loud shout of victory arose from the throng amid jumping, waving of fists, and gleefully vicious smiles peppered with laughter. "Let it be upon us! Let it be upon us!" they chanted.

I shivered suddenly, and then it struck me like a bolt of lightning out of a clear sky. Jesus of Nazareth was to be executed in my place. *My* place. I was a murderer and a thief. I had abandoned my family. Jesus was a teacher, and, if the rumors were true, a healer. He had never harmed anyone. He had never shed blood. And yet his would be spilled while mine would be spared. To what purpose? Why would God countenance such a thing? And why would my people demand it? My weary mind could find no answers, and while I should have felt peace, I was deeply unsettled.

Pilate barely spared me a glance as he turned and left, a disdainful, disgusted look on his face that I doubt was meant for me. As he passed the centurion, he gestured toward Jesus and said, "Take him to the Praetorium and prepare him."

The centurion saluted, then barked out orders to soldiers who jumped to comply. Then he turned toward me, the repulsed look on *his* face causing me to instinctively cower.

"You are free, scum…for now. But I will be watching, and I'm sure we will meet again."

I've always had a hard time telling that part of my story. That day was at once starkly unforgettable and an indiscernible blur. When I think about how I found myself outside the walls of my prison, a free man once again, I shudder at how little I knew—at how little I *still* know—about the redemption I have so earnestly and yet often unknowingly craved.

The Roman guards tossed me onto the dusty street outside the prison like a cartload of refuse. At first I wandered aimlessly, probably in circles. Part of me wanted to flee the city, escape into the hills, hide in a cave, and get that long sleep I so desperately craved. But another part of me felt…something bigger, something momentous and powerful, something dreadful and inevitable and…hopeful? I had realized I was becoming delusional, perhaps mad, before the first massive peal of thunder nearly knocked me to the ground. When the rain started falling in sheets and the earth rumbled beneath my feet, I thought maybe I actually *had* died, that maybe my mind was just blocking the memory of my execution.

How I found myself at that cursed place I do not know. It was very dark, and the tempest had recently calmed. All was quiet except for the sounds of soft weeping from the women who remained. They shouldn't have been there. It was long past time for them to be safely home, though two men stood silently to the side, heads bowed, shoulders slumped, seemingly oblivious to the fact that they were drenched and it was unusually cold. The Roman soldiers had withdrawn, but a few might still have been watching from a shelter nearby.

It was hard to make myself look upon those three crosses, especially the one in the middle, but with some effort I did. There was the man who had taken my place, the famous Jesus I knew so little about. The crude sign nailed to the top of his cross mockingly proclaimed him King of the Jews in three tongues, and some had said he truly was. But he was dead. Perhaps, I thought, if he had lived and I had died, he could have rallied enough of the people against their Roman masters. Perhaps he could have been the Messiah that would lead the long-suffering Jewish people to victory over all their enemies and make them once again the most powerful and prosperous nation under heaven.

But his own had turned on him, and I suspected Roman stratagems may have been involved as well, despite Pilate's seemingly odd actions. Some Romans were haughty and stupid, but most weren't. They knew the Jews didn't like them, and they were always looking to either expose rebel plots or infiltrate the resistance and turn those plots against them. I had been a victim of such an infiltration—betrayed by my brethren for Roman coin, the remembrance of which had made me seethe with anger until I in turn had betrayed others.

I stared at the lifeless body of Jesus, and soon hot tears trailed down my cheeks. The great Jesus of Nazareth was dead, the rebellion I'd fought for was rudderless and fragmented, and I was without hope and direction. I was alive, yes, but what was that worth? My parents and sisters would be waiting for me, but only out of duty. I expected no love, nor did I deserve it. With that last somber thought tumbling around in my mind, I turned my back on the grisly hill of hopeless death and made my way toward the place I used to call home.

CHAPTER 1

But the natural man receiveth not the things of the Spirit of God: for they are foolishness unto him: neither can he know them, because they are spiritually discerned.

1 Corinthians 2:14, KJV

I was a restless and curious boy, but that wasn't unusual. Most children are rambunctious. But I was endlessly, obsessively fascinated with the arts of war. Ironically, as a boy I idolized the Roman centurions whom I would later come to despise and even hate. I always had something in my hand that I imagined to be a sword—shields were for sissies, of course, and the centurions didn't carry them. When I was with my friends, I always assumed the place of Primus Pilus, the senior centurion of an entire legion, and sometimes in our fanciful games I would use my vine rod—usually a small, gnarled stick fallen from an ancient olive tree—to enforce discipline. I enjoyed that too much, I think.

My father was at first indifferent, but by the time I was nine he was becoming annoyed by my idolization of the Roman officers. I had even learned to sound like them in their own language when I wanted to. Father berated and shamed me for my obsession with the Romans, warning me that I was becoming a traitor to my people. He was not a man of many words or much learning—a basketmaker by trade—but he was a man of fiery passion once aroused, to which I can bear clear witness.

My mother was never happy that I played the Roman soldier, either, even as a little boy, but she didn't mind that I learned the 'true' Roman language of Latin. I already spoke Greek in addition to Aramaic, because it was expected, and she thought I possessed some great gift because I could learn a third language as well. She had high and misguided hopes that perhaps I could become a teacher or a scribe and speak fluently the holy language of Hebrew. I suppose I could have, but such a path never interested me. Her daily encouragements toward scholarship never deterred me from my boyhood fantasies, but they did begin to irritate me. By the time I was just thirteen, I became so resentful of both my father's attacks and my mother's lectures that I left. I cursed my parents in a fit of teenage rage, betrayed our family bonds, and left!

It was stupid, and if I could choose a single point in time to do over, it would be that moment. In those days I could barely see past my belly and my loins, and I didn't use my head for much beyond trying to look and sound like a Roman centurion. My passion was much like my father's, and it completely overpowered what kindness I had learned from my mother. After a week, I almost returned home out of hunger and want, but my pride didn't let me, and by the grace of Jehovah I found a man who would apprentice me—or rather, *he* found *me*, wandering despondently and begging for food near the Essene Gate in the southwest corner of the city. I wouldn't have chosen to become a tentmaker, but that was Master Iddo's trade, and it was better than being a scribe. So I learned to make tents, big and small, fancy and plain, costly and meager. He must have somehow obtained my father's permission, because there were never any protests under the law about my apprenticeship. Every month or so my mother, sometimes accompanied by my sisters Salome and Mara, would come by to see how I was doing, but we rarely spoke. I behaved awfully toward them.

Adah was Master Iddo's wife. She was a stout, stern woman, and she didn't much care for me at first, vehemently protesting my presence in her house. Her heart soon softened toward my pathetic existence, however—God alone knew why—and she began to teach me what she knew of letters and the Law. I couldn't train in the synagogue as a runaway orphan, of course, nor did I want to, but it was enough that Mistress Adah taught me, for I was never meant to be a scholar.

Her sons and her daughter were already grown and moved away when I arrived. One son was a tentmaker in Hebron, enchanted by a young woman from that area who had become his wife. Another son was studying under the Pharisees and hoped to become a great teacher—he was apparently Adah's favorite and visited at least once a week. The third son had wandered into Syria chasing dreams of great wealth as an artificer in gold and silver, and he was seldom heard from. The daughter was the youngest—just eighteen when I arrived—and she was a respected chef for the household of a member of the Sanhedrin. Adah sometimes seemed conflicted about her, perhaps because few of the common people possessed great love or respect for the Sanhedrin, though that made little sense to me at the time.

I don't recall exactly when I began to harbor resentments against my former Roman heroes, but as an apprentice to a tentmaker I sometimes heard things from our patrons, some of whom were reputable merchants or minor Jewish nobles. At first I dismissed their stories of Roman abuses and whimsical excesses without any real thought, but over time the tales of mockery, arrogance and cruelty sank in. By the time I was fifteen, I started to see myself as a real Jew and to understand what that meant. I still didn't go to synagogue very often, though my master encouraged me to, and when I went I didn't understand much. I made a few friends, though, most of whom were older than I was, and they treated me with respect.

I also noticed that becoming a man meant that the Roman soldiers viewed me differently than they had when I was a child. A young boy—even a Jewish boy—could elicit a smile, and maybe even a sweet, from the occasional toughened Roman soldier, whereas a man—especially a Jewish man—was usually viewed as a potential threat, and a filthy potential threat at that.

Early in my seventeenth year my education in life took a great leap forward. One of my friends, Alon, was two years older than me, the son of a cloth merchant named Isaac and well-advanced in his own apprenticeship to his father. His family lived just three doors down from Master Iddo's household, so I saw him often. He was small for his age, and I was large for mine, so it was difficult to tell the difference in age between us. He was the funniest, happiest person I'd ever met. He hated the cloth-trading business, and I was not enthralled with tentmaking, so we had much to commiserate—and rib each other endlessly about. Alon was devout in the faith of the Fathers, but he never judged me and never put me down for not going to synagogue with him, though truth be told I went more frequently when he was around. He traveled often with his father, mastering the trade he was resigned to inherit.

Alon was intensely curious. He loved learning about anything, whether it was cultures or architecture or animals or even rocks.

He would have made the wonderful teacher and scholar my parents had wanted me to become. In his travels he would seek out the places of learning and absorb as much as he could from scrolls, plates, tablets, and conversations. It was always a great day when he returned from a trip, because he would excitedly share his newfound knowledge with me, as much as he could. Sometimes he would even have some exotic artifact or trinket to show. Because of Alon, I became more aware of the broader world, and I was constantly amazed at the rich variety of people, customs and behaviors he told me about. Sometimes I was alarmed and angered by the stories of corruption and tyranny, and I came to understand more clearly the dim place the once-mighty Jewish kingdom occupied as both a vassal state to Rome and a disposable buffer to Rome's enemies to the east and north.

Alon had a younger sister who was two years younger than me. Chanah was as bright as Alon, and bubbly in the way of girls. At first I didn't notice her much, but a few weeks before my seventeenth birthday she entered the tentmaking shop wearing a Persian Cyclamen in her rich, black hair. Suddenly I realized she was near to being considered a woman, and she looked the part. After that I couldn't stop thinking about her. She liked me, too, but she was coy, and sometimes I wasn't sure what to do or say around her. I could tell that her mother Sariah was none too happy with what she saw, and Isaac also did his best to limit our interactions. Alon, however, thought it was endlessly hilarious, often joking that Chanah would be better off with a snake-bitten mule than with me. He was amused that his parents took it so seriously.

I wish I could have had a serious conversation with Alon about his sister, but the Romans made sure that never happened. It was Fall, and the Feast of the Tabernacles was approaching. Alon and his father had joined a small caravan traveling to the Parthian city of Ctesiphon, on the mighty Tigris River. On their return, shortly before crossing into the Roman province of Syria, they were attacked by a large group of bandits. The drivers pushed the animals hard for the Syrian border, and it appeared they would escape. But the Roman garrison guarding the crossing stopped them and wouldn't allow them to pass. As the bandits pillaged the caravan, the Roman soldiers just watched, some even laughing at the few pathetic attempts at resistance shown by the members of the caravan.

I wish Alon had not been so brave, and yet to this day I admire him fiercely and am proud to have been his friend. Instead of watching the bandits loot his father's goods, he fought, first with his hands, then with a dagger he took from a bandit. A few of the drivers were inspired to join him in the resistance—until a Roman arrow took him in the back and a bandit finished him off with a knife to the throat. Alon's father went mad. He had been pleading with the Roman officer to assist them, but instead the soldiers seized him and bound him. The bandits finished their evil work, and the last thing they did before leaving with the loot and the camels was transfer a hefty, clinking bag of tribute to the officer, who tied the money at his waist and sent the dazed remaining members of the caravan home on foot—a journey of more than a fortnight. Perhaps he had been sure they would die along the way, and he had likely been proud of his brutal treatment of the Jewish dogs.

Life is a cruel but effective teacher. Alon's father survived to relate his heartrending tale, but he didn't return home until he had made pleas for justice under Roman law to multiple Roman officials in both Caesarea and Jerusalem. None would listen with any real intent to pursue justice on soldiers so far away, and so justice died swiftly.

The night I learned of Alon's death, I paced my small room in barely-restrained fury. I nearly rushed out of the house to attack a passing Roman patrol with my bare hands. I'm still not sure why I didn't, because I don't remember feeling afraid.

The next day there was no work to be done, for Alon's family and all of their friends, including Master Iddo's household, were in mourning. The grief was particularly deep and bitter given that Isaac had been forced by the Roman soldiers to leave his son's body behind to be desecrated by bandits and wild animals. I heard him cry aloud the next night, shouting from his rooftop terrace, asking God if he had done something wrong to be punished so severely. I excused myself from Master Iddo's house before sunrise the next morning and wandered the hills around Jerusalem the entire day. I had to keep moving while my mind tried to process everything—not just Alon's tragic death, but my own confused existence as well.

When I returned, with the sun low in the sky, Chanah greeted me at the head of our street, her eyes rimmed red with tears. I stopped and lowered my eyes, not knowing what to say.

"He was your best friend," she said. "I'm sorry."

I was stunned. She had just lost her brother, her parents were consumed with grief, and she was worried about me?

"Thank you," I mumbled. "I'm sorry he was your brother." I instantly knew I'd said that horribly wrong, and I looked up to see her reaction. She apparently knew what I'd meant, because she just nodded. "I loved him. He was a good man. God will take care of him."

I knew that must be true, even though I didn't really understand it. Alon was the son every parent wanted to have. Perhaps, I thought, he was too good for such a harsh, senseless world.

"Is there anything I can do to help you?" she asked sincerely, and I gave her a confused look. Part of me was amazed at her empathy, but I admit that part of me was offended that she would ask. Wasn't I supposed to be helping her and her family?

I didn't know how to help, though, so I mumbled a decline to her invitation and then shuffled off to Master Iddo's house to find my sleeping mat, there to stay until the next morning. Sleep did not come, but various scenes in my mind of how Alon died at the hands of bandits allied with Roman soldiers did, and no amount of kindness from Master Iddo's family or Alon's younger sister could stop those terrifying images.

Two pain-scarred days later I was on my way north to Scythopolis, the leading city of the vaunted Decapolis, the cities that promoted Roman culture and tradition. I had run away again, abandoning those who had shown me kindness, leaving no indication where I was going. I wasn't sure what I was going to do yet, but I thirsted to do something violent. I considered assassinating the ranking Roman centurion in the city, and then, if I got away with it, traveling to another city in the Decapolis and doing the same. My other option was to join a rebel mercenary band, which, word had it, could be found if you talked to the right people. That seemed the better option, as it would let me exercise my anger longer and more often. Despite the vaunted *Pax Romana*, there were always cities and regions rebelling against their Roman masters, and some of them paid handsomely for new recruits. I was their man. At almost seventeen, I was already larger than most men, and thanks to the abundant whiskers growing on my face I could pass for someone several years older.

Those two options were enough for me. But on the road just outside of Scythopolis I stumbled upon a third. It was nearing midnight on a cool and overcast night. I was deep in thought as

I approached the city, and it must have been an impish fate that caused the sound near the road. I stopped and looked to my right, my eyes straining against the darkness. I took two steps in that direction, and then I heard it again, a bubbling groan like a brook whistling over the rocks. Several more steps took me off the road and into some low grasses, and that's when I saw them.

I took a long, slow breath as I comprehended the scene. There at my feet were two Roman soldiers. Based on the stench that enveloped them, they'd been drinking heavily. In the dim light I determined that they were *milites*—common soldiers with no special training—each wearing a simple leather *cuirass* with scale-plated shoulders, baldric and sword, deep-red tunic, arm guards, and greaves. Their helmets had been tossed nearby in the grass, along with their spears, though their satchels were still strapped around their shoulders. They had probably feared to enter the city and have their drunkenness discovered by an officer, and so had laid down to rest.

I considered them for several seconds, images of Alon being struck down crashing against my consciousness in waves. Then I looked up and down the road to see if any other late travelers plied that path. Seeing nobody, I grabbed the closest soldier under the arms and dragged him farther from the road, up and over a small hump in the landscape. After pausing to see if either of them was waking, I quickly did the same with his fellow, and then I made sure all their equipment was cleared away as well. An idea had been forming in my mind, driven by those boiling images of Alon's death. By the time I had the soldiers nestled away from the road, I had worked up the necessary courage and rage to carry out my plan.

Never had I killed another human being. During my pretend battles as a child, I had often wondered what it would be like, but

I'd always imagined killing in the chaos of battle, overcoming my enemy with strength of arms for the good of my family and people, or at least for the good of some fair maiden. I had never pictured taking the life of an unconscious man, and I hesitated, crazed though I was with anger. But I told myself that there must have been a purpose in me finding these soldiers. Part of me reasoned that finding them like that was a test to see if I would show them mercy, but that voice was weak. I could think of no better purpose than to avenge Alon.

I drew one of the soldiers' swords from its short sheath and tested the edge. It was sharp, which meant it was either well-maintained or seldom-used. With a hand over the first soldier's mouth and a knee on his chest, I pierced the man's jugular with his own sword.

That was when I realized my mistake. Blood was soaking the top of his tunic, and I had no means to clean it so that I could wear it and look like a Roman. Luckily there were two of them. Before killing the second soldier, I removed his armor and clothing, hoping desperately that he wouldn't wake up, since my body was shaking at what I had just done. I steeled my courage again and killed him as well, then quickly donned his uniform. It fit me well, even the *caligae* for my feet. His *loculus* was too ornate—probably a family gift and something that would stand out—so I retrieved the satchel of the first soldier. After searching both satchels, I found myself the grim owner of two tent spikes, a short length of rope, a brass wire bracelet probably purchased for a girlfriend or a harlot, half a loaf of hard bread, one *sestertius* and ten *quadrans*, plus my own clothes and the meager few coins I had brought with me. I couldn't tell which Roman emperor's head adorned the *sestertius*, and I didn't care. That much money was a fortunate find.

After calming my shaking somewhat, I was about to rise when I heard movement along the road. I immediately flattened myself to the ground, my heart thumping loudly as I felt a rush of new adrenaline. After a few moments of near panic, I peeked above the small rise in the soil, straining to see. Two Roman cavalrymen were walking in front of their horses and conversing in low tones, coming from the direction of the city.

The marrow in my bones froze as I watched them draw closer. I was no match for them, and I couldn't outrun them. My heart raced faster, my stomach churned, and my muscles were taut to the point of tearing. My mind, however, suddenly focused, and it came to me that I should consider the wind. There was a light breeze, and thankfully it was blowing in my face. If the wind shifted, though, the horses would smell blood, and while they were trained not to shy away from it, they would likely react. The soldiers, too, would recognize the unmistakable stench of so much blood and investigate.

After an endless minute, the cavalrymen passed by none the wiser and continued on their way, perhaps wondering when they would happen upon the two careless soldiers who now lay dead behind me. They might even have been friends with them, and that thought produced a brief pang of guilt that I determined to forget. I waited a few minutes more before getting to my feet. Then I moved away from the road more than a mile into a small orchard which would provide better concealment as my body recovered and I worked out a new plan. I didn't dare enter Scythopolis, though from Alon I'd heard many amazing things about the majestic city with its broad colonnaded cardo running its length from north to south, its multitude of exotic shops, its fine theater and hippodrome, and its ornate synagogues. The Jews there had become intoxicated with Roman opulence, and it was better that I spend no time there, anyway. At best I had a couple of days before the bodies were found, one out of uniform.

That third option, which I decided upon after killing the two hapless soldiers, was to travel to the border between Syria and the Parthian Empire, the very same border that should have been strongly secured by Roman guards when Alon and his father had arrived there and requested aid. I intended to find the company of soldiers that had betrayed that caravan and exact my revenge directly upon them. It would take some time, but how much more satisfying would it be than just killing random Roman soldiers?

I covered the nearly forty miles north to Chorazin in a day and a half without incident and found lodging at a tiny inn. I ignored the few stares I got from people who likely thought I was a Roman deserter, and I avoided any contact with actual Roman soldiers. I had planned as I walked, knowing that Syria was a rebellious province with more numerous Roman garrisons. By the time I arrived at Chorazin I had decided I would buy common merchants' clothes instead of wearing my rough laborer's garb, plus a mule to pack the armor and supplies—that *sestertius* truly had been an amazing find. I had also created a plausible backstory.

Upon finding the right Roman border garrison, I would sell the mule, don the soldier's attire once again, dirty and bruise myself up, then straggle into the camp with a harrowing story of kidnap by Jewish rebels from a location south of Hebron near the fortress of Masada. I would explain that my captors had carried me all the way to Syria to sell me as a slave to the Parthians, but that I had escaped before the transfer could take place. I was sure I would be accepted, at least while runners took news of my ordeal and transferred it south almost five hundred miles. By the time word came back that my story was false, that a *milite* named Ascanius Severus didn't even exist, much less was kidnapped and transported to Syria by slavers and rebels, either my grisly work would be done or I would already be dead.

The journey north and east beyond the borders of Damascus was uneventful. Because I was big and strong and carried a spear—the adornments of which I had removed to make it look more common—nobody cared to bother me. The mule turned out to be even-tempered, too, so I traveled quickly. Within a week I had crossed the Syrian desert and arrived at the great trading stop of Palmyra—the Bride of the Desert, as she was called. The border was not many miles hence, so I was sure the garrison would be based nearby.

After renting a room and selling the mule, I began making inquiries. I was careful, and I usually broached the subject by telling a story about the gallantry of the Roman soldiers who had once protected my uncle's family after they were harassed by the Parthians. I also claimed I had a brother who had gone to join the Roman army, and that I had last heard he had been sent to a camp in Syria.

Palmyra was a beautiful city, and while small it was filled with the pleasurable abominations that weaken men's wills. In my angry and godless state, I partook of some of them, though I was careful not to spend all of my plunder on wine, women, and dice, as I would need it to continue along my path of vengeance. That determination probably saved my life, since I was alone. Had I allowed myself to become too inebriated or isolated, I would surely have fallen victim to the deadly thugs who roamed the back streets at night, away from the Roman patrols.

My break came as I was inspecting some dried meat at a vendor's shop on the cardo of Palmyra, which was decorated along almost its entire length by hanging flowers and fluted columns—a mixture, I was told, of famed Greek and Roman architecture and the legendary hanging gardens of Babylon. The wide street was busy that day, as a large caravan from the west had just arrived and its owners were replenishing supplies. The dozen or so rough-looking caravan guards who had accompanied it stalked around looking for victims—men to intimidate or women to cajole—though they stepped cautiously when the Roman patrols passed by. Cowards. None of them would dare do what I was about to do. Likely, none would dare to do what I'd already done. They looked like nothing more than paid bullies to me.

"They are fools."

Startled, I looked at the woman tending the shop. She nodded toward a particularly scruffy-looking pair of the merchant guards.

I smiled, removing the deep scowl I had been directing toward the ruffians. "I agree. But they are hungry, no?"

Her smirk was tinged with disgust. "Their master pays them too well, but I will indeed take their coin." She sighed. "It used to be that the caravans didn't need so many guards. That was before this new Roman captain arrived. He claims to have taken the battle to the brigands, and that they are fighting back. He promises he will finish them soon. But the attacks continue. I do not trust him. I hear he was an *optio*, but his centurion released him."

I lowered my voice. "When did this Roman captain arrive?"

"The better part of four months ago." She rearranged some strips of meat hanging near the front of her shop. "He brought a mangy squad of ruffians with him and declared that the city was under his protection and would be safe if we all 'cooperated' as the blessed vassals of Rome we were expected to be. If you ask me, he's as pompous as the Emperor himself. I recognize stuff and nonsense when I see it, and that man is full of it…and of himself."

"When was the last attack?" I ventured.

She thought for moment. "Near a month ago, but at least a day's journey north, along a minor road that some traders use to avoid a higher cost of passage. He has men up there, and he goes occasionally to visit a certain harlot. He's there now, I hear."

I thought through what she was saying. It couldn't be that simple, could it? Had I already found the man I was looking for? Was he at the place where Alon had been killed? All I knew was that it was an isolated border crossing and that it was north of the Bride of the Desert. Was my luck that good?

"How long does he usually stay?" I asked, perhaps being a little too daring. I didn't want to arouse suspicions, but this woman seemed no fan of the Romans, unlike many in this festering city. I was happy I hadn't been pretending to admire the Romans while in her presence.

"Two weeks, sometimes three. He really likes that harlot."

I nearly chuckled at that, but merely smiled again. Then I purchased enough meat for a two-week journey.

CHAPTER 2

*For godly sorrow worketh repentance to salvation not to be repented of:
but the sorrow of the world worketh death.*

2 Corinthians 7:10, KJV

I played well the part of an escaped prisoner of the dirty Jewish rebels. I was so convincing, in fact, that Ovidius—the harlot-chasing Roman captain—had his men armed, organized, and ready to hare off after the supposed kidnappers and slavers within an hour of my arrival at their slovenly encampment of about forty men. However, since I pretended not to be sure where my captors were, thanks to my wandering in the desert with little water and no food, they had no idea which way to march to find the phantoms of my vengeful imagination.

They nursed me back to strength over the next two days, and I recounted my fantastical story—in near-perfect Latin, of course, that gift of tongues bearing ironic fruit. I embellished it with tall tales of my bravery and imbued it with open contempt for my ignorant, uncivilized captors. I related the blow-by-blow scene of my escape to a hushed audience around a small cooking fire—how I had lured one of the rebels near and knocked him unconscious with my forehead, then cut my bonds with his dagger and wreaked havoc in the camp during the night, frightening the hapless beggars near to death and stealing back my sword, spear, and armor from dead Jews.

I had initially fled south, so I said, but after two days I became weak with hunger and thirst and aimlessly drove myself onward with true Roman grit and determination. After the fourth day, I stumbled upon their camp and blessed the gods, and now I wanted revenge on the rebels, wherever they might be found. Ovidius and his men believed every word of it.

The morning after I arrived in camp, two runners were sent to carry the message of my glorious escape to my garrison and bring back orders for me. That would take weeks, so I made sure to seize every opportunity to talk with the soldiers when they were deep in their drink, plying them for information about what their duties were and what kinds of actions they had been involved in recently.

Finally, the night before the captain was planning to return to Palmyra, one of the senior soldiers half-drunkenly recited a story of how they had recently watched a caravan of Jews plundered by Parthian bandits and had all profited handsomely from it. He even told me which of the men had fired the fateful arrow that led to 'the noncompliant Jewish boy's' death. He made me promise not to tell the captain he'd told me, because they were supposed to keep such secrets safe on pain of execution. I vowed to keep his secret very, very safe.

So I knew the truth. Captain Ovidius had led the carnage, and many of the men in the camp had been involved in the treachery. I had little time to exact my revenge.

I volunteered for guard duty on the fourth watch that night, and to my amazement I was paired with the man who had launched that vicious arrow. I almost began to believe that God might care about me and my quest, though I knew that couldn't be. Still, I rejoiced, and when the time for the watch came, I tried to appear as relaxed as possible, fearing that my excitement would show and draw his attention.

He was a slothful soldier. He struggled to stay focused and awake as we sat in the dim light of dying embers near the edge of the camp amid scrub brush and small boulders half-buried in the sandy soil. The cool air carried the soft sounds of scurrying critters and chirping insects, but the most peaceful time of the desert night had arrived. It was easy to pull out my dagger and start sharpening it. When his eyes finally fluttered and his head lolled back, I reached around him with one hand to cover his mouth and then slit his throat. It seemed to happen in slow motion, and like I wasn't in full control of my movements. He died with no sound and only a brief struggle. After his breath leached away, I looked around the dimly-outlined group of scattered tents to make sure none of the soldiers had been awakened.

When I was sure nobody had stirred, I made a beeline for the captain's tent, spear in hand. Just in front of the entrance flaps I froze, realizing I had seen the harlot go in there with him earlier. I listened for a moment, and I could hear two even but distinct breathing rhythms. I couldn't kill her. I couldn't. She was innocent—at least of murder, and I couldn't imagine myself killing a woman under almost any circumstance.

If I'd had more time, perhaps I could have been stealthier. But each moment that passed pressed harder on me. I needed to get it done. So I ducked into the tent, which was taller than the normal soldiers' tents, found the captain lying on blankets with the harlot sleeping softly beside him, and thrust my spearhead toward his throat.

My aim was true, and he barely had time to gurgle and thrash before I was dashing out. The harlot woke immediately, but the shock of what I'd done must have delayed her reaction, because I gained a precious few seconds to sprint out of the camp and disappear into the brush before her screaming started. I fervently hoped the waking soldiers wouldn't figure out what had really happened for a couple of minutes, and that mobilizing a pursuit would take additional time.

I alternated running and walking for the next two hours, changing direction often, trying to cover some of my tracks and occasionally stopping to listen for pursuit. I was generally headed north, and I knew where I wanted to go. As daybreak was nearing, I arrived at the small village I sought. There I bought supplies, some new clothes, and another satchel. I had abandoned my Roman armor and Roman sword about a mile from the village, but I still had dagger and spear. My funds were low, but I didn't care. In my righteous rage I felt Alon would be proud, and maybe he would even put in a good word for me on the other side.

After two months of hiding in the hills and barely surviving off the land, I had made my way to the bustling port city of Tyre, in Phoenicia. I quickly became comfortable there, selling my labor to another tentmaker and spending my wages on a meager subsistence and cheap wine. I made a few friends, too, though not the good kind. Our target was trouble, and our aim was pretty good. Within a year, there was a bounty on my head. I'd ransacked an inn with two other men and stolen a dozen head of sheep to impress a coquettish young Phoenician woman who kept pressing me to see how reckless I would be for her. Too late, I realized how dangerous the game had become. I had to flee Tyre.

I ended up in Ptolemais—not far down the coast and still in Phoenicia—with one of my new friends, Yacob, the firebrand son of a spice merchant from Sebaste, a city in the heart of Samaria. It seemed odd to me, since Samaritans were so disrespected by proper Jewry, but he hated the Romans even more than I did and was determined to see them kicked out of Israel and Syria both, alive or on death wagons. I tried to pry his secrets from him, but even drunk he wouldn't reveal the source of his hatred.

In Ptolemais we found others willing to join our cause, and before I knew it I was one of the leaders of a sizeable rebel band. We amassed weapons and trained regularly for battle, knowing that desire alone wouldn't beat the Romans and their well-drilled pagan hordes. We were careful to mask our activities, and as the days and weeks passed we became confident that we could have an impact.

At first, the other members of the group were all impressed that I had actually killed Roman soldiers, and close inspection of the spear I owned was proof enough for them that it was true. But as the confidence of the group grew, my behavior became more prideful and erratic. One day I even challenged the guard of a Roman merchant to a fight in the middle of a busy street, and Yacob nearly punched me in the head before dragging me away.

I realized I had become drunk on bloodlust and power, though I felt incapable of controlling it. I'd wanted to be a heroic rebel fighting for the freedom of my people, but instead I was a killer, a rage-mad fool who had come to believe he was invincible and the master of all around him. Yacob and others tried to reason with me, urging me to master my rage and focus on the long-term goals of the band. But I was impervious to their arguments. I had lost my humanity...and with it my true identity.

Fortunately for Yacob and the other Ptolemais rebels, my recklessness caught up with me one night at an inn near the docks. I had suffered a long day of being goaded, ridiculed, and even spat upon by haughty Roman legionnaires who laughed at my impotence. One even rapped me sharply on the side of the head with the butt end of his spear to the hearty approval of his fellows after he said I'd given him a 'look.' I had been alone and maddeningly powerless at the time, just trying to buy bread.

As I ate in seething, solitary silence in the inn amidst the peaceful backdrop of dulcimers and harps, a Jewish man at the next table commented on the tune and noted that it had been composed by a Roman musician. "That there is as fine a piece of music as has ever been written," the stranger proclaimed loudly to the small group of men with him, all minor merchants by their look. He wasn't drunk, but he was getting there.

"You have been too long away in Rome, Malachi," chided one of his friends. "I fear they have filled your head with bees."

His other companions laughed heartily.

"Nay, Simon," objected Malachi, who didn't seem embarrassed. "There is complex and yet simplistic genius to this piece that comes from a deep appreciation of many masters across the empire. Only a man approaching the divine mind could meld them together into a symphony so sublime that its equal cannot be found in all the lands of Abraham, nor yet anywhere else."

His friends paused to think about that, a couple of them cocking their heads, and then one of them let out a hearty laugh and slapped the table hard.

"Lights above, Malachi!" he shouted. "Did you rehearse that? There are no Roman spies here…nor any of their gods!" He laughed even harder, most of his companions joining in, causing everyone else in the common room to turn and stare at them. Even the dulcimer player missed a beat.

Malachi looked flustered and angry, and when they were all finished laughing and had taken another drink, he wagged a fleshy finger at them. "Laugh if you want, but the Romans keep the peace, uphold the law, and generally let us worship as we please. They also excel in arts and entertainments, and we should feel proud to be a part of that."

Now that was an interesting statement. Malachi really was a Roman toady. He wasn't alone, of course, and that made me furious. There were far too many sycophants like him, who through greed or cowardice continually sought the good graces of their masters and even came to worship them.

Simon raised a hand to calm everyone. "Malachi," he said, his tone moderating and his voice so low I had to strain to hear him, "the Romans are indeed impressive, and they are the pre-eminent power among the nations at present, but we are sons of Abraham, and our people the children of the covenant. God *will* return to us. When the Messiah comes it will be different, and no unhallowed hand can stop it. Those who oppose us then will be swept aside with the besom of destruction. His kingdom will be greater than David's, and greater than Rome's." He sat back and puffed out his chest, looking at the others around the table, who all nodded their agreement. I liked this Simon.

Malachi was about to reply when another man at the table spoke. He had been calmer than the others, though his eyes were intense now. He seemed to be the most senior of the group, with gray at his temples and flecking his beard.

"Perhaps he already has," he said, his voice also low. "I know several followers of a new rabbi who they claim has come to fulfill the prophecies. They aren't crazed zealots like those who once followed Theudas or Judas of Galilee—some of them are sound men of Jerusalem. They are sober and wise, they work hard, and they work together. There are many fine artisans among them, and fine musicians, too. They are composing new songs, and what I've heard so far rivals even this." He waved toward the inn's musicians, but his eyes remained focused on Malachi.

The Rome-lover looked confused for a moment, but then slapped both hands on the table and roared with his own laughter. "You can't be serious, Barnabas. Another ragtag band of delusional lepers who claims to have found the Messiah? Blasphemy! If the Messiah were already here, Ananais would know it, because he would have come to Ananais first."

Barnabas nodded. "You might be right, but my point is that some of them are breaking out of our stale traditions, including those regarding music." He lowered his voice again and spoke with an even tone. "And your infatuation with the Romans bothers me."

Malachi took that as a challenge. "I am a son of Abraham, which means I am a survivor. Our god is powerful, but the Romans have powerful gods as well, and you would all—" he cast his gaze around to include the entire group "—do well to remember that. If we manage our affairs right, we can become brokers of power across the empire. If we must share control of Israel, so be it. And if we have to lose a few of our brethren to appease our weaker-willed Roman taskmasters, God will see the right of it and our children will prosper as in the days of Solomon. The Messiah will not come if we show weakness or stupidity. He will only come if we show strength and unwavering purpose."

I stared at this Malachi as my mind re-processed his words. Here was a man without honor, driven purely by greed. Here was a man who would sell his own people for power and pleasure. Here was a man who could stand by while Roman soldiers put an arrow through the back of a boy because he dared resist tyranny and treachery. Here was a man who dishonored the prophets and blasphemed God!

I stopped thinking at that point. My rage became a bonfire, and instead of being focused on the minor harassments of that day, it aligned on an image of Alon, bravely resisting the barbaric demons to his last breath. Malachi himself might as well have nocked the arrow that slew him.

The next few moments will forever be etched in awful, eternal remembrance across the wounded chasms of my soul. It pains me to recount them, but I must.

I stood and stepped toward Malachi's table as I raised my heavy stone mug high in the air. The men at the table turned their attention to me, unsure what I was doing but unconcerned. "Jehovah be praised," I said loudly, still moving closer. Most of the men looked confused, and one even smiled as he whispered something to the man next to him. When I had reached the traitor's side, I brought the mug down with all my strength on his head.

I knew instantly that I'd killed him, and it hit me then like an avalanche on Mt. Hermon how far I'd fallen, how loathsome I'd become. I'd lost control of myself completely. I'd savagely killed an innocent man, an unarmed Jew, and in the presence of dozens of witnesses. I would be swiftly and severely punished unto death.

My outrage evaporated with the man's life. Then my courage failed, and I ran out the front door so fast I couldn't even hear what was going on behind me.

It was night, and I was desperate. I ran under cover of darkness until I was nearly spent, with no destination in mind. Running was what I was best at.

For two years I bounced around, mainly along the coast south of Mt. Carmel—Dora, Crocodilion, Joppa, Jamnia. At one point I made it as far south as Agrippias, almost to Gaza. I shaved often and kept my hair shorter to alter my appearance. I introduced myself to some few as Simon the Tentmaker from Derbe, a citizen of Cilicia, and I found customers for my tents by surreptitiously avoiding the trade guilds and offering lower prices for my work. For short stretches of time I was diligent at my trade so that I could eat well, but I found no joy in it, and not joining the local guilds meant that I had to move often so that I wasn't seen as a threat to their markets. Word spread, though, and I knew that eventually Jewish authorities would get involved.

In Lachish, some few miles inland from Agrippias, I started to hear rumors about another great rabbi, who had arisen in Galilee of all places. Similar to what the merchant Barnabas had described, some believed this rabbi was the long-promised Messiah, come to save Israel. I dismissed the claims without a flicker of hope, knowing it was just the fevered imaginations of a beaten populace with no backbone to stand up on their own and forcefully throw off the Roman oppression.

Besides, I was a man without a people or a god, a murderer of Jew and Roman alike. If the Messiah came, he would not save *me*. And so I maintained my existence by the sweat of my brow, turning my mind toward the happy and miserable day I would die. How long would it be? And who would care?

Though I told myself I had no interest in whisperings regarding the Great Teacher in the north, I unconsciously began to migrate slowly in that direction, following the winds of hearsay and hope. In Nicopolis, and then Gophna, then Sychar, and finally Nain on the southern edge of Galilee, I plied my wares and kept my peace, my curiosity growing while my desire to disregard the man they called Jesus of Nazareth waned. By the time I reached Nain, this Jesus was being spoken of by most people I met as if he really were the Messiah. In my barren, twisted mind I wondered if perhaps, just perhaps, their vain and foolish hope could be used to ignite the hearts of the Jews to battle. Maybe they could finally be convinced that the so-called protections of Rome were nothing more than the pillaging of the poor by arrogant elitists.

I didn't look for this other Jesus, but I tried to gauge his influence as I began to hatch new schemes of bloody mayhem. It was by chance, then, that I saw Jesus of Nazareth once, in the synagogue in Magadan, which overlooked the Sea of Galilee, the Kinnereth. I was to meet a man one afternoon in front of the synagogue who needed a tent made, and as I waited a loud argument began inside. Curious, I stepped through the doorway to see what was happening.

"Doing good does not include healing on the Sabbath unless a life is in immediate danger!" shouted a man near the lectern. By his long peyot and meticulous attire he appeared to be a Pharisee of significant age and rank. Two other Pharisees flanked him to either side, heads nodding approvingly. There was a scattering of other men in the room, and at least two of them didn't appear to be siding with the Pharisees.

The man the Pharisee was shouting at kept his hands calmly folded in front of him. "Have you healed someone in immediate danger on the Sabbath?"

The Pharisee huffed in derision. "No, *Rabbi* Jesus, but that is irrelevant to your blasphemy. You used the power of the devil to heal a man here in God's house on his holy day, claiming to be 'doing good.' You will be condemned, punished, and forbidden to teach."

The man nodded, eyes narrowing. His response was louder this time, more authoritative. "A generation of vipers seeks to condemn the Son of Man for doing the will of the Father. The Sabbath was made for man, not for God. Well might you seek to push back the waters of the Great Deep as oppose His will. Many of the Romans you pretend to hate are more righteous than you, and they will receive more mercy from the Father in my name."

Authority and power thrummed through his voice and countenance, and I could see the Pharisees cringe, which seemed to anger them even more. Before they reacted, though, the man looked at me, and I was undone in his presence.

It felt like thousands of bee stings drilling deep into my flesh and getting hotter with each wave. My muscles quivered, my heart fluttered, and panic filled my mind. I took an involuntary step backward, then another and another until I was outside in the full sun. I bumped into a man standing near the doorway, and he steadied me with a soft imprecation. When I was finally able to break the grip of Jesus's gaze, I turned to find my escape, forgetting about the man I was supposed to meet. I hobbled up the street in a shambling, lurching run, resisting the urge to scream. I kept going for several minutes until finally, after what seemed like two eternities, my heart calmed, the pain subsided, and the panic dissipated.

The dread, however, remained.

O loathsome, murderous man that I was! Whether this Jesus was the long-awaited Messiah or not, he was a far better man than I, powerful in his righteous purpose and faithful to Almighty God. I was a diseased rat in comparison, and I hoped never to see him again, lest the fire of Elijah come down from heaven and consume me.

It took me a few days to fully recover my mind after that experience, and re-stoking my hatred for all things Rome helped, despite what Jesus had said about some of the Romans being more righteous than those Pharisees. With new determination and a promise to myself to keep my rage in better check, I searched out others who shared my passion. They were easy to find in the Galilee with its active Zealot movement, and that gave me renewed purpose.

Within a month, a group of about thirty of us wreaked havoc on two small Roman garrisons in hit-and-run attacks. Our success made us too confident, though, and we underestimated our enemy. Had I had the common sense to realize that the Romans would surely try to place more spies among us, I would not have taken information from a relatively new recruit like myself. But I did, and I feverishly encouraged us to attack a small six-wagon Roman supply caravan guarded by less than thirty men, traveling north toward Caesarea Philippi.

The hastily-prepared plan called for us to attack near the end of the third watch, when the sentries would be least alert. We would come from two directions, rising up from among small stands of trees to fire a volley of arrows at the sentries before charging in among the low tents with swords and spears to hack, slash, and stab anything that moved. In less than a minute we would break off, disappearing into the trees and low hills and easily outdistancing any pursuers.

The time came, and our anticipation was high.

As we released our volley of arrows, though, the plan fell apart.

The Romans were all awake. Several soldiers leaped out of tents and drew fletching to cheek as we raced toward them, while others drew forth shields hidden in the wagons and prepared a defense. About a third of our number turned and ran, which was wise, as we'd lost all tactical advantage. The rest of us increased our speed and barreled into the fight, using our momentum to some benefit.

It wasn't nearly enough. Roman blood was spilled that night, but wreck and ruin were the ultimate outcome for us.

By the next morning I was secure in a Roman prison cell, awaiting sure judgment of death.

And then, just weeks later, Jesus of Nazareth died instead, and I was unexpectedly on my way to a very uncomfortable reunion with my family.

CHAPTER 3

For the wrath of man worketh not the righteousness of God.

James 1:20, KJV

When I arrived at the door to my parents' house and knocked, I was wet and bedraggled from the hard rains. My only possession was the ragged prison robe I wore—I didn't even have sandals. My sisters opened the door, and I barely recognized them. I was twenty-one, which meant Salome was eighteen and Mara sixteen—both women where girls had once stood. They just stared at me until my mother arrived. Bless her soul, she at least tried to appear happy that I had returned alive. She escorted me inside after a brief and awkward hug, and then set about to find me some clothes and prepare a meal. I think taking care of me gave her something to do and distracted her from the shame I brought to the family, so I let her minister without objection.

My father would not embrace me, nor would he speak to me, but I could see the emotions at war behind his eyes, and I couldn't tell which were winning. Was he at least happy that his boy who had so idolized the Romans in his youth now defied them? Or was I simply and forever the unfaithful lout who had abandoned his parents and his sisters and gone off killing, pillaging and whoring? Someday, I feared I would need to tell him my full story, though perhaps it would be better to bury it.

At supper the day after I arrived, he finally spoke to me, though without using my name. "Two centurions came to the house before you arrived yesterday. They were angry. They said you were a murderer and a rebel who didn't deserve to be free."

I blinked at him, then took a long, slow breath before nodding. "They're right. I don't deserve to be free."

"Yeshua," chided my mother. I was glad she had used her nickname for me, because being called Jesus was painful, even though it was a common name.

"Did you kill a Roman?" asked my father. I couldn't tell from his tone what answer he hoped to hear. I glanced at Salome and Mara, who looked down at their plates, then at my mother, who was staring at her hands in her lap.

"Yes." I focused on my father and tried to measure that war in his eyes again. "Several of them, including two of those who murdered my friend Alon." I thought I would feel pride in those last words. I didn't. I looked down at my own plate, which was filled with so much more than our meager meals at the prison, so much more than I deserved.

My father was still for several moments, then pushed his plate forward and folded his hands in front of him. "Did you father any children?"

"Abbas," my mother objected, but then she looked at me with worry in her eyes.

My sisters continued to stare at their food.

"No," I replied. "Well, I don't believe so." I couldn't look at my mother. I didn't want to see her disappointment at having such a lecherous son.

My father nodded without emotion. "How long do you intend to stay?"

I honestly had no idea. I could have tried to strike back out on my own instead of returning to my parents' house, but I had neither money nor tools. I didn't even have shoes.

And I was so very tired.

"I don't know," I replied after a few moments of intense silence. "My fate is obsidian to me." I had heard an old man say that once, maybe in Joppa, and it seemed to fit. "I will…I will figure that out soon."

For the next six months I didn't do much tentmaking, even though Master Iddo came and invited me to assist him, exhibiting unwarranted sympathy. I made a few tents with him, but I spent most of my time attempting to sow the seeds of sedition in Jerusalem and elsewhere, in some cases trying to capitalize on the crucifixion of Jesus, which had caused a considerable stir.

I had lost the temper of my edge, though, and I failed to make many converts. Collectively we accomplished next to nothing. I found one centurion who wasn't as cautious about his own security as his companions, but as I studied him I discovered that he was incredibly kind and generous to everyone he met, Jew and Roman alike. He had an *agnomen*, an honored nickname—Egyptus—which set him apart as a hero for some great deeds done in the lands of the pharaohs, and yet he wasn't a smug Roman champion who kept his vassals and vanquished foes under his heel. Weren't the dirty Jews his enemy? It didn't make sense, but little in my life had.

My father died that autumn of a failure of his heart, and my pathetic little rebellion came to a final close. My mother and sisters needed the income I could bring as a tentmaker, and for some other reason they seemed to want me there, inexplicable as that was. And so I returned to making tents full-time with Master Iddo, reminding myself constantly that making tents was the only value I possessed.

Within the year, I completed my apprenticeship with Master Iddo and became a journeyman tentmaker, which allowed me to open my own official shop in the space adjoining our house where my father had done his basketmaking. I worked long hours, and my mother and sisters showed a remarkable knack for finding customers, so we lived as comfortably as the working class in Jerusalem could generally expect.

It was not many months after becoming a journeyman that my mother started pestering me to find a wife. The new challenge seemed to please her immensely. I was nearly twenty-three, an infamous pariah, and beginning to seem like a leper since I hadn't married already. I hadn't given marriage much serious thought, because I was convinced that no woman would—or *should*—want to be with me. It didn't seem right that anyone should be subjected to living with me, much less bearing my children, who would grow up under a shadow of shame. So I did my best to ignore my mother and hoped she would ease up. Of course, as is the way with all mothers, the opposite happened.

I was working in my shop on a crisp, clear, late-winter morning when I heard a soft rap at the inner entryway. I lifted my head to look, and Chanah, who I hadn't spoken to since running away after Alon's death, stood in the doorway, a hesitant yet proud smile faintly discernible on her lips. She wore an elegant cream-colored cloak over a long flowing tunic that was nearly as purple as the finest Roman garment. But what really caught my eye, what caused my heart to skip in its beating, was that her dark hair was down and braided in the way of some of the Greeks. She was twenty-one, a grown woman, and showing herself to me with her hair down!

I had, of course, seen many women in my time who let their hair down outside of their homes. I'd even spied a fair number of prostitutes with their hair shorn shorter than a man's. But I had never seen this, exactly. Here in my mother's home stood a veritable green-eyed goddess, demanding that I notice her in all her divine beauty, which indeed I did.

All thought fled my mind while my heart struggled to regulate itself and my loins stirred rebelliously. I had all but forgotten about Chanah. I had seen her occasionally since my return, but whenever I did I turned away in embarrassment and sorrow. I had heard she was becoming a fine seamstress, sought out by many of the nobility. She spoke better Greek than I did, and some Latin as well.

She didn't say a word, just looked at me. As I studied her face, it became clear, even without any words, that she was not offering herself to me. She was demanding me. What had my mother told her? Why would Chanah do this? She knew I had abandoned my family, that I had been a brigand and a whoremonger. I shuddered to think that she would likely have learned I was a murderer as well. She knew, as did all the city, that I had been the spotted lamb set free in the place of the crucified King of the Jews. The Sanhedrin, to please the Romans, had made sure my name was to be loathed.

I was bewildered beyond reckoning. I was horrified beyond measure. I was elated beyond belief.

I finally stood, as was proper, and bowed my head. "Chanah." I kept my gaze on the floor in front of her. "Why have you come?"

There was a long pause, as uncomfortable as untreated ram's hair against the most tender skin. I was finding it hard to focus my vision, and my chest was compressing.

"Your mother invited me several weeks ago, Jesse Bar Abbas—" I was glad she used my new name of Jesse "—but I was not ready yet."

"Ready?" I asked in a whispered croak.

"I didn't come because of your mother's wishes. I came because of mine." She took a step toward me, and I looked at her face.

My knees felt weak, my feet unsteady. My mind was swimming in waters as thick as the Dead Sea.

"I have thought about you many times since the day we learned of Alon's death," she said. "I know you mourned him deeply, as did I. I know you sought vengeance for him. I know you've suffered. And I know…" She stuttered, but when she continued her voice was strong. "I know that you have caused others to suffer."

Tears came to my eyes as I nodded. "I am a wretched man."

"No." Her voice was firm. "You are not. I see how you treat your mother and your sisters, Jesse, and I see that you have begun to master your anger."

I laughed at that, though the sound lacked humor. "I have mastered nothing. I am a broken vessel. There is no longer any oil to fire my anger, that is all."

She took two more steps forward, and before my mind could register it, she had my face in her hands, holding me as a wife would handle her husband.

"We are all broken vessels, Jesse, but we can be remade. This world is cruel and difficult, but we can overcome it. You have proved that to me. You came back and endured your shame, when most would not have. You take care of your mother and sisters, and you deny yourself much...of what you could have."

My heart was on fire, for I had caught the suggestive pause. But how could it be? Of all the men of Israel on the earth, why would she want *me*?

The tears began to flow freely, dripping down my cheeks and onto her hands. I should have tried to wipe them away, but I felt frozen in the moment. Chanah was crying as well, but less than I was. "I massacred the Romans who killed Alon. I have murdered others as well, including a Jew who simply said something in favor of the Romans that offended me."

She nodded, and her hands pressed more firmly on my face. She didn't act surprised, though. "That is the past, Jesse, and your future is different. I have seen it."

I have seen it. Those were the words of a prophetess, but I barely registered the thought. I was too harrowed up by my sins.

"Jesse." Her tone was both imploring and authoritative. "I wish to be your wife. I want you for my husband."

I was so shocked my sobbing suddenly stopped.

"Do you hear me?" she asked.

"But...but your father," I finally said. "We have no contract, and I cannot pay him yet."

She smiled, locking my eyes with hers. "We will have the *ketubah*, but my father does not require payment. I have discussed this with him, more boldly than a daughter should, but God wills it, and so do I."

I thought I had known Chanah before, but now? She was Esther in her glory, boldly saving her people. And I was...I was not worth saving.

"But why me, Chanah? I am not...I am not worthy of you, or of anyone."

"Be careful not to compare me to 'anyone,'" she said with a chiding smile. "I know what I know. Do you not want me?"

That was unfair. Of course I did. No man on earth could have looked at Chanah at that moment and denied her. It was impossible. Unthinkable.

"I do want you," I said reverently, "but I still don't understand."

"You will, my betrothed. Prepare your groomsmen."

To this day I'm surprised she went through with it. Given who I was, and the many others she could have chosen, it is still inconceivable. I prepared the *ketubah* for my soon-to-be father-in-law to sign, and I cobbled together a payment as well, though he objected. It wasn't as much as it should have been—not for her—but it was all I could give at the time. And Chanah insisted that we not wait any longer.

Re-living the seven days of our honeymoon celebration has carried me through many a dark time since. She was an angel, a jewel in the crown of heaven, and yet she deigned to be my wife. My mother was overjoyed, as were my sisters. Chanah and I moved into the new room I prepared in the home of my mother, and I worked hard in the hope of becoming a master tentmaker. I was still a wretched soul, but I wanted to do well for her, and that desire drove me as nothing else ever had—not even my fury toward the Romans.

I didn't tell Isaac about the vengeance I had taken for his son until several weeks after the celebration, and I wasn't sure how he would react. I think he was pleased, though, and it seemed to give him some closure. Sariah was not as gratified when she found out, though she said little and accepted the outcome. She worried for her daughter, and I didn't blame her. Chanah's parents didn't see me as the best option for their wonderful, beautiful, talented daughter, and indeed I wasn't.

We welcomed our first child—a girl we named Hannah—a year later. We buried her after only a week. An infection had attacked her lungs, and the physicians could do nothing to help. At least she wouldn't be cursed with having me as a father, I reasoned, and while that should have made me happy, my precious Chanah was heartbroken to lose her little Jewish princess. At the sight of her tears on the first day of mourning, I went into a rage that lasted two days and nearly destroyed my small workshop.

But while Chanah was deeply saddened, she seemed to understand better than most people that such was the way of life. She allowed me to release my grief and then kindly asked if I would help her deal with hers. I felt the selfish fool, then, and I did my best.

Our next baby came two years later. Joel lived just two hours after opening his eyes and beholding his radiant mother, and then his heart stopped beating. Jehovah was surely his God, and he was only willing to give us Joel for a short time. Again I raged, though this time after ensuring Chanah was okay.

Indeed she was, and it perplexed me deeply. She talked often about how merciful God had been to her, and how she trusted in his plan. That was incomprehensible to me, though I had no standing from which to argue. She renewed her work with vigor, as I did mine, and she coaxed me to the synagogue with her on many occasions. Four months later, she entered the workshop at noonday and announced in nearly breathless tones, "I have met a man."

My blood froze. I had dreaded that such a moment would come. That she'd met someone better didn't surprise me. That she'd tell me so frankly, though, and as if I might somehow welcome the news, was unexpected. Fear and shock kept my voice soft while my heart pounded. I could only manage, "What?" Then I braced for what would come next—her request for a bill of divorcement.

"Jehovah! He came, Jesse. He was here, in the flesh."

She had met Jehovah? *The* Jehovah?

"It was him, Jesse." Tears ran down her cheeks as she rushed to my stool and cupped my cheek in her right hand. "Jesus who was crucified, he is Jehovah, the great Messiah, and he arose from his tomb as foretold by the ancient prophets. Afterward he appeared to his disciples, and they now spread his fame and his word throughout the land. One of those disciples is Saul of Tarsus, a student of Gamaliel who once persecuted those who believed in Jesus. I met Saul today, Jesse—and through him, Jehovah—and my soul cannot be contained for joy."

I still felt confused. Had a man of God just stolen my wife from me or not? It felt like what I deserved, but I wasn't going to be happy about it.

"Then you should go to him," I said. "You deserve to be happy."

She cocked her head like a sparrow interpreting a strange sound, and then clapped both hands on my shoulders. Her laugh surprised me almost as much as her initial words had. "No, my dear husband, you adorable jester. You do not understand. Saul is a personal witness of Jesus, whose disciples call him the Christ. He is Messiah for the whole world, not just the Jews. He appeared to Saul almost two years after his crucifixion, and he...well, you need to hear Saul's story yourself, Jesse. It will heal your soul."

So she *wasn't* leaving me? She was only trying to...'heal my soul?'

I took her hands off my shoulders and squeezed them lightly. "My heart is glad that you have found this happiness, but I cannot bear to hear such a story, nor would it be of any benefit to me. This Jesus—the Christ, as you say—suffered in my place. It should have been me who died that day."

Chanah freed her hands and cupped my face in them, leaning close and focusing intensely. "He knew he would die that day, Jesse. He could have prevented it—even Pilate knew that. Before Pilate was exiled he confided to many of his servants that he expected Jesus to free himself. But Jesus needed to suffer and die and live again so that we might all be redeemed from our sins through faith and repentance and live forever in the presence of God. I don't understand it all yet, but he didn't just suffer for you. He suffered for all of us, and my heart is near bursting at the blessed salvation he offers us. He *won*, Jesse. The Messiah fulfilled his mission and secured the greatest victory of all time. And Hannah and Joel? They are with him in paradise. *Our* children. We will see them again, Jesse. Death is no barrier to us now. I felt it, and Saul confirmed it today."

I looked at her for several seconds, blinking as I tried to think. I felt warm inside, but I ascribed that fully to the joy *she* was feeling. I really did want her to be happy. The thought of approaching these disciples of Jesus, though…I couldn't do it, and no amount of coaxing—even from Chanah—would change that.

"I will need some time, dear wife," I finally said, removing her hands from my face and gently kissing each of them. "Be happy for what you have found."

I expected her to press, but she stood straight and nodded with a knowing smile. "God is altogether good." She smiled brightly as she turned and left the workshop.

For the next four years, Chanah was unable to conceive. The physicians determined she had become barren, and I resigned myself to this fact. It wasn't fair to her, but it seemed merciful to any potential children. Chanah was often discouraged, but she prayed day and night, patiently importuning the Lord for another child and expressing gratitude for the two she had already been given. That still made little sense to me, but if it gave her strength and hope I was satisfied.

She continued to meet with the Christians, who had gained no small notoriety, especially after two of their leaders healed a lame man at the temple and then miraculously escaped from prison. Soon after, she stopped attending the synagogue, which alarmed her parents at first, though she slowly but surely reassured them that she was both sane and happy. She even invited the chief 'apostle' of this band of messianic zealots, a man named Simon Peter, to her parents' home to teach their family and friends, including my mother and sisters.

I didn't object, of course, because I had no authority in any faith. Chanah was so much the better of us—in charity, humility, intelligence, kindness, faith, and courage. Neither could I join her, as I explained repeatedly. If indeed Jesus of Nazareth was the Messiah, he had no need or desire for me. I was embarrassed to even hear his name. My life was built on sand in a fierce hurricane, the house barely standing. She was a mountain, firm and immovable in the storm.

CHAPTER 4

*Because the foolishness of God is wiser than men;
and the weakness of God is stronger than men.*

1 Corinthians 1:25, KJV

As the confusing new doctrine of the Christians swirled about me, I focused on my craft and worked harder. I wasn't a true master, and only the lesser nobles showed any interest in my work, but I was becoming skilled enough that every few weeks a desperate family would send one of their boys to me asking for him to be apprenticed.

I refused all such requests, despite Chanah's objections, and for a time they stopped coming. But one day a dirty but determined young boy showed up at my door, and he watched me intently for a few minutes without saying a word as I worked on reinforcing a seam. His hair was dark as night, but his eyes were a startling light blue that unnerved me to look at.

"Who are you?" I finally asked gruffly. "Do you have an order to convey or a message to deliver?"

The boy shook his head, seeming to wilt under my rough manner. Then he straightened and looked me in the eye. "No, master, I come…I come to learn. I want to be a tentmaker."

I shook my head and returned to my task. I thought he would go away after a few minutes. Didn't everyone know by now that I didn't want an apprentice? But he was still there when I finished the seam. "Sorry, boy," I said, trying to take some of the edge off my hard tone. "I work best alone, and I'm no master."

"I will do whatever you ask, and all of the cleaning," he offered, undeterred. "I am strong for my age, and I don't eat much, and—"

"Hold on." I lifted a hand and stood up from my stool, towering over him. It was time to be more forceful so I could get back to work…and back to forgetting the past, which would be nigh on impossible to do with an apprentice to remind me of the innocent boy I used to be. "I told you I don't want—"

His eyes captured mine. They weren't pleading for pity or demanding anything, as children's eyes often did…and even those of many adults. They were hopeful and resolute. The boy bravely stood his ground. He seemed to emanate determination, tinged by desperation.

I felt a chord of my heart being plucked as if by a great finger. I narrowed my eyes and shook my head, resisting the thought forming deep in my mind, the thought that I could make use of an apprentice if I really wanted to.

"You never gave me your name." I was buying time, but my words were sterner than I'd intended.

"My name is Elhanan," he replied softly, as if ashamed, though it was a fine name, meaning 'God is good.' It seemed a mockery, of course, that a boy by that name would show up at my workshop. I had once had a friend by the same name. The Romans had caught him stealing and beaten him until he was crippled, and he had hung himself. That had been seven years before.

"How old are you?"

"Ten...almost eleven."

My eyebrows rose. He looked nine at best. "And who are your parents?"

The boy shook his head. "I have no parents."

"An orphan?" I asked, surprised. "Where do you live?"

"Outside the walls," he said, then cast his eyes down.

In the hills? Surely the boy could have appealed to the priests, who could have found him work as a house slave for a noble or a wealthy merchant. Why would he come by himself to the tent-makers' quarter of the city looking to be an apprentice?

"Who *were* your parents?" I asked, my curiosity peaking.

Elhanan looked back up at me and shook his head again. "I was very young when they left. Two, I think."

"When they left?" There was a big hole there somewhere. "Where did they go, and who took care of you?"

He shrugged. "A family took me in for a while, but then I left to...to find my parents." He looked down again, but not before I caught the tears forming in his eyes. The room became very silent, and even the street outside seemed hushed.

"You didn't find them." He didn't affirm it, but I knew. "And then you decided to live on your own? How did you survive?"

He didn't answer at first, just stood there studying his slipshod feet. When he looked up at me again, his eyes still glistened. "I followed Peter the Apostle of Jesus of Nazareth, and I helped people...and they gave me food."

Jesus of Nazareth again? Would I never get away from him?

I whistled softly as I shook my head. This boy had traveled all over Israel, without a family, following the acolyte of an itinerant preacher who claimed he was the Messiah, and he was *nine*? For the moment I forgot Chanah's strong beliefs about this Jesus.

I forgot how he had affected me the first time I had seen him. "You know Jesus is dead, don't you?"

"No, master, he's not," said the boy with a spark of fire in those sharp blue eyes.

I had to admire his persistence, but I nearly chuckled at his naiveté. "I saw him die, boy." I was jolted with the realization that Chanah believed as this boy did, and that I would never say such a thing to her.

Elhanan nodded almost imperceptibly. "So did I, but I was only four." He didn't blink, didn't turn away, didn't cry, didn't frown—just stated it flatly and with the gravity of a wizened cleric.

Now there was a riddle. How many four-year-old boys would have been out that night in the storm, much less near Golgotha? And how many would be able to remember it? Was Elhanan mentally unstable? Or was he just so desperate he had come to believe whatever adults with food to share had told him? The thought struck me that he might be lying about not having a family—that he might be a runaway—and I could be in trouble if I took him on as an apprentice without their knowledge and consent.

"And how do you know he's alive?" I challenged him. I had asked Chanah the same question, several times.

He shrugged. "My heart knows it's true, and I've met most of the people who saw him…um, resurrected."

I didn't believe that, of course, but for some strange reason I liked this plucky boy. Part of me wanted to accept him, despite the risks. But I couldn't, and if the Christians were helping him it wasn't like I would be sending him away to starve. I was about to tell him that when Chanah stepped into the workshop through the door to the house.

"I thought I heard you speaking with someone, dear husband, and it sounded like—"

As I turned she stopped, having noticed Elhanan. Her brow furrowed slightly, and then a hand went to her mouth as her look changed from puzzlement to surprise to…something I couldn't quite describe. Something tender and protective.

"It's a boy. I *dreamed* this." Her words were nearly a whisper, said to herself. After a moment of silent reverie, she looked at me and tilted her head. I was trying to come up with some sort of introduction when she walked over to Elhanah and grasped him by the shoulders. "Where did you come from?" There was awe in her voice.

Elhanan looked up at her shyly. "I came to be an apprentice tentmaker."

"That is good." Chanah gave a little laugh as if the most joyous thing had just happened. "We have been waiting for you."

My mind spun, and I could only watch helplessly as she brought him in for an embrace. I was about to object when the words caught in my throat. Chanah was veritably glowing, the joy on her face a wonder to behold.

Finally, Chanah released him. "I'm sorry, dear husband. I should not make this decision alone. We could use an apprentice, though, correct?"

Hope leaped in the boy's eyes, and my heart cringed at the thought of crushing that hope. Between that and Chanah's excitement, all my reasons for turning him away evaporated like the dew. So I nodded, trying not to show resignation.

Before I could say anything, the boy blurted out "Thank you!" and rushed from the doorway, springing down the street like an excited hare. "I'll be back in the morning," he yelled over his shoulder before either of us could think to stop him.

Chanah headed for the door as if she were about to race after him. She stopped at the threshold, though, and turned to me. "Thank you, Jesus Barabbas." Her use of my original name seemed purposeful. She strode forward and caressed one of my cheeks with a hand. I felt boundless joy at that touch, and nothing else mattered.

"Good morning, Master Barabbas," said Elhanan cheerfully.

The boy stood in my doorway once again, as promised, the pre-dawn light barely making his face discernible. I was on my stool looking at a sketch made for me by a minor merchant of growing repute. He'd commissioned a festival tent. It would be a challenge, reflecting his ambitions, and it wouldn't be cheap. I had taken a risk in accepting the job, but my confidence in my craftsmanship was growing. My family would greatly benefit if I could pull off something like that.

The boy looked so thin. I hadn't noticed the day before. "It's Jesse, not Barabbas."

"Oh, I'm sorry, master." He bowed his head.

"It's okay. Have you eaten, boy?" My voice sounded like I already considered myself his teacher.

He nodded. "Some roots, master."

Some roots. I knew what it was like to eat roots. "Go into the house and get some breakfast, and then come back and we can talk."

He rushed to obey, his eyes wide with betrayal of his hunger.

I returned to my inspection of the sketch. Within a few minutes he was back.

Chanah followed him in, a small smile playing at the corners of her beautiful lips. She nodded at me as she approached.

"He was very hungry." She tousled his hair, and then tousled mine, shattering the master-student image I was trying to create. On purpose, I was sure.

I motioned Elhanan toward the only other stool in my workshop, trying to look authoritative.

Immediately upon sitting down, he looked at Chanah and apologized. "I didn't mean to eat so much, mistress."

I almost smiled but caught myself.

Chanah laughed lightly, resting her hand on my shoulder as she studied the small waif staring at us with wide, guilty eyes.

"You didn't eat too much, Elhanan," she said gently, "but I hope you saved room for dinner tonight."

I could almost see him salivating at that, and his eyes went even wider.

"And of course you will be staying with us. We have room." The boy's jaw dropped, and Chanah laughed again as she reached forth tender fingers to lift it back into place. Then she turned to me and whispered, "I am with child, dear husband."

Then *my* jaw dropped. She whisked away without another word, as if she had just told me the weather was fair. She was in the house before I could recover. I tried to splutter something, and Elhanan's eyes narrowed as if he were trying to solve a puzzle. I scowled and tried to think. How was she pregnant? Wasn't she barren? Had the doctors been wrong? Why was she so happy? Shouldn't she be scared of the same tragedy repeating itself? I knew that *I* was afraid…and mainly for her.

After a few moments I could feel Elhanan's stare, so I motioned him over to stand next to me. He leaped off the stool and was at my side in two heartbeats.

"First lesson," I said, "is how to tell a good sketch from a bad one. If the plan is bad, the tent will be, too."

Two weeks later, I found myself nearly passed out with exhaustion after staying up all night to finish the merchant's pompously-complicated tent. I had sent Elhanan to bed hours before, and it seemed all I could do to make it to my own bed, with the first glimmers of dawn showing outside. As I shuffled across the front room of the house, I noticed something odd, and then I realized there was a stranger there, along with my mother.

"Who is this?" I asked, squinting in the dim candlelight at the shadowy, slim figure crouched in the corner as if she were afraid of me. My mother was stooping near her, retrieving a clay cup from the floor.

"She did some mending for us and brought it over," replied my mother, straightening but not looking at me, as if that were the most normal thing in the world to say at that time of day.

"We do our own mending," I said, leaking a bit of annoyance into my tired voice. "We don't need to pay anyone else for that." I rarely asserted myself that way, but sometimes I forgot who I was, and how miraculous my present circumstances were.

My mother turned and gave me one of the kindest looks she'd given me since I was a young teen boy. "Business is good, your work sells well, and we can afford to help another. This is better than just giving alms. She wants to work."

That gave me pause, but I was still agitated and exhausted. "I already have an apprentice to help us, and Chanah is an expert seamstress."

My mother carried the cup toward the small table in the opposite corner, ignoring my objection. "You were up all night working. Does that mean the tent is complete?"

"Yes." I turned to study the woman again. She looked older than my mother, though probably not by much. She wouldn't look at me, instead staring silently at our well-swept floor. My mother returned and crouched beside her.

"Fine." I didn't have to force gruffness into my voice. "But who is she? I haven't seen her before." At least I didn't think I had.

"Her name is Jarah bat Elizur. She has recently come from Bethany. She was widowed at the time of the crucifixion, and she sews a fine seam."

There she went again, mentioning *that* crucifixion as if it were the only one that had ever occurred. There were still crucifixions happening, though they weren't as common as before. This Jesus they called the Christ certainly hadn't died in the hearts of a great many people, including my mother and my wife. And Elhanan, of course. He knew he was forbidden to talk about Jesus with me, but I heard him talking with others. The boy was a firebrand for that so-called martyr. I had started to worry about him getting crosswise with one of the local rabbis, though Chanah just seemed enchanted by the prattling blue-eyed charmer.

I didn't like remembering that particular crucifixion day. It still made me feel like a coward, doubly so because I hadn't truly returned to the revolution afterward. Instead, I had made only a weak effort, then given in and taken up my trade. I was an obedient Roman subject.

I sighed, my mind not working well in its sleep-deprived state. "I hope she wasn't married to one of the thieves hung up next to that Jesus."

Dead silence invaded the small space, and I cringed as I realized I had probably just said a very foolish thing. But how could I have known? I was about to excuse myself when the woman spoke.

"My husband was no thief," she said softly but clearly and with a touch of raw emotion. "And no Roman hung him."

Now I was even more confused. "Who else but the Romans?"

A sharp intake of breath from my mother told me I'd unknowingly set my foot in it again. Why had I opened my mouth? Who was her husband? How did he die on that hill, if not by the Romans? And when was I going to get to my bed and sleep?

The woman hesitated, but at a nod from my mother she swallowed and rose to her feet. She was tall, nearly as tall as I, and as broad-shouldered as many a man, which I hadn't noticed when she was hunched on the floor. "His name was Judas, called Iscariot," she said softly. Her voice was louder when she added, "And it was Jesus who betrayed him."

She stopped abruptly, her shoulders drooping, then added a few more words in barely a whisper. "Or at least it seemed so at first."

My mother looked at the woman with glowing compassion. "Jarah, I know this is difficult for you, and seeing the man who was released in Jesus's place brings back the anguish." She moved to stand next to me and patted me on the shoulder, still looking at Jarah. "Now tell us again from your husband's own account what happened."

Wait. Judas called *Iscariot*? Suddenly I remembered. The man who had betrayed Jesus to the chief priests. The man who had taken thirty pieces of silver to deliver his master into their hands. The man who had hanged himself a week later. Some said he had returned the money. Others said he had used it to attempt to bribe his way into a Roman heiress's arms. There were at least a dozen other stories, all of them grotesque or sultry. All I knew was that Jesus had been exposed as a powerless Messiah, and that the Romans still preened and postured about it as they lifted their noses at all of Jewry.

Jarah was about to begin when my mother held up a hand and turned to me. "Where is Elhanan? I wish him to hear this."

My mother was certainly in command that morning, but instead of complaining about it I simply shrugged. "I sent him to bed. He should wake soon." No sooner had I finished than Elhanan came rushing through the outer doorway, skidding to a stop before us, panting slightly.

"Done, master," he said, bowing his head. "The new cilicium will be delivered before first watch tonight.

I was momentarily baffled. "What?"

"The dyed camel-hair cloth you talked about with Master Belem. The deep blue you wanted. I know his apprentice, and he's up even earlier than I am, and so…" He stopped, apparently unsure whether I was pleased or upset. I wasn't sure what I was. Who was this strange kid?

"Oh, yes, um…well done, Elhanan." I hadn't actually asked him to order it yet, though I had planned to that very day. "Now why don't—?"

"Good morning, all." Chanah swept into the room looking positively radiant and regal, which was probably because she hadn't had to sleep next to me and endure my snoring and occasional nightmares. She cupped my face in her left hand and kissed me on the cheek, and all my thoughts turned to how beautiful and perfect she was. She greeted my mother, then Elhanan, and then Jarah, whom she obviously already knew.

"Who is our visitor?" asked Elhanan eagerly, addressing Chanah, not me.

Chanah smiled at him like…well, like his own mother would, I supposed, and I wasn't sure that Elhanan wouldn't be claimed one day by Chanah as a son. She had already come to love that boy fiercely, though sometimes I wasn't sure whether a big part of that was their faith in Jesus Christ and his controversial teachings.

"Listen to mother Jarah's story first." So, she'd been listening.

She lifted an arm, and Elhanan slid underneath it. I was left with nothing to say, and I felt like a foreigner to the entire situation anyway, so I sat on a nearby stool and pretended attention. In truth, I was thinking about how I was going to work that cloth—an exotic blend that I would use to trim the command tent of a high-ranking centurion. When Jarah spoke, though, there was something in her tone and bearing that drew me in.

"My husband was one of the first to heed the call to discipleship from Jesus of Nazareth," she began, staring through our southern window at something far, far away. There was a note of proud nostalgia in her voice, and the words flowed as if she had repeated them many times. "He heard him preaching in a synagogue in Capernaum with authority so great that the Pharisees could not confound him, and even the unclean spirits obeyed him." The memory of my first encounter with Jesus flashed brightly in my mind, and it was hard to shake off the powerful terror and helplessness I'd felt, especially when I considered my own status as an unclean spirit.

"He witnessed as Jesus healed the sick in that city, and then immediately pledged his fealty to the man he knew must be the long-awaited Messiah. He followed Jesus diligently, taught with him, and protected him on more than one occasion from mercenaries sent by the Sanhedrin to kill him. He saw him raise the son of the widow of Nain from the dead—a mighty miracle that was!—and then was given charge with Thaddaeus of spreading the Messiah's message in all the areas around Hebron.

"It was in Hebron that my husband first cast out a devil, and he himself became a mighty teacher, convincing many that the Messiah had truly come, that the time of our salvation was at hand. He healed a woman of trembling, mended wounds without leaving a scar, and commanded a lame man to walk. I know, because I was there with him, tending to the sick, helping to feed the poor, and comforting those who mourned. It was a glorious time, heaven's own light shining brightly upon us. But then many of the chief priests in the city became worried.

They began to arrest and question any who professed to be disciples of Jesus."

Her eyes hardened. "My husband was not afraid, and he would not stop preaching Jesus. He and Thaddaeus endured much suffering after being themselves arrested, but they finally convinced a few of the priests that if the Messiah truly had come, it would be wiser to side *with* him than against him. This caused great rejoicing in the city, though not among the scribes and the other chief priests, who were jealous of Jesus...and of Judas called Iscariot, my faithful husband. They could not oppose us, though. No, they could not!" She was very dramatic, and I couldn't decide whether to be annoyed or impressed. Perhaps I was simply too tired to judge it.

"For nearly three years," she continued, "we toiled and taught, first in Hebron and then throughout all of Israel, and after my husband witnessed Jesus cleansing the temple for the second time, he rushed to our home proclaiming that the time had come. The salvation of Israel was at hand!" She raised both hands high, palms upward, her eyes glistening in victorious joy.

She slowly lowered her hands, but her smile stayed. "I was one of the first to greet Jesus when he triumphantly entered Jerusalem to declare his kingship. My daughters laid palm fronds along his path. My sons carried messages to the faithful and made sure the streets ahead were clear. I will never forget the feelings of that day." Her expression suddenly became solemn. "Nor will I forget the feelings of the days that followed.

"My husband supped with Jesus and the other apostles in the upper room of the mansion of Omri the Just. There were plans to be made, and we had pledged our all to see them through. My Judas came home very late that night, and I could tell he was disturbed. He had left that morning with his mind bouncing in the clouds, so I was confused at the change."

I grunted, completely forgetting my manners, which earned me a scolding stare from my mother.

Jarah looked at me, too, so I said what I was thinking. "He was excited about betraying Jesus in the morning but had second thoughts later that night? It is a hard thing to kill a man, even if you think he deserves it."

The room went dead silent, and my mother's stare turned from scolding to a strange mixture of horror and compassion. For me? She knew I had killed before. She had known for a long time, and at one point had resigned herself to the fact that her son would be executed. I hated the look she was giving me, though, and I wished for an outright scolding instead. Why couldn't I just go to my room and sleep?

I looked at Elhanan, who was studying me as if I were a strange new bug.

"My husband never wanted Jesus dead," Jarah said softly with a touch of defiance and…pride? She clearly believed that, despite the facts that proved her wrong.

"He made sure he died, didn't he?" I didn't look at Chanah or my mother after those words slipped out. I truly was tired.

"Did he?" my mother asked. "If he knew, as did the other apostles, that Jesus had more power in a lock of his hair than the entire might of Rome, how would delivering him to a scraggly band of second-rate priests and poor conscripts put him in any danger? I've heard the account of the boy—now a young man—who saw them that night, and the apostles who were there confirmed it. The soldiers were backing away from Jesus. They were rightly afraid of him. The soldiers ran the boy off without any clothes after Jesus healed the soldier's ear, and then Jesus meekly delivered himself into their hands."

My mother had ascended to one of her religious fervors, and it was no use trying to talk her down from it. I could either leave—which would be even ruder than I had already been—or I could hear the story out. At least there might be some entertainment value in hearing the rest. I might even be able to pass the story on to a few of my customers and get both a hearty laugh and some good coin. There were lots of jokes going around among the Jewish nobility regarding the 'false king Jesus,' and I could use that to my advantage.

I wouldn't, though, and not because it was a terrible thought. I didn't like *any* references to that man, so none would come from me, insulting or not. I sighed in resignation.

"You didn't know my husband, Barabbas," challenged Jarah.

Of course I didn't. And it didn't matter.

She continued. "He was a true believer. He knew Jesus was indeed the Son of God, the prophesied Messiah. He endured great persecution for his belief, but he stood strong." Her eyes were like molten gold in the rising dawn, and I had to admire her passion, even if it bordered on crazy. "Those final weeks were hard on him, with all the talk—by Jesus himself, mind you—of his death and that it was somehow necessary. My husband couldn't bear to see him die. He knew there had to be another way. He became convinced that Jesus could find another way, and he pleaded with him for many days."

"I guess I don't blame him for that, Mistress Jarah," I said. "If Jesus truly was the Messiah, as you say, then he would have freed us from our Roman slavery. What possible use could his death serve? We've had more than enough martyrs to warm our blood." My blood was warming as I spoke, the rage which bubbled inside me threatening to take control. But I wouldn't let it. That part of my life was over, and I had accepted it, weak man that I was.

She shook her head slowly, sadly, and then stared at the floor. "I have learned much since then. I, too, thought that when Jesus cleansed the temple again the week of the Passover, my husband had convinced him. Judas was giddy as a young boy at festival that day…and then the next day he was changed." She put her face in her hands and sobbed. My mother sat by her and gave her a comforting embrace. Chanah had tears welling in her eyes as well, which made me feel even smaller.

"We committed a great sin!" she wailed after a few moments, shoulders shaking, face a reddened mess of tears. "But we could have repented! I told him that. I pleaded with him to reconsider his plan to take his own life, but he had sunk too low." Her voice dropped to a whisper. "And then he left me, and I pray for his soul every day, though I don't know if there is any hope or not."

"There *is* hope, Jarah, for both of you," offered Chanah without hesitation. "I do not speak for God, of course, but…have you spoken with Simon Peter about this?"

Jarah looked up with a bewildered, almost horrified look on her face, but then it faded to dull resignation. "I dare not speak of it, but Peter has shown me some kindness, as have a few of the others. They do not speak of it, either."

Chanah looked at me as if I might have some wisdom to add to this most ethereal and confusing conversation.

I just shrugged my shoulders, feeling acutely uncomfortable. I had no idea what I could say that would make sense, much less be helpful.

Chanah stared into my eyes for a few moments and seemed to reach a decision. She turned back to Jarah and grasped both of her hands firmly. "You need to speak with Simon Peter. He will have wise counsel to share. He has admitted his own failings that night as well. He will listen, and I believe he can help."

I waited for Jarah to reply, and she might have nodded slightly, but she seemed utterly spent, and before I knew it my mother was ushering Jarah out the door and accompanying her into the growing morning light, Chanah following. I looked at Elhanan and frowned. The boy's eyes were glistening, but he wasn't looking at me. I was profoundly perplexed, and so I chose not to think about it. It was well past time for sleep, anyway.

CHAPTER 5

*That in every thing ye are enriched by him,
in all utterance, and in all knowledge;.*

1 Corinthians 1:5, KJV

Many days later I left to deliver the tent trimmed in dark-blue cilicium to the centurion. I mocked the man in my mind for his color choice, which was obviously an attempt to get as close to purple as possible without it actually being purple. True purple would have been seen as presumptuous. Roman politics were as mad as a demon-possessed pig, though I had to admit that Jewish politics weren't much better.

I smiled at the image. Chanah had told me the story of the swine who had run themselves off a cliff to rid themselves of demons, and I sometimes chuckled as I pictured them as Romans, rushing around in frantic confusion playing their grand game of back-stabbing nobility and pillaged largesse.

The centurion was stationed in the fortress at Alexandrium, a nearly two-day journey on foot, though he was being promoted and transferred to Caesarea, which must have been why he needed the grander travel tent. Chanah wanted Elhanan to stay behind, so I traveled with our mild-mannered donkey pulling our small cart.

I found lodging in Ephraim the first night, planning to eat a simple supper and retire. However, while the innkeeper was delivering my meal, a middle-aged man with a dark cloak and a tall staff entered the room and sat near me. He greeted the woman, who apparently knew him, and then leaned back and closed his eyes. He hadn't asked for anything, so I watched for a few moments, curious, but then shrugged it off and began to eat.

No sooner had I taken my last bite than the man's eyes popped open and he looked straight at me. I paused before swallowing, taken aback. I had thought him asleep.

"I don't know who you are," he said, "but I was sent to fetch you. And that's odd."

My eyebrows rose. I was sure I had never seen this man before. I had hardly ever been to Ephraim and didn't have any acquaintances there. Nobody had known I was coming.

"Elder, you must be mistaking me for someone else. I am passing through on business, and I was not expected here tonight."

The man nodded. "Yes, I figured as much. But the man who bid me find you was quite certain you would be here tonight. He described you perfectly, so I knew you were him. I let you finish your dinner out of courtesy." He nodded as if that were a satisfactory explanation.

But it wasn't. A cold knife of fear struck my heart. Perhaps some of the rebels were trying to reach out to me. I couldn't allow that to happen, not now, not with Chanah expecting.

"No," I said, shaking my head. "You're mistaken. I am a simple tentmaker, and I leave to deliver my wares in the morning, to the fortress at Alexandrium." I hoped that mentioning a commission from the Romans might scare him off.

"Yes, yes." The man nodded. "He knew this, too, but he wanted me to take you to meet his mother and sisters. I'm not sure why. His mother's name is Salome."

He placed emphasis on her name, and his look intensified as he waited to see if I would react to it. Salome was a very common name, but it seemed clear that *this* Salome wasn't common.

"I am not a rebel," I said, my mind still working the riddle. I recalled one rebel band using their mothers' names as code words or pass phrases, but they wouldn't use a name so common as Salome.

The man chuckled. "Of course you are, just not in the way you think. I'm not that kind of rebel, either, and neither is Salome."

I was growing more unnerved by the second, thinking seriously of leaving that inn and finding another, even if it was the middle of the night before I could lay down my head.

"I'm sorry, Elder," I said, trying not to be offensive, "but I cannot come with you." With that I rose, gathering my cloak and turning toward the stairs to the second floor. After my first step I heard the man rise, too, but I resisted the urge to look back at him. There were a handful of other patrons in the room, so I wasn't overly worried.

"I'm sorry, young man," he said, "but I—"

"It's okay, Thomas."

That voice. It was a woman's voice, melodious and kind, though with a somber mien. It demanded attention, and so I stopped and turned. The man who had offered the strange invitation was bowing to her, and he seemed to be searching for what to say.

She stood just inside the door, looking not at Thomas but at me. Her robe was soft, whiter than most, but her cloak was the most striking robin's egg blue I had ever seen. It bore no tassels to comply with Mosaic law—a bold statement. The veil covering her hair was white and rimmed with gold, and her face was uncovered, something my parents would have considered scandalous in this setting. Unless this was her home? She seemed about the same age as my mother, perhaps a few years older.

"Mary." His lips froze, his face turning bright red as he looked at me, then back at her. "I mean, Salome, what are you doing? You should not be out alone like this, night or day."

She smiled patiently. "It's okay, Thomas. John is with me, but I asked him to wait outside. You can imagine how much that pleases him, especially when I ask you now to do the same."

"But—"

She held up a finger, and he hushed, then turned to look at me again. It was clear he wanted to say something more, his eyes gathering thunderheads, his cheeks reddening. I could well imagine the threats he wished to utter about harming this Salome who was really named Mary. Instead, he mumbled something to her and walked out of the inn.

She patted him absently on the shoulder as he passed, her gaze already pinning me in place. Then she walked to Thomas's table and took his chair.

"Sit, please," she said. "We have things to discuss."

I clumsily moved to the table and sat as requested, wishing I had already left to find another place to bed down for the night.

"Barabbas. That is what they call you."

I could only nod dumbly. I was still trying to figure out if I was in some kind of danger, but my thoughts were sluggish. Who was this woman and how did she know me? Had I ever seen her before?

She continued. "There was a brief time that I resented you, though it was neither logical nor any of your fault." Her voice was still melodious, but the words were somber. I dreaded what would come next, something about *that* day, most likely.

"You have suffered much."

That was not what I had expected to hear, nor had I anticipated the deep empathy with which she said it. I risked a glance at her eyes, even though that was improper. There was no anger, no judgement, and strangely no pity. There was wisdom, though, and a mix of both melancholy and hope.

She smiled, and I found myself unable to look away.

"There is no sin in looking upon my face, Barabbas," she said. "That is a foolish tradition of our stiff-necked priests. I, too, have suffered much, but how can you know that unless you see it in my eyes?"

I didn't know whether to answer the question or not, but I couldn't have articulated an answer anyway.

"I have spent too much time being bitter," she said. "I don't know how he forgives me for that."

"Your husband?" I asked, and suddenly I was worried. If I were seen alone with this woman, and her husband found out, I could be in serious danger, as could she.

She laughed lightly, not seeming worried at all. "Him, too, I guess. Joseph is a good and faithful man, though he has passed from this life to a better. No, I speak of my son."

"This is the son who, um, wanted me to speak with you?"

She cocked her head slightly, a question in her eyes for just a moment, and then she nodded. "Yes, it is. I am Mary, the mother of Jesus who is called the Christ."

Time stopped, and I felt myself redden as the shame rushed to my face. This was *the* Mary, who had watched her son die on the cross in my place? I had seen her, though I hadn't looked closely enough to remember her face. Cold fear locked up my heart, but I had no urge to run. If I was a dead man, part of me was relieved that it would finally all be over.

She must have known what I was thinking. "I bear you no ill will, Barabbas, despite what you may believe. Nor do my son and his true father. I've felt strongly the last few days that I needed to speak with you, but I'm curious as to why."

I gave her a perplexed look. How could she not know why, and how was I supposed to help? What had she meant about her son Jesus's true father? That didn't make sense. If this really was the same Mary, she had only married once according to Chanah. She had no children by another man…unless, of course, the rumors spread by the chief priests were true, which I had a hard time believing of this woman, though I couldn't say why. Of course, maybe they had adopted. I already knew Chanah wanted to adopt Elhanan, so I supposed they might have adopted Jesus.

"There is no reason to talk to me," I answered, looking away.

"Curious," she said, nodding. "Well, my visit is important. Why he wouldn't tell me the real reason is…never mind. I am here to bear witness of something that you need to know, whether you want to or not, whether you choose to do anything about it or not. My son, Jesus of Nazareth, is alive."

That saying was not new. Chanah, my mother, and Elhanan talked about it incessantly. But what did it really mean? It was common to say that an ancestor still lived on in his or her descendants, but she'd made it sound different, unique.

I shrugged uncomfortably. "I don't know what that means."

She nodded knowingly, then continued. "It means that he voluntarily gave up his mortal life on that cross. His physical body was indeed without life for a time. It means, as he had so plainly told us many times, though we refused to understand it, that he took up that same body again in a glorious manner that we cannot yet comprehend, so that we could *all* live again. It means that we can enjoy an abundant life, both here and in the eternities, if we will follow his teachings, which are the teachings of his Father. *Our* Father. I have seen him, Barabbas. Recently, even. I have touched him, embraced him, and felt his tears as he wept for his mother—tears of sadness for what I have suffered, and tears of joy that I finally understand why he came, and why I was chosen for my task.

"Mind you, while I was chosen to be the mother of the Son of God, I was not forced into it. The choice was presented to me—with a warning of how difficult it would be. I chose to accept. And then I bore a son without ever knowing a man, and that miraculous child was and is Jesus the Christ, the Savior of the world, the Messiah of all people, Jew and Gentile alike."

I remembered a little of what Chanah and others had said about Jesus's fabled *virgin birth*. I was as skeptical as ever. "With all reverence for your loss, good woman, I'm sure your son tried, but he hasn't saved us. I have tried, too, but that is in the past. We are still as dogs before the Romans. I don't know when the true Messiah will come, and I honestly don't know if the Messiah really will come. I doubt we deserve it."

Mary had leaned in, nodding as I spoke. When I finished, her eyes sparkled, and she smiled. Again, it was not what I was expecting.

"Oh, he did come, my new friend, and he did save us. The Romans claim power over life, and they often exercise that power, but they have no power over death, though they sorely wish they did. My son's death led to his victory over death, not to defeat at the hands of the proud Romans or Jews. His suffering became the healing balm for our troubled souls. Oh, Barabbas, I wish you could see and hear what I have seen and heard. I am no longer sad but hopeful, no longer distraught but determined. I am a follower of the Christ, and a teacher of his ways. I wish I had more time to teach *you*, but I am called elsewhere. There is a man named Gideon, however, in Jerusalem. I have asked him to teach you, but you must seek him out. It must be your choice. And know this—you are far more than you think you are. We all are. It isn't easy, but once you discover that, your life will change."

I didn't know what to say to that. I felt the strangest warmth and peace. It was like nothing I had ever felt, and yet I couldn't process it. I had been sure I was going to die again, that this grieving mother whose son had been crucified by the merciless Romans had found me and was going to have her revenge. Such was the way of the world. And yet she was ministering to me as an honest rabbi might.

She didn't demand an answer or a promise from me. She just smiled again and rose with stately dignity. I rose with her, bowing slightly.

"Think on it, Brother Barabbas." She left, and I was so astonished by our conversation that sleep eluded me most of that night.

I started my journey to Alexandrium earlier than planned the next day. It was a beautiful morning, nearly cloudless, and the soft, steady breeze made the temperature comfortable. In the back of my mind, I wondered if it could be a sign from God that Mary was right about everything, but as often as the thought came up I pushed it aside. It seemed too simple.

As the day wore on, though, I realized that the novelty of the prior night's experience was not diminishing in my mind. In fact, the event had begun to intrude upon my thoughts with such tenacity that I was getting annoyed. I contended with those feelings, hoping to argue myself out of whatever mental enchantment Mary had cast upon me. In the midst of that internal struggle, I almost didn't notice the pair of bandits as they prepared to leap upon me.

Despite my surprise, my instincts were immediate, my mind instantly clear. Both had small clubs in their hands, and I spied at least one knife tucked into a sash. The fight would need to end quickly if I was to survive. For their part, they would want it to end quickly so that other travelers wouldn't happen upon their perfidy. Since they both came from my right, and my donkey was to my left, I stepped forward and pivoted underneath the donkey's neck to get to his other side. Then I brought the end of my walking staff over the top of the donkey's neck and rammed it into the forehead of one of the bandits. He hadn't been expecting me to strike while hiding behind my donkey, and he staggered backward with a muffled, incredulous curse. His partner instinctively ducked and brought his club up to shield his head. Taking advantage of his pause, I pulled the donkey's lead rope and pushed his rump to turn him, then kicked him softly in the sensitive part of his belly.

The bandit saw what was coming right before it happened and tried to jump out of the way. But even a glancing blow from an angry donkey's hooves can incapacitate a man, and I felt as much as heard at least one of the man's ribs crunch. I quickly moved around the front of my indignant donkey and finished both men off with a few quick strikes of my staff. I didn't kill them, though I could feel the bloodlust rising. I swallowed hard as my hands trembled—not at the shock of being accosted, but at how close I had come to taking another life—and I rushed away, leaving their fate to others who would be passing by. At least they wouldn't be causing any more trouble for a while.

I headed off the main road, part of me illogically fearing pursuit, but also knowing that a random Roman patrol could scoop me up in their net for an indeterminate period of time until everything was sorted. My donkey kept pace willingly, and soon we found a different path, one that I was sure would bring us into Alexandrium on time by another way, since it was only a few miles off. I couldn't stop thinking about the two bandits, and while I was glad I hadn't killed them, I didn't feel bad about how severely I'd injured them. Which led me to the obvious conclusion that I wasn't becoming a good man. I wasn't on a path to redemption, as I had hoped. No, I was just a bad man who had become afraid to kill.

When I arrived at the gates of the fortress, the soldiers made me wait until it was almost sundown to pass through, despite the token given me by the centurion's servant when the tent was requested. It was pretty standard behavior. I was a Jew.

Finally, I passed through and was led to a place where I could unload my cart. Two servants—one Jewish, one Ethiopian—helped me carry the tent materials to the private storage room where they would be kept. A third servant stayed with my donkey. When we reached the storage room, which was on the second level of the inner keep, there was an aide waiting to inspect my craftsmanship. I was surprised when he noted that everything was acceptable. He led me deeper into the keep and one floor higher to a large wooden door banded in blackened steel. He knocked once, then heaved it open and let me in.

The room beyond shimmered as the last light of the waning day invaded through the broad window openings. Torches had already been lit on the otherwise bare interior walls of fine-hewn stone. A simple but well-made bed occupied one corner, while table and chairs of darkened hardwood sat on the other side of the room. Various chests lined the long wall opposite the windows, large and small, some stacked on top of each other.

A tall, light-skinned man with shockingly blond hair stood near one of the windows, intently studying something in the town below. His hands were behind his back, buried beneath his long, red cape. He wasn't wearing any armor, but his tunic was a deep ocher bordered in brilliant and very expensive white. His well-oiled leather sandals were laced intricately up his calves.

The aide left and closed the door.

"You're here for payment," said the man, who I presumed was the centurion who commanded the fortress and had requested the tent. I hadn't met him and didn't even know his name.

"Yes, master," I said.

"My aide indicates it is of acceptable workmanship."

"It was my highest priority."

"I wanted it last week."

I almost wobbled, my mind racing to remember every scrap of the conversation with his servant, which had occurred more than a month before. I was certain I had gotten the date correct, even in the Roman system. I couldn't have been off by a whole week! How could I respond? There was little hope in arguing against a Roman centurion, even before a magistrate.

"You may leave the tent here, but I will not pay you. Next time, remember to deliver on time. Now come and let me show you something."

My heart sank. I could make a plea to the local priests, who might be able to do something if they cared, but this was almost worse than the highwaymen. After a moment I obediently shuffled over to stand next to the harsh centurion.

He pointed out the window, but at what I couldn't tell.

"What do you see?" he asked.

I strained eyes and mind to figure out what he might be meaning, and all I could come up with was, "The day is ending, and the town prepares to sleep."

"That is childish," he chided. "What you *should* see is the open insolence of Roman subjects, beneficiaries of Roman progress, refusing to respect their masters as they cease their labors of the day and begin their rebellious and murderous plotting. Much as you do, *Barabbas.*"

I froze as if encased in a great block of ice from the far north of the world. His servant had known me as just Jesse. I hardly dared breathe, and instead of embracing death I felt panic. I was in the custody of a Roman. *A Roman!* I didn't want to die at the hands of a Roman. Not that my preference would make any difference to the heavens.

"I have been looking for you for some time, as have others. I can see now by your reaction that I have indeed found you. Barabbas the rebel, murderer of Roman legionnaires. I know you were pardoned by the governor, but you were *not* pardoned by me. My brother died in the last caravan attack you and your friends staged, and he was a good man, far better than I. My assignment here has kept me busy, so I was not able to conduct a proper search for you, but then a handful of weeks ago, who do I hear about in Jerusalem but a man who recently bought a tent from the craftsman many call *Barabbas*. It took me only a short time to track down that man, and then I found you.

"You should have stayed hidden. You should have fled Judea." He chuckled softly. "But you didn't. Bold or stupid, I can't decide which."

He turned away from the window, leaving his entire back exposed to me.

I had my knife at my belt. They hadn't even bothered to search me, so pathetic I must have looked to them, despite my size. My hand twitched, my blood jumping to a full sprint. I had the advantage, and I knew where to strike. And then…

I'm not sure what happened. My body calmed. My heart stopped racing, my thoughts became more ordered, and my arm relaxed at my side. No, I would not kill this Roman, or anyone else unless they threatened my family, which this one hadn't.

He finally turned to face me, and the opportunity was over. He had an amused look in his eyes, but he also seemed slightly confused…or maybe disappointed.

"When did you kill your first Roman?" he asked. "I'm curious."

I looked at his knees, not caring to look at the face of my executioner. "More than ten years ago now."

"That long? Where was it?"

I lied. "North of Palmyra, near the border." I couldn't bring myself to mention the first two I had killed outside of Scythopolis, drunken and passed out and unknown to me.

"And why did you kill him? What made you spill blood that first time? It is no easy thing, despite what some may claim."

"Ovidius was his name. The other I don't remember. They accepted a bribe from some bandits across the border and let them rob the caravan of my friend's father. When my friend resisted, another Roman sank an arrow into his back. The rest watched it happen, their swords sheathed." I was angry as I remembered, my tongue becoming looser. I had just insulted the brotherhood of Roman soldiers by accusing some of their number of keeping their swords sheathed when innocents were being assaulted. But I was already a dead man, so what did it matter?

"Ovidius," he repeated. "I have heard that name. He was a wastrel and a disgrace. How do you know you killed the right man?"

"Because they bragged of it. They viewed my friend as just another slaughtered pig."

The centurion nodded pensively, his amusement gone. "And then what did you do, after killing Ovidius?"

It was no use holding back. "I fled and joined the resistance. I killed many more times before I was caught in a well-laid trap. And then...and then I was freed. I should have died that day. The world would surely have been a better place." I turned my back on the vengeful Roman and looked out the window again. The light was nearly gone, the day spent. I waited for what seemed a long time, expecting the blow or strike or stab to come, but it didn't.

"Face me, Jew," the centurion said.

I turned and looked him in the eyes. I would die with an inkling of honor.

"Why did you not strike me earlier? You knew I was a threat, and I exposed my back to you."

I breathed deeply, savoring the air for the last time. "I am done, spent. I am already a murderer, and a thief, and a shame to my people. I hope for the mountains to fall upon me and bury my disgrace. And...and I met Mary, the mother of Jesus of Nazareth last night."

I don't know why I said that last part, but her words had burned into me. Logically, I couldn't have successfully struck him anyway—he had exposed his back on purpose, hoping to goad me into the attempt.

He cocked his head. "I've heard of Mary. And Jesus, of course. Why would that be important?"

"She claims he lives, and she wanted me...wanted *me* to become one of his disciples." My eyes lowered again as I heard those words ring mockingly in the air. Me, a disciple of a holy prophet? Well, perhaps. I had refrained from killing the bandits and striking this Roman, and I had worked hard for my family the past few years, so perhaps my eternal fate had improved, if only slightly.

He folded his arms and nodded. "Yes. His disciples stole his body, and I still can't figure out how." He shrugged. "We searched for weeks, but of course they destroyed it so it couldn't be found. They needed to keep the myth alive that he had mysteriously risen from the dead. It was a clever plan. There are many Jews who believe that he really was the Messiah, and now that he's 'risen' from the dead he will raise an army of the dead to lead the Jewish people to victory over all their enemies." He laughed. "I have been many places, Barabbas, and heard many strange things, but this is as strange as any of them. Ha! An army of the dead!"

I hadn't heard that story, so I remained silent.

"Well," he finally said, "I appreciate your company, Barabbas. I needed to enjoy a hearty laugh. And now, of course, it is time to die. The bandits I sent couldn't do the job, but I didn't blindly trust it to them. I would prefer to execute justice with my own hands, anyway. It is truly a pity that you killed my brother."

As he drew out a long knife, I closed my eyes. So, this was it. Why did I feel so calm? God was about to strike me down by the hand of this Roman and send me to my eternal fate, and I didn't feel…anything. I knew Chanah and our unborn child would be well cared for by my mother and sisters, and perhaps they would have a better life without me. As the time drew out, that became my one firm hope.

After what seemed an eternity, I opened my eyes. The centurion stood before me, knife raised.

"Why do you not strike?" I asked.

"Why do you not defend yourself?" he countered.

I shook my head. "I am guilty. If this Jesus that my wife believes in can truly forgive sins, he won't forgive mine. Not all of them, anyway. I have earned my just reward in the deepest pit of Sheol."

Inch by inch, the knife lowered, the centurion staring hard at me until he seemed to make a decision. "It seems to me that you will suffer more here than if I were to send you to the afterlife," he said, his voice hard. "And I will not sully my honor by striking you down defenseless. My brother, who had more honor than I do, will forgive me. And perhaps this is the gods' just idea of a joke, making us act out this tragedy. Go, Barabbas. Your life is spared today."

I took a moment, trying to determine whether I was dreaming or not, but I came to no conclusions. As I turned to leave, he said, "Wait!" and I turned back.

He retreated to a small, travel-worn chest at the foot of the bed, kneeling to rummage through it for a moment. When he returned, he handed me a small jute bag that clinked with coinage.

"For the tent," he said. "I am a man of honor, and since you did not merit death, I must pay you what I owe."

I was perplexed, my jaw slack, but I took the bag.

"Now, don't go out the door. I will lower you through the window. Your cart and donkey will be returned to your wife by one of my servants in two days. Make sure he does not see you. I will tell my household that you attacked me and that I killed you, and that I had your body removed privily so that none of the Jewish leaders would find out. They are prickly, incessant with their twisted pleadings, and treacherous."

"I know," I said, nodding.

His eyes rounded. "You…know?" He shook his head slowly. "There is more to you than I thought. You like neither the Romans nor your Jewish leaders?"

I shrugged.

He laughed. "That is rich. This barren, forsaken land never ceases to amaze me. Come, I have some rope."

CHAPTER 6

That they should seek the Lord, if haply they might feel after him, and find him, though he be not far from every one of us.

Acts 17:27, KJV

The next day and a half were a haze as I hid during the day and traveled carefully at night, but I made it home without losing either the money or my mind. I arrived only hours before the centurion's servant returned with the donkey and a story about brazen bandits having killed me on the road near the fortress. I was thankful to have spared my beloved Chanah the pain of that cruel lie. She only had to act distraught upon hearing the sad tale from the man.

Several days passed before I could truly believe I had avoided execution by this enigmatic centurion. More than a month passed before I could sleep soundly again. I couldn't decide whether God had mocked me or protected me, but as the memory of my near death faded, that of my strange encounter with Mary magnified.

It was another two months after that before I decided to accept Mary's advice. I'd told Chanah of my encounter with her, and instead of nagging me incessantly to search out Gideon—whom many referred to as 'Father' due to his age and his leading role as a teacher—she patiently encouraged me. She was, of course, eager to answer my questions when I posed them to her, and she knew where Father Gideon could usually be found. Elhanan, on the other hand, would have pestered me without end if not for Chanah's intercession.

I didn't tell Chanah my plan to finally seek out Gideon. One Sabbath evening I waited until my household had left for their worship meeting at the home of one of the apostles. After a few minutes I departed, heading in a different direction, my emotions bouncing between hope and fear. I couldn't decide what I really hoped for, nor could I tell what exactly I feared. I almost turned back several times, but each time I thought of Chanah, and the light of her confidence guided me. I was determined to at least try.

When I arrived at the house where Father Gideon normally taught, I hesitated at the threshold. My heart was beating faster, and I wondered again if I should be there. I could make a strong tent, and I was grateful for that skill, but could I be *redeemed?* My stomach felt like roaring liquid lead, my feet like large stones. I could clearly hear the voice of a man teaching, and by the amount of rustles and murmurs I guessed there were at least twenty other people inside.

It seemed like several minutes before I forced my feet across the threshold. I was hoping to go unnoticed and find a seat in the back, but from the far corner of the large front room, the man who was teaching spotted me immediately. He appeared just as Chanah had described the famed Father Gideon. Most of the three dozen people in the room were seated on the floor and had their backs to me, intent on him, soft torchlight dancing softly across their attentive forms. But when his preaching stopped, of one accord they followed his eyes, turning to stare at me.

It was the worst possible entrance. I thought seriously of backing out and leaving, but Father Gideon stood immediately. His wide grin surprised me, even partially hidden as it was by his bushy brown beard. It was as if he knew me and was elated to see me. I couldn't fathom how either could be true. He stepped carefully between a few of the worshippers as he approached, and then unexpectedly leaped over the shoulders of the last two men sitting between us, surprisingly agile for a man with such strong girth. He took my hand in a strong grip, though I hadn't offered it.

"Welcome, brother. It is a delight to finally meet you." He winked. How did he know who I was? He gently drew me toward an open spot of floor that had mysteriously opened up near the front, and I sat. I didn't look around at the others. I just swallowed, wondering what I had gotten myself into. I was there, though, and I would listen to Father Gideon's sermon. And then…and then I knew not what.

"Master," came a whisper from my left, and I started. I turned my head and saw Elhanan a few feet away. Chanah and my mother were right behind him, my sisters on either side. Chanah shushed Elhanan, then smiled slyly at me. She had known! *How* had she known? She was supposed to be at the house of Andrew the apostle.

My mind was spinning. I looked back toward Father Gideon, who was still beaming as he sat again in front of the group. I sensed that at least most of the eyes had refocused on him, but that was small comfort.

"Brothers and sisters in Christ," Father Gideon said, his warm smile and twinkling eyes taking in the group, "we have another son of our Heavenly Father who wishes to learn more of our

Savior and Master. We welcome you, Jesse, son of Abbas, husband of our sister Chanah." He met my gaze and nodded. "We hope you find peace here this night, Brother Jesse."

I was grateful he had called me by my new name, and 'son of Abbas' was more anonymous than the infamously unflattering Barabbas. Still, some in the room would surely figure out who I was, if they didn't already know.

Father Gideon renewed his sermon, and the focus of the room shifted back to him. At first I was overwhelmed, but the kindly old preacher's voice drew me in, and within a few minutes I was mesmerized. He didn't speak as the priests and rabbis, using archaic and elevated forms of speech and reading long passages of scripture. Instead, he spoke of daily practicalities, of using scriptural teachings to overcome common challenges, and of keeping what he called the 'two great commandments.'

By the end of his sermon I felt at peace. He was a marvelous teacher, and I could understand his words plainly. I became nervous again when he concluded, though, not wanting to garner any more attention. He asked my sister Salome to offer a prayer for the group, which was odd to me, but she seemed happy to do so. Afterward, everyone rose and began to mingle reverently, discussing the sermon and how they could use it in their families.

I got up and moved toward the back, avoiding eye contact. Chanah and my mother passed by me on their way to the doorway, but neither spoke to me. Chanah squeezed my hand and smiled up at me, and my mother followed her lead as they exited. My sisters didn't look at me, and I could tell they were wondering if they should say anything.

As I turned to follow my family, Father Gideon was suddenly at my side, taking my elbow in a surprisingly firm grip. "You will stay a few minutes?"

Phrased like a question, it was clearly a command, and I had no will to argue. I nodded, then let him lead me out of the main room, down a short hallway, past his wife to whom he offered a short explanation, and into a smaller room, where we were alone.

He nodded at the blankets covering the floor, and we both sat. Then he asked me a question I was conflicted how to answer.

"Are you glad you came tonight, Jesse?"

I started to nod but stopped myself. "I enjoyed your sermon, but I doubt I am worthy to be a Christian. Perhaps this was a mistake." I was about to get up when his hand was on my arm again, gently holding me down.

"Your guilt is misplaced, Jesse."

This man had no idea how broad and deep my guilt was. How could he? In any case, I wasn't sure how much of what I was feeling was guilt and how much was profound resignation. I was a murderer. My fate was already written, wasn't it, despite how desperately I wanted it to be different? "It is not my guilt that is misplaced, Rabb—um, Father. *I* am misplaced. I should not be alive. If I had died in Jesus's place, then all Israel would be rejoicing, and the Romans would be ruined instead of ruining us."

There was great sadness in his eyes as he tilted his head to consider my words, which I was sure he knew to be true.

"My son," he said in a surprisingly warm and tender voice, "Anything the Romans can ruin, God can repair, and what God repairs, the Romans cannot ruin. Jesus showed us that with his own body, and he continues to prove it to us by his sparing hand. Besides, Jesus didn't come to ruin the Romans. They will ruin themselves eventually, though some will follow him and be saved. Some of the Jews will follow him, too, though I fear it will not be many." The sadness in his eyes strengthened.

I wasn't sure about what he'd said, but I had no arguments to offer.

He sighed. "You feel irredeemable. That is not an uncommon feeling, tragic as it is. But the Lord's sure promise is that if we are faithful in seeking truth and righteousness under his guidance—and he will not force us—there isn't a power in, above, or beneath the earth that can touch us if he does not will it. I have seen the truth of that myself, and so has his chief apostle, Peter, whom prisons cannot hold, no matter how deep or well-guarded. Far from defeat, the path to victory is open now to all of us. Can the Emperor raise the dead? Can the Emperor wash your soul clean and lead you to the heavenly courts of glory? Nay, he cannot, not with all his legions behind him. Only the Messiah can do it, and what has Rome to say to that?" His eyes sparkled triumphantly.

My blank stare took some of that sparkle away, but he was undaunted.

"I know it's hard to understand. I had my own doubts. Indeed, many who were present this evening have doubts, and many of those doubts come from stubborn Jewish pride—that was one of my stumbling blocks, too, and probably still is." He smiled ruefully. "But God doesn't expect you to believe based on my word alone. He wants you to ask him yourself. He wants you to humbly knock at his door and receive his answer through the Holy Spirit, which testifies of truth.

"All Israel *should* be rejoicing as we speak. Indeed, the Romans should be rejoicing also, because God loves them no less than us. Now there is a hard truth for a Jew to accept." He chuckled. "Of all the people in the world, the Jews should recognize the meaning of his life and sacrifice from their own scriptures, and yet most of them still do not. Oh, Jesse, son of Abbas, he *lives*, and I was one who saw him and spoke with him in person both before and after his miraculous resurrection."

Eyes glistening, Father Gideon gripped my arm again, willing me to comprehend his words. But it was too difficult. I didn't know how to ask God anything, and I had no confidence he would listen. I had never felt the Spirit of God to know what it was like. Was it even real? There were more people who didn't understand it than those who claimed to feel it. Asking a priest or a rabbi to define it was like asking them to paint the wind. And where was this hope that should cause Israel to rejoice? Weren't we still under the iron heel of the Romans? Weren't most of our chief priests and scribes corrupted and consumed by their lusts? What good did Christ's resurrection—if it were true—offer us? Father Gideon had also spoken of full and permanent forgiveness of sins in his sermon, and that Christ made that possible, but even if somehow he had made forgiveness possible for others, surely it wasn't meant for me.

Father Gideon loosened his hold, and he seemed to be waiting for me to speak.

I cleared my throat, then swallowed. "I am happy for you, and for my family. But I have never felt the Spirit of God, and I doubt I ever will."

Father Gideon smiled. "You felt it this evening."

I blinked, thinking back, then shook my head. "I don't know what I felt."

"That's okay. You will, in time. The Spirit is usually a still, small voice, as Elijah experienced on Mount Horeb when he longed to die, believing he had failed Israel. It is peace, understanding, and goodwill. It is love and hope. It is often courage as well. Jesse, you have a work to do, and you cannot do that work until you're free of the torment from your own mind. Do you remember the thief on Jesus's right hand as he hung from the cross?"

I shook my head, though I had briefly witnessed the scene and heard the story.

"The thief on the right rebuked the other thief for mocking his Savior, and Jesus promised that first thief a place with him in Paradise. Though the thief had sinned during his life, he recognized his Lord at the point of his own death, and he defended him. Jesus saw the change in his heart and forgave him. Think of that, for it is real. I have received forgiveness as well, and the peace that comes from being right with God. I continually seek forgiveness through repentance and faith."

I leaned back, breaking his grip on my arm. "I believe you. But you don't know me. I don't deserve God's forgiveness. I would settle for peace to continue providing for my family, and for their happiness. That is enough."

Father Gideon's tone became more earnest, his eyes drilling into mine. "You are mistaken, Jesse. Intelligent, but stubborn and mistaken. Jesus *is* Jehovah, the same who spoke with Abraham, Moses, and Isaiah. He is our God, sent to us by Father Elohim, and he has power to forgive your sins. He had power to do whatever he wanted here—to build or to destroy, to grant life or to take it. To raise Lazarus and others from the dead. To raise us all now. Even when he was standing before Pilate in chains, he could have called down legions of angels to aid him and destroy his persecutors. But he wouldn't betray us. He wouldn't leave us behind. Not even you.

"Behind all that power was a purpose, and the purpose was us. It was *always* us. He chose to humble himself and suffer, Barabbas, for you and for me, out of the purest love this world has ever witnessed. He could have leveled these hills to a plain and avoided his mission, and he himself would still have been God. Do you not wonder why the earth trembled and the skies raged when he finally allowed his mortal life to end? Because he had offered himself as the last and perfect sacrifice to fulfill the law of Moses and provide us a way back to heaven. He did not falter or fail. He did not lash out in pride or anger, even as the very souls for whom he was suffering mocked him and led him to his death. The heavens wept at his anguish, but not at his death. Oh, how they rejoiced at his choice!"

There was such feeling and authority behind Father Gideon's words that I turned away. I felt their impact from my head to my bowels and thence to my toes, and I didn't doubt he sincerely believed what he was saying. For an instant I thought that I, too, might believe, might accept that I was redeemable. But I still couldn't see myself there. It didn't seem possible. I could see my family there, however, and I vowed in that instant to protect Father Gideon and the Christians with my life. That was a purpose at least as worthy as making fine tents. I might be a fool, but I could at least be a valiant fool for a righteous cause.

Chanah encouraged me to pray with her occasionally after that day, and I did, though never as the voice. It seemed foreign to me that we would be praying in our home without prescribed recitations and precise mannerisms. She tried to teach me, explaining that there were certain general forms to follow while the words should come from my heart, but my mind resisted. Despite my inability, though, I could feel the power in our home when she prayed. She addressed Elohim as if she were a high priestess of old, and she poured out her soul in thanksgiving and praise, in confession and contrition, in pleading for forgiveness and mercy, in asking for strength and wisdom. She called down the kindness and blessings of heaven on our household, and on the child growing in her womb. I almost wept in awe sometimes. I wondered often how she could remain with a fallen man like me, even though I was faithful to her.

I attended many of Father Gideon's lessons. I struggled with my right to associate with these brave Christians, who were constantly harassed by the Jewish leaders and ridiculed by the haughty, amused Romans. Then again, I had vowed to protect them, and how could I protect them if I wasn't with them?

As the next few months passed, leading us toward Spring, I learned to sit calmly through the lessons, and I began to understand some of the concepts of the doctrines. I would never partake of the sacrament, of course, for it didn't apply to me, but I saw how happy the remembrance of the Savior's sacrifice made all who ate the bread and drank the wine.

I was there when Chanah went into labor near the end of one of Father Gideon's lessons. A terror, long held at bay as the pregnancy had progressed, gripped my heart. Two midwives rushed her to a separate part of the house. Several others in the room left as well, some to take news to Chanah's parents, some to secure supplies that might be needed, one to seek a physician.

I sat on the floor amid the momentary stillness of the room. Then I bowed my head and prayed silently. To my surprise, the words came. Father Gideon began to pray aloud, though his words receded into the background as I poured out my heart to God, pleading that he would hear me despite my sins. I begged him to strengthen Chanah and her baby, that they both might live. Tears ran down my cheeks, and I sobbed softly.

I don't know how long my private prayer lasted, but when my emotions were nearly spent I felt I hand on my shoulder, then another, and then several more on my back and arms and head. I glanced up, noting that several men and women surrounded me, and that among the hands on my head were those of Father Gideon. He began a different prayer, invoking the ancient priesthood power he often spoke about, the same that Jesus wielded. His words were intense, his tone serene. I had heard him speak before of the laying on of hands by the elders of the church, but I had thought it only applied when someone was sick.

Peace settled over me, and I was awestruck at the power of it.

The prayer ended in a final appeal in the name of Jesus, the Son of God, and then Father Gideon dismissed the group. He invited me to another room where we could wait. His kind wife offered us refreshment. We passed the time solemnly, speaking little, listening attentively to what was occurring in that other part of the house. There seemed nothing out of the ordinary, but after a few minutes peace failed me and my heart started to pound. When all went silent, I thought it would burst from my chest.

Finally, the sound of a baby's frantic birth cries filled the house.

I cried tears of joy. But my happiness was tempered with the memory of our first two children and how short their lives had been. Anxiety wove a web around my heart as it struggled to rejoice. The same thing would surely happen, I thought, and my sobs began anew. They must have changed in timbre as well, because Father Gideon offered comforting, hopeful words. He knew our history with children. But how much could a man like me dare to hope? If there was truly any hope, it was because of Chanah, and maybe Father Gideon.

We took our newborn son home on the second day of the week, the birth having taxed Chanah more than the previous two. We named him Matthew, after the apostle. It was a fine name, meaning gift of God. Matthew was a handsome, well-formed boy with strong lungs, for which we were grateful.

A week passed, and then two. Matthew ate well and was strong. It was miraculous to me, this improbable birth of a healthy boy, and the light that shone constantly from Chanah's eyes was enough to illuminate all of Judea on a moonless night. My mother and sisters were giddy with joy, as was Elhanan. For a while, it was all I could do to focus on making good tents. Just a short while, though. My son needed me.

Matthew's first birthday was a marvelous milestone. I hadn't believed it would come. He had experienced no major illnesses, and he was growing strong and sound. Chanah was the best mother Israel had ever produced, save Mary the mother of Jesus. Her energy seemed inexhaustible, her love limitless.

News had reached Jerusalem the week prior of a new Emperor—a new Caesar called Tiberius Claudius. Eight years had passed since Christ's resurrection. I wouldn't have thought much of the news until Andrew, the brother of Peter, showed up at our house as we were celebrating. He'd come to speak with Chanah, of course, given her remarkable faith and her ability to share that faith with others. Many of the apostles, the Seventy, and the elders had come to meet with her before, some to give assignments, some to seek her counsel, and others, I was sure, to find out if she'd had any success taming the strange animal she kept as a husband. But Andrew I had never seen.

He announced his presence humbly enough, which wasn't always the case with some of the others. "Good Jesse and Chanah, greetings I bring from the Twelve and from the Brethren and Sisters. May I enter?"

Chanah bounded to her feet. She was always delighted to see one of the leaders of the church. I wondered sometimes if I should be jealous. "Brother Andrew, welcome to our home on this joyous occasion of the anniversary of our son's birth." She looked at me, her face beaming, and I glanced at Matthew, who was sitting on my mother's lap, waving his pudgy arms up and down, clearly excited about something. He was looking at Chanah, and when she was happy, he generally was, too.

Andrew smiled at the baby, then spread his hands before him. "I apologize for intruding. I can return tomorrow."

"No, it's okay." Chanah looked at me. "Right, Jesse?"

I nodded instinctively, and as Andrew expressed his gratitude Chanah showed him to a seat next to Mara, who was clearly excited to be sitting by an apostle. Chanah and I took our places between my mother and Salome, nearly across from him. Elhanan plopped down next to Salome.

When we were seated, he took a deep breath and began.

"You have heard there is new emperor, yes?"

"Yes," Chanah said. I simply nodded.

"As you know, the reign of Caligula was becoming ever more despotic, and the repercussions across the empire were multiplying. He made Christ's church feel his tyranny as well, here in Jerusalem and elsewhere. We feared he would choose the saints as a target for one of his purges, and we were putting plans in place for that possibility. His assassination at the hands of the Praetorian Guard was a great relief, though we were uncertain what would follow.

"The ascension of his uncle Tiberius Claudius was a surprise, and yet we had known it was a possibility. It brings a blessing we had sought with much fasting and prayer."

Chanah tilted her head, and Mara said, "How did you know it might be him?"

Andrew nodded. "Two months ago we received a brother from Tarsus with a report from Paul, who—"

"Is he well?" I blurted out, then blushed. I had never met Paul, once called Saul, but his story of conversion to Christianity was legend. That had been about six years ago. I didn't consciously place much day-to-day interest in him or his activities, but the account of his fateful trip to Damascus sang to me. I had traveled that very road. The Lord had not appeared to me, but I was not Paul.

Andrew smiled. "Paul is well, and the messenger he sent to us was valuable and knowledgeable. The man is a trader who has much business in Rome, and also many friends there, some of them well-placed. He told us of growing intrigue among the Guard and the Senate, which together sought to reign in the power of the Emperor. He went so far as to predict that they would choose Claudius as the next emperor if some harm were to befall Caligula, because he would be more manageable due to his physical deficiencies and lack of clear ambition."

Chanah straightened. "The messenger—he is Aristarchus, the Macedonian?"

"Yes." Andrew smiled, eyebrows lifted in surprise. "A most remarkable man, and already quite useful in the work of the Lord. His ships have provided safe and swift passage to many of the apostles and brethren as they have begun to preach to the Gentiles and the far-flung Jewish communities, going even so far as Hispania, Britannia, and the eastern shores of the Black Sea."

Chanah had spoken to me about the various journeys of the apostles. At first she had expressed worry that they were going too far, spreading too thin. I had heard others talk of this as well. Shouldn't the church build its strength in Israel first? How could far-flung colonies of believers prosper if they had so little contact with their leaders? How could they combine their resources when needed? They would be isolated, easy prey for Jewish and Hellenist antagonists, among others.

And yet resolute Peter would calmly explain that this was what the Lord wanted, that if they weren't prepared to follow his counsel they couldn't claim to be his disciples. This made sense to those like Chanah, whose faith was deeper and more brilliant than the fires of the finest ruby. Outside of the apostles, though, others still argued.

Andrew continued. "He also told us that he had counseled with Paul and the elders in Tarsus on the matter. They were of the belief that if Claudius ascended, he and the Senate would seek to repair relations damaged by Caligula and that there would be a greater adherence to equity and justice under Roman laws. This would allow the work of the church to continue apace, and even accelerate. We of the apostles in Jerusalem—including Peter—have discussed it, and all are agreed. We don't know how long this time of relative peace for the saints will last, so we must move quickly to take advantage of it."

He paused, letting us take this in. I was wondering how this applied to us when Chanah asked my question. "Why would you bring this news to us, Brother Andrew?"

Andrew took another deep breath as he swept his gaze across us, including Mara seated next to him. "We have a request for you and your family…and it will require some sacrifice."

Sacrifice? I shifted in my seat as I took in that word. "What is it, I asked?" Chanah placed her hand on my forearm, leaning forward expectantly, as if she were excited. I, on the other hand, felt anxiety rising in my chest.

"There is a place at the edge of the empire, in Armenia, called Artaxata. It is near the Roman commerce hub of Kainepolis, not far from Lake Sevan. Matthew has been there, as has Thaddaeus, and there are a few strong believers in the area already. It is an important place, for reasons we do not fully understand. We feel strongly that you and your family could be of great service there."

I was stunned.

Chanah's hand squeezed my arm slightly, but otherwise she seemed calm, deliberative.

My mother gasped and put her hand over her mouth, while my sisters shifted their gazes from Andrew, to me, to Chanah, and to my mother.

"You may, of course, take a few days to decide," Andrew offered carefully.

Days? I would need weeks. I stared at nothing for a few moments, my mind rapidly stitching seams that just as rapidly unraveled. It would be wonderful to leave Jerusalem and start a new life where nobody knew me as Barabbas, but my business was thriving. There were very few of the saints in Jerusalem who treated me as a pariah any longer. On the other hand, there were still many Romans who despised and hated me. The centurion I'd met in Alexandrium, who had moved to Caesarea, could change his mind at any time, too. Armenia was far away—perhaps out of his reach. But what would it be like? How would we be accepted? Salome and Mara would need to find good husbands, though both had resisted to that point for reasons known only to them and perhaps my mother.

Questions and possibilities were still spinning in my mind when Chanah squeezed my arm again and turned to look at me. "Jesse," she said tenderly, "my husband, what do you think?"

I folded my hands in front of me and scrunched my shoulders. "I do not know," I replied softly. "I cannot tell what is right."

"He has not the gift yet," offered Andrew.

"He is my husband," Chanah retorted, a reprimand in her voice that startled me. "We are one—someday in the covenant, too—and we must decide together." Had she just spoken to one of her beloved apostles that way? In her eyes I saw calm authority, and my heart swelled as I felt her love and devotion. To *me*. I nearly cried.

Andrew was startled as well, and I thought he would be offended. But instead, he bowed his head slightly, a look of contrition on his face. "Yes, you are right. I am sorry, to both of you."

Chanah locked her gaze on mine, her voice softening. "Jesse, I see your hesitation, and I feel it, too. I do not think it is right for us to go, at least not at this time. I feel it strongly."

I blinked, trying to comprehend. Was she saying *no*? Was that allowed? I sneaked a glance at Andrew, who was frowning pensively.

"Where you go or stay, I go or stay, dear wife. You have more wisdom than I could ever dream of."

"Oh, stop it." Her look was not amused. "You are a son of God, Jesus Bar Abbas, with far more potential than you will let yourself admit. You'll realize that someday. I promise it."

I didn't know what to say to that, and apparently neither did anybody else.

My mother broke the uncomfortable silence. "I have a voice, too," she said, "as do Salome and Mara. If Jesse and Chanah do not go, can my daughters and I accept the call and take the journey? I would take Jarah bat Elizur, Judas Iscariot's widow, as well."

That was a bold request, and my mother seemed to think so as well. She held the apostle's gaze, but she seemed to shrink as she waited for his answer.

Andrew was thoughtful for a few moments, then said, "We had not thought about that, but perhaps we should have. You can go, of course, on your own, and if you carry an official writ from the Quorum of Apostles it will go better for you when you arrive."

He returned his focus to Chanah, and I expected a lecture on obedience. But it didn't come. Instead, he said, "I have been trying to learn not to be surprised at the directions in which the Spirit moves us and at how poorly we sometimes interpret that guidance. Even we apostles have much to discover. We thought the call was for you, Chanah, but perhaps it was instead for Ruth, Salome, and Mara. Jarah I am not sure about, but that may be beyond my wisdom to judge."

Beyond his wisdom? Here was a man of great authority in the church, which was growing rapidly in power and influence, and even worldly means. I knew how men endowed with great power usually reacted when challenged by those of lower status. I had seen only one great exception, and that in the strange centurion who had spared my life. Andrew appeared to be a second.

Chanah nodded, and I could see tears forming in her eyes. Elhanan had squeezed in beside her, hugging her as if he thought he might be sent to Armenia with my mother and sisters.

"If my husband is agreeable, we will stay," she said. "Elhanan, too," she added, kissing him tenderly on the top of his head.

It was my turn to speak, and my thoughts turned to my mother first. "How will they make the journey? Will there be others? And how will they live when they get there?"

Andrew nodded, acknowledging my concerns. "There are others going as well, from Jerusalem and other areas. Your mother and sisters will be safe. And the saints in Armenia will help them find work and a place to live after they arrive. We have given detailed instructions. They will be well cared-for, Brother Jesse."

I nodded, satisfied. "We will stay then."

Andrew smiled broadly, shaking his head. "There is a great mystery here, and it is good." He turned to my mother and sisters. "Ruth, Salome, Mara, you are called on this missionary journey. Will you accept the call?"

My mother looked at her daughters, tears flowing down her cheeks. Both nodded, crying as well, and when I felt the first tears in my own eyes I tried to blink them away. My mother and sisters were leaving? Would I ever see them again?

As if she had heard my thoughts, Chanah wrapped her arm around my waist and hugged me. "We will see them again in this life, dear husband. I know this to be true."

How did she know? How could she truly know? It was more than my mind could manage, but I resolved to trust her.

Within the week they were gone, accompanied by several others, including a member of the Seventy and his family. We said our farewells, trusting in God to protect them.

CHAPTER 7

Then Peter said unto them, Repent, and be baptized every one of you in the name of Jesus Christ for the remission of sins, and ye shall receive the gift of the Holy Ghost.

Acts 2:38, KJV

The next two years were busy for us. We prospered, though not all happened as we wished. I was making more tents, employing Elhanan's growing skills and maturity. Some of our tents were elaborate, multi-roomed structures, and they were well-received. I soon required a larger shop, and so we acquired the home next to ours for a fair sum and utilized its entire ground floor for my work.

My studies with Father Gideon and other Christian teachers continued. Occasionally they would ask when I would be baptized—as would Chanah—but I was comfortable with things as they were. I still didn't believe baptism would benefit me. I also didn't want to make a sacred commitment that I wasn't sure I could live up to. I was happy to be a student and not an official adherent. Besides, if any of my wealthy customers asked if I were a Christian, I could truthfully say that I was not, though I always added that the Christians I knew were good, honest, hard-working people. I viewed it as doing my part to help the cause, creating good will toward the saints.

Chanah didn't see it that way. She overheard me speaking to a Jewish noble one day, and she was not pleased. It was difficult for her to raise her voice to anyone, but she did with me that night. I argued with her, believing I had done the right thing, but she cut every argument to ribbons. I was more careful afterward, and we seldom spoke of it. But I could tell that my intransigence with regards to truly becoming a Christian made her sadder than before, even given the reasons I had offered. She said it was my choice, though, and she prayed harder for me.

After Matthew's second birthday had passed, in the early part of summer, Chanah gave birth to another baby girl, whom we named Miriam, the prophetess who was the sister of Moses. She was a beautiful child, but she lived just two days. I felt sick with grief for Chanah, but she refused to dwell on her sorrow. I felt like I had further disappointed her. *Was* it my fault?

By the next summer we accepted that we would have no more children. Matthew was three, and he continued to be a strong, happy boy. We also found a rabbi who would declare our adoption of Elhanan despite the fact that we were a family of 'mixed' religion—one Christian and one Jew, since I was still technically considered to be of the Jewish faith. The adoption wasn't necessary, since Elhanan was almost fourteen. But it was important to both him and Chanah, and so we were officially able to call him our son.

As fall was approaching, Father Gideon invited us to witness the baptisms of several Samaritan families near Bethel. I was sure Chanah had planned it. I had never witnessed a baptism—not even Chanah's. I resisted, but she begged me so sweetly and incessantly to accompany her and Elhanan that I agreed despite knowing her subterfuge.

Two days later, I asked her why we couldn't just see a baptism near Jerusalem, and she said that people were afraid to join Christ's church in Jerusalem because of the power of the chief priests and scribes. I wasn't sure that made sense, since it seemed to me that many of those who claimed to be Christian still attended the synagogues and lived their lives in the same way they had lived them before what she called 'conversion.' Why would the chief priests care?

Expressing that sentiment nearly earned me a slap from my gentle wife. Many Christians, like her, renounced their Jewish faith, and new members were all encouraged to do so. The fact that some of them didn't had no bearing on the faith of those who did. Jewish leaders often made note of it, though, and behaved accordingly, which usually meant badly.

We were eating supper the evening before we were to leave when there was a knock on our door. I was expecting a messenger regarding a potential tent order, so I rose to answer it. Instead of the messenger, I saw a slightly-stooped middle-aged man with thinning hair on top, fidgeting with his fingers. He looked up at me and gave a hesitant smile.

I was about to ask who he was when my breath caught. Could it be?

"Uncle Levi?"

The man nodded more confidently. "Yes. You are Jesus, right?"

I nodded, but said, "It's Jesse now."

"Oh. Is my brother's wife—your mother—here?"

I didn't immediately answer. I couldn't believe it was my Uncle Levi. He was a leper! Or rather, had been. He showed no signs of it now, though instinctively I backed up a step.

He raised his hands in a calming gesture. "It's okay. I am fully healed."

Chanah appeared at my shoulder. "Healed of what?" she asked.

I turned to her. "Dearest, this is my Uncle Levi. He's…I mean, he *was*, a leper. For a long time." It sounded ridiculous coming out of my mouth. How was it possible?

"Oh," she said matter-of-factly. "Well, invite him in. I will prepare another plate."

An awkward few seconds passed before I finally ushered him in and offered him a place to sit, trying not to feel so worried about contagion. As we waited for Chanah, I introduced Elhanan and Matthew and told him briefly where my mother and sisters had gone. His face fell at that news but brightened as Chanah returned with his food. He looked emaciated.

Chanah sat, and she didn't seem worried at all. "I have heard of you, from Ruth. She thought you may have died already. I think she felt badly that she didn't try to find out if it was so."

Levi paused to swallow his first bite of food. "I'm glad she stayed away. Hell is an awful place to visit."

Chanah looked at me, prompting me with her eyes.

"Uncle Levi, how were you healed?" I asked.

He shook his head. "I cannot say for certain, and I don't know why. I was near death. I accepted that. The others in the leper colony knew it, too, and they left me alone. Then, today at the noon hour, a man and a woman entered the colony, completely unafraid of being infected. They walked straight up to me. The man called himself Matthias. The woman didn't give her name, but she let too much of her hair show. She had eyes that pierced my soul. She pronounced that I should be healed. When they reached out their hands, I thought I *had* died, and that they were there to guide me to the heavenly place where my suffering would be at an end. The rush of fire and wind through my body as our hands touched seemed to confirm it.

"But then they pulled me to my feet, and I looked around. I was still in the leper colony. Wails of agony and despair still surrounded me. Then I wondered if they were demons, but I looked at my hands. They were as whole as they had been before my leprosy. I touched my face, and even my beard was restored. A few others had seen what happened, and they began to whisper among themselves. Several approached, though most did not. And some of those who came would not allow themselves to be touched, one shouting that it was a hallucination. But those who were touched were healed. All of them. Then we leaped and danced and shouted with joy, praising God.

"They asked me to follow them, and of course I did. I would have accompanied them to the gates of the Roman garrison and attacked the guards if they'd commanded, because I knew their power could not be opposed. They led me here, naming this the home of my departed brother's family."

I had no words. I had *seen* him as a leper. His case had been severe. His wife had called the authorities to take him to the leper colony when she had first noticed his skin lesions, fearing she and the children would be infected. That had been fifteen years ago.

Then another thought struck me, and I was on my feet and racing out the door. I looked up and down the street, squinting to identify people further away. But she wasn't there.

Chanah rushed up behind me, concern in her voice. "What is it, husband?"

My breath was coming fast. "I think it was Mary who healed him, but she's gone."

"Of course it was," she said, and I turned to stare. "She's always showing too much of her hair—well, too much for the

Jewish leaders, but they dare not punish her for it. And she has the gift of healing."

I was still nervous, but Chanah insisted Levi stay with us for a few days. We had plenty of room. She also invited him to the baptisms, though he was confused by what that meant.

The new day dawned, and we made our final preparations to leave. Levi demanded he help, and he was surprisingly energetic given his many years in the colony. They did work there, but they didn't have the same motivation or opportunity. The governing councils, both Jewish and Roman, made sure they had food, basic shelter, and cloth scraps to make clothes. It was called charity, though it often looked more like keeping them in their place.

I marveled at Levi's sanity, too. Many lepers went mad. It was understandable. But he seemed normal. It was almost like he had never been there at all. Had Mary healed his mind as well?

When all was ready, Chanah gathered us in our front room to pray. She asked Elhanan if he would lead us in that prayer. We knelt together on the floor and bowed our heads, and then Elhanan began.

"Grandma!"

Even I knew that a prayer never began that way. My head snapped up as I twisted to my feet to face the doorway. Had Chanah's parents come? Had she invited them without telling me? She visited them often, but they rarely made an appearance at our home.

My jaw fell as my eyes beheld my mother framed in the doorway. She looked two years younger instead of two years older, and her faced beamed with joy.

"Jesus Bar Abbas, my son," she said, tears flowing. "God's mercy is upon us this day." She threw her arms wide and rushed toward me, embracing me with a great squeeze. Then she turned toward the others, who had all risen...and noticed Levi. Her eyebrows jumped, one hand going to her heart while the other covered her mouth.

After a moment she cried out, "Levi, is that truly you?"

He nodded, his face mirroring the awe on hers. "It is, though I don't know how."

Though it was improper, my mother walked over and embraced him as well, praising God as she did. Chanah joined them, and then Elhanan. Matthew, not wanting to be left out, toddled over and grasped one of Chanah's legs, then closed his eyes and smiled contentedly.

I stood apart, watching in amazement. I had many questions, but I waited. Before we were all seated on the floor, though, it was Chanah who asked the first question.

"How did you come here, Ruth?" My mother shrugged and then sat down, as if it were no big thing to travel for weeks across rugged territory. "I joined a caravan. It was Mary who arranged it."

I squinted, incredulous. "*Mary* asked you to return?" I looked at Chanah, who was staring at Levi, who seemed like he was confused but didn't know where to start.

My mother nodded. "Mary said I was needed here, but that my daughters—and their husbands—should stay."

Chanah squealed so loudly my ears rang, and then clapped in delight. "They both found good husbands?"

Mother's beaming smile returned. "They are very happy, and their husbands are both good, faithful, Christian men, one a Jew from the tribe of Dan, and one a gentile from Armenia. And both Salome and Mara are with child."

"God be praised!" said Chanah, nearly in a shout. Matthew was startled by the outburst, but then laughed and started to clap as well, seeing his mother's obvious joy.

I couldn't help but grin. I reached over and picked up Matthew, setting him on my mother's lap. She held him gently as Chanah peppered her with more questions, and he soon settled into her embrace.

"So why did she say you are needed here?" asked Chanah a few minutes later. "Did she give you an assignment?"

My mother shook her head. "She didn't explain, but she said I would discover it. Her letter to me was a shock. I was very engaged in the work of the church in Armenia, and there was even talk of building a temple in Kainepolis soon, if it were approved by the apostles."

"A temple?" Chanah's excitement rose again. "So soon? The temples in Damascus and Alexandria continue to see delays, and the one in Antioch has only just resumed construction. There is much opposition."

My mother nodded. "The prelate in Armenia has been favorable to the Lord's church and has even met with Thomas the apostle, who tarried in the region for several months. There are rumors the prelate may even be baptized...but, of course, those are just rumors—people get excited, you know."

Chanah grasped my mother's hands. "Your daughters and their husbands may soon have the full blessings of the temple, something we don't even have here in Jerusalem. They must be so very happy."

I had heard Chanah and others explain how the temple in Jerusalem had been defiled for centuries and only partially cleansed by Jesus. I could see how those who ruled it lacked the authority to operate it properly, and that dire prophecies had already been sealed upon it. But I didn't understand why it was so important, though Chanah had explained it several times. Perhaps my mind was just stubbornly closed to it.

"They are," my mother said, "but they know it will be a difficult road. Much sacrifice will be required before the blessings can be harvested. Judas, Salome's husband, is a skilled stonemason, and Mara's husband Marcus a talented craftsman in all types of wood. They are eager to help."

There was a brief pause, and then Levi finally spoke. "Who is Mary?"

Chanah and I locked eyes, apparently both feeling the same jolt. We hadn't told him that we thought it was Mary who had healed him. Chanah nodded at me, inviting me to answer.

I looked at Levi, wondering how to begin. "Mary is the mother of Jesus of Nazareth. Have you heard of him?"

He wrinkled his forehead, thinking. "Rumors only. It was said he could heal all manner of diseases, including leprosy, but I never saw him. Some claimed the Sanhedrin kept him away from our colony so that he couldn't perform miracles there."

That was sickening, but it made some sense. "Well…" I looked at Chanah, hoping she might take over, but she appeared not to notice my hint, "…um, this Jesus was crucified by the Romans at the request of the Sanhedrin. Chanah and I have both met his mother, and she is a remarkable woman. We think it was she who healed you yesterday."

Chanah looked disappointed that I hadn't explained more about Jesus, but it passed quickly. Levi just nodded and said, "Mary." His tone was reverent. "I am glad to know her name. Thank you, Jesse."

Then he frowned, looking sad.

"Uncle," I said, "is there something wrong?"

He focused on the floor, waiting several seconds. "I must ask something, my nephew, though it shames me."

"Of course. Ask it," I said.

"My family has abandoned me. Phoebe claims that only demons would have healed me, and that it won't last. She believes I carry a great curse, and so she has asked for a writ of divorcement, which I will grant her."

I knew Phoebe was a devout woman, but stubborn as the wind. She was a harridan, too, awful to behold when her ire was raised. It would be futile to oppose her.

"I would ask," he continued, "that you allow me to join your household, Jesus, son of my brother Abbas."

I had a hard time wrapping my mind around his request. This was the man who had cursed me for running away from my parents, even threatening to have me thrown into prison. I hadn't thought about that in a long time, though. I glanced at Chanah, who was smiling at Levi as though my answer should be obvious.

I supposed it was, and I cleared my throat. "It would be our honor to have you."

"Thank you," said Levi in a near whisper.

Chanah wiped a tear from her cheek. Then she got up and lifted Matthew into her arms. "Okay, everyone, we don't want to be late. It's time to be heading for Bethel."

My mother looked around as everyone else rose. "I've just arrived. Why are we going to Bethel?"

The road to Bethel was in poor shape, but our mule didn't seem to mind, and we hadn't brought our cart. The weather was warm, but not hot, so we made good time. When we arrived in Bethel just before the last rays of the sun disappeared, Father Gideon was waiting for us. He found us accommodations, advising us that the baptisms would take place the next day. Rain had been plentiful that year, so the reservoirs were still reasonably full, making this strange practice of baptism by full immersion easier to do without having to travel to the sea or one of the greater rivers.

We stayed in the home of a kind elderly couple. They bubbled over with excitement about the 'Gospel of Christ' and claimed to have been among the first in Bethel to join the Lord's church. Their home was simply adorned but immaculate. Colorful carpets and curtains cheered us throughout, and while the wooden furniture wasn't of the finest hardwoods, it had been polished until it shone like clear topaz. We dined on roasted lamb and an impressive variety of fruit and bread, and I wondered if someone passing by might complain to the local rabbis that we were feasting so extravagantly on a non-feast day.

Mid-morning the next day, we headed for one of the small reservoirs on the outskirts of the town, discovering that it was well-secluded thanks to both the low hills that surrounded it and a small barn. There were about twenty people gathered when we arrived, including Father Gideon, who stood next to a shorter man in a nearly white robe and a fine red belt. The man looked almost like a Roman, and Father Gideon seemed to be taking some instructions from him.

Curious, I wondered who this man might be, and then Chanah nearly shouted, "It's Paul! Paul has come!"

A strange sensation came over me. I was elated to finally meet Paul, and yet I wished he wouldn't notice me. It was childish, but I was Barabbas and he was Paul. He had persecuted the Christians, but the Lord himself had appeared to him, and he had repented and been forgiven. I could not say the same. He was a powerful and brave preacher with a high and holy calling, and while we both made tents, tentmaking was the only thing in which I could say I exceled. Not even that centurion who had lured me to his fortress intimidated me as much as Paul.

Chanah's arm firmly locked with mine as we all approached, keeping me from lagging. Paul looked at us, and his face broke into a wide smile. He strode toward us, arms extended. He greeted Chanah, Matthew, my mother, and Elhanan warmly, then paused to spend more time with my uncle Levi, looking deeply into his eyes and whispering something so softly I couldn't hear it above the breeze rustling the hard grass and tough shrubs. He finally turned to me, his smile moderating as he nodded.

"Barabbas," he said.

I lowered my head, then backed away a step.

He chuckled. "You have nothing to fear from me, tentmaker. I am a humble servant of God and an imperfect man like you. I was hoping you would come, but I didn't believe you would. You have surprised me."

I glanced up, and he took a step toward me, holding my gaze.

"I know you have heard this before, but you are about to witness the making of sacred covenants with God our Father through his Holy Son, Jesus the Christ. These covenants open to us the straight and narrow path of eternal promise, and with the guidance of the Holy Spirit we can continue along that path until we are able to live with our Lord forever in his glory. The world may blindly persecute us for our choice, and we may even be called upon to give our lives for the cause of truth, but the only person that can destroy our promise is us."

I had indeed heard it all before, but I still didn't fully comprehend it. When I dropped my gaze again, he took me gently by the shoulders. Something about him touching me—me, such a sinful man—forced my gaze up again. If he was going to lower himself to touch me, the least I could do was look him in the eye.

"You will also witness the power of the Savior of the world to forgive sin. If you have repented of your sins and committed to follow him, your sins are washed away at the time of your immersion, and you begin again as a new creature, accompanied by his spirit and the power of his might. I know this to be true, as I have been raised from great depths to see the light of his merciful countenance. I was lost, Barabbas, so far lost that only the Lord himself could find me. How I treasure the stark memories of that day!"

The power that emanated from Paul both made me warm and caused me to shiver. I felt like a gnat, though, and from every pore of my body oozed the desire for him to remove his focus—and his hands—from me. Thankfully, after a few seconds he released my shoulders. Then he turned and walked over to the small group of people gathered at the water's edge.

Paul and Father Gideon talked for several minutes to the people waiting to be baptized, but I was far enough away that I could discern only pieces of the conversation. I counted eight men, ten women, and four children who looked to be at least nine. They all had cherubic countenances, eyes riveted on their teachers. I looked at the water, too, and while it wasn't stagnant, it wasn't very clean. How could a proper baptism be done if the water was not clean?

Paul waded into the murky water, but before it had reached his knees he stopped and threw both hands into the air. He had seen something. "Secundus!"

A man was hastening toward the pool from the far side. An elderly but spry woman followed closely. They were both caked in dust from a long journey.

Paul exited the water and rushed toward the man. He threw his arms around him when they met, then slapped him on the back several times.

"How did you find us?" Paul asked. Then his brows lowered. "And why are you here? Is there something wrong?"

Secundus paused to catch his breath as the woman stepped up next to him. "Mary knew where you would be. We dined with her the night before last. We have come with as much haste as we could manage. I have news, and God be praised that we found you."

"Very well, brother. I'm glad you have come." Paul focused on the woman who'd followed Secundus. "And who have you brought?"

"This is Laelia." Secundus took her hand. "She is with the house of Cornelius, whom Peter baptized some time ago, as you know. She was away when Peter was there, but she was a believer even before her master sent the invitation to him. She sent a letter to Peter later, but perhaps it was not received. I met her in the marketplace in Caesarea, and without having ever seen me, she claimed she knew I was a Christian. She begged me to help her find one of the leaders of the church."

Paul looked puzzled. "Is Cornelius not able to baptize her himself, or someone in his household? There are some who were ordained, is that not so?"

Secundus shook his head. "I do not know. She says only that Cornelius encouraged her to seek the elders, which would need to come anyway to anoint her with the Spirit."

Paul nodded slowly, frowning slightly. "I thought we had discussed this already. There are elders among the Gentiles now, and there should be more. I thought that included Cornelius."

Secundus shrugged. "I have not met Cornelius and only know what Laelia has told me. I found no elders in the city, either, though it was rumored some would be there."

Paul nodded thoughtfully, forehead creased in apparent concern. But then he looked at the woman and smiled broadly.

"Sister," he said, "your faith is as the guiding star. I have seen very few that can match it. You are Roman, I presume?"

She nodded. "I am Phrygian, and born Roman. I searched many years for the true God, and then I dreamed about Peter coming to see my master, and I knew that somehow this man would lead me to God. I didn't know when he would come, though, and so I missed him. I thought at first I had displeased God, but the desire grew in me, and so I begged him to come again. When I saw Secundus, I knew he was the answer to my prayers, for I had dreamed of him the night before."

Paul's eyebrows rose, and he looked at Secundus. "Did she tell you this?"

He shook his head. "No. She just claimed she knew I was a Christian and said she wanted to unite herself with the Christians. She seemed very anxious about it, so we came as soon as we could."

I'd taken a few steps closer to hear the conversation, and I was nearly at the water's edge. The scene was captivating.

Paul nodded once and took the woman by the hands. "Laelia of Phrygia, do you believe that Jesus of Nazareth is the Son of God and that he atoned for our sins?"

"Yes," she said with a vigorous nod.

"Do you believe that he died on the cross and took his body up again after three days, and that he lives?"

"Yes." Tears formed in her eyes as she stared at Paul expectantly.

"Do you believe that he ministers still today, and that he guides his church through his apostles, who were given authority by him to baptize with water and with the fire of the Holy Spirit?"

"Yes." Her tears were flowing now, and I noticed my own vision blurring. There was a burning feeling growing in my chest.

"Do you covenant that you will follow Jesus the Christ, keep his commandments, provide aid to the poor in body and spirit, and be his witness to build his kingdom on the earth wherever you go?"

"Yes. Yes, I do, with all my heart and soul."

Never had I heard such a strong plea accompanied by such firm determination. Her fervor bespoke both peace and valor.

Paul stared into her eyes for several moments, and then smiled again. "Then you shall be the first today. Come, sister, and I will baptize you in the name of the Father, the Son, and the Holy Spirit." He led her toward the pool.

As they entered the reservoir, the water seemed to…change. Perhaps it was my eyes or a trick of my mind, but the water seemed clearer, cleaner.

I watched in growing fascination as Paul raised his arms in the air and prayed for the woman. Then he grabbed both of her wrists in front of her and plunged her backward into the water. When he pulled her back up, she beamed and shouted praises to the heavens in a language I didn't understand, though it sounded vaguely Greek. Paul laid his hands on her head and prayed again, this time pronouncing eloquent blessings, both temporal and spiritual, upon her.

When he was finished, she stood trembling for a moment, gazing heavenward.

The onlookers silently watched, some with hands over their mouths, some crying.

Then she turned toward me, looking straight at me as if no one else existed. A thunderbolt of indescribable power struck my heart as she raised her arm and pointed at me.

"It is your turn, young one," she said, her voice carrying all the authority of Elisha and his fiery chariots. Yet I had never seen her before.

My skin tingled, my breath became shallow, and my heart quavered.

But then Chanah was there by my side, placing her hand on my back and whispering gently in my ear. "You are called, Jesse, and our Redeemer does not call him whom He cannot qualify. Join me in this, my husband. I love you."

I didn't know what was happening, but after a moment of panic everything suddenly became clear. I knew it was all real. It was real, and I wanted the peace, the joy, and the radiance that had fallen upon that strange woman more than anything in the world. I didn't want it for me. I wanted it for Chanah and Matthew, for my mother and Elhanan, for my faraway sisters, even for my uncle Levi. And I wanted it for the Messiah, the man who, though he was God, took my place on the cross.

Slowly, with tears coursing down my cheeks, I walked into the water.

CHAPTER 8

*God is faithful, by whom ye were called unto
the fellowship of his Son Jesus Christ our Lord.*

1 Corinthians 1:9, KJV

I wasn't sure I felt everything the others claimed to have felt. They rejoiced openly when they were baptized, which seemed appropriate to the occasion. But even though it was Paul who baptized me, and even with Chanah's exuberant and joyous tears, my emotions weren't entirely clear. I was as happy as I could ever remember being, but it still seemed like I was missing something. Part of me felt that was appropriate. I was Barabbas, after all, and it would take more time.

Laelia was the only one who received the blessing of the Holy Spirit while standing in the water, but when we were finished Paul and Father Gideon laid their hands on each of us and pronounced the same blessing. Again, there was much exultation and rejoicing, and while I clearly felt the power that was wielded by these extraordinary servants of God, my joy was muted by comparison.

Regardless, I was now officially a Christian, and I was happy with that. My heritage was still Jewish, but my faith was heretical, even though both Chanah and Father Gideon explained to me that we weren't denying the Law of Moses. We were instead witnessing that the Messiah had fully complied with the ancient law according to the prophecies so that we could live his higher law. They described how the Law of Moses actually pointed toward the 'New and Everlasting Covenant' that Jesus had instituted, how the great Isaiah had seen our day and rejoiced, and how Moses himself had predicted that the lesser law would have its fulfillment in Christ.

I was no scholar or scribe, but when we gathered for dinner that evening Chanah showed me various passages of scripture, urging me to ponder and pray about them. She also asked the old couple in whose home we would abide another night if they would allow me to offer a prayer for the group. The request seemed to delight them, and even though I had reluctantly agreed ahead of time, it didn't thrill me. Shouldn't someone with more experience do it? Chanah would have been the best choice, and while that violated the well-established customs of the synagogue, we were on a new path. I stumbled my way through it, feeling distinctly uncomfortable, and Chanah seemed perfectly pleased with the effort.

Shortly after we returned home, instructions came from the apostles that we should vary our meeting times and places on the Sabbath. Our teachers would rotate more frequently as well. Roman authorities in Jerusalem—likely influenced by the Sanhedrin and by King Agrippa—were apparently ascribing no small threat to the growing congregations of Christians. Both Chanah and I felt a growing impression that real danger was imminent. I supposed that made sense, since the Romans could be prickly when it came to any kind of gathering they didn't understand. They viewed everything as if it could become a potential threat to Rome, and the mismanagement of local affairs by the various governors only increased their paranoia. Had they understood what little threat we Christians posed to peace, and what hope we had to offer, they would have *guarded* our meetings!

I looked most forward to Father Gideon's visits, and not just for his teachings. His administration of the sacrament seemed to transport me to another realm, though it was so different from the traditions of Jewish atonement. There were never any blood sacrifices, since Christ's blood was the last to be shed in sacrifice. There was no bleating of anxious lambs gathered for the ritual slaughter. There were no squeals of pain as throats were cut and blood drained. There were no gory messes to clean up afterward. I had always liked the great fires, but I could live without those.

Within a month of my baptism, I baptized my uncle Levi. I had been granted priesthood authority to baptize by Father Gideon, which felt most strange to me. It was all I could do—with Chanah's encouragement—to bring myself to believe that I was worthy to baptize my uncle, and I scarcely understood what I was doing. But Levi was happy.

A few weeks later, my mother accepted Levi's marriage proposal.

This, too, was new. Under the law of Moses, she didn't have much choice, no matter which pharisaical authority was followed. Under the New Covenant, the choice was hers as well as his, and as she saw the faithful progress of my uncle she grew to care deeply about him.

Perhaps I was growing accustomed to the new practices, because their marriage, performed by Father Gideon, wasn't a strange event to me. I was learning about the higher covenants of the temple as well, and the pieces began to fit together more firmly.

My business continued to thrive. The addition of Levi and his tanning skills provided the opportunity to create more exotic tents at a better cost, making our household more prosperous, even with Chanah focusing less on her work as a seamstress and more on educating both Elhanan and little Matthew.

The following spring, we learned Chanah was with child again, confounding anew the local physicians and midwives. Simon was born to us, another strong, healthy boy. He brought much joy to his mother and brothers, who doted on him as if he were a Babylonian prince. I was happy, too. Truly happy. I didn't let it carry me away, though. I was constantly aware of how easily I could slide off the path of righteousness, but at least I could laugh again without restraint, as I used to do with Alon.

News came before Simon's first birthday that the temple in Antioch had been completed, and that a temple in Kainepolis in Armenia had been approved by the apostles. The church was experiencing rapid growth in the number of followers, and the devotion of the saints was increasing amidst the opposition of the adversary. Work was progressing anew on the temples in Damascus and Alexandria as well, and all of this news brought great joy to the saints in and around Jerusalem. In fact, it was as if a lightning bolt had struck Israel. Everything sizzled with energy.

New missionary expeditions were arranged, and soon saints—often entire families—were departing for places across the empire like Rome, Gaul, Cyrene, Macedonia, Thracia, and Bithynia, with two intrepid elders and an apostle even taking a ship for Britannia, where Rome's authority was still weak. Others traveled outside the empire for the first time, aiming for Ethiopia, Mesopotamia, and the northern reaches of the Black Sea.

I sat on my stool one day the next spring, Simon speaking gibberish on my lap as he watched the people passing by through the window. Chanah slipped into the shop and wrapped her arms around us from behind, laying her head on my shoulder. She didn't say anything, just squeezed softly and gave a contented sigh.

I was amazed every time she did that. How could I have been blessed with someone like her? She was the best person I had ever known, Peter and Paul included. This was my heaven, and if it was the only one of which I would ever be worthy, it was enough. After a few moments of blissful peace, she spoke.

"I love our family, Jesse."

"As do I," I replied.

"There is a group of saints traveling to Antioch after next week's Sabbath to worship in the temple. I would like for us to join them. We would go by ship from Joppa to make the journey faster. Can you have your current work completed by then?"

I pondered for a few moments, thinking through my projects and the extra hours Elhanan and I could devote toward meeting that goal. It would be difficult, but doable, and it would be worth it for her happiness.

I finally nodded. "Yes."

"Thank you, dear husband. It is not large, but I have heard that the temple is the most beautiful structure in Antioch and that even many of the Greeks are jealous of it." I could feel her smile on my shoulder and hear the reverence in her voice. I didn't understand it as deeply as she did, but I knew it was special.

"Jarah bat Elizur will be joining us. She is back from Armenia and brings a new husband with her, a recent Jewish convert from Rome. He is said to have once been a professional gladiator and that he could have been a notable trainer if he had not become so disillusioned with the sport. He had performed throughout Cilicia, Syria, and Armenia, and decided to live in Armenia after retiring."

"Why did they come here, just to travel back up to Antioch, when a temple will be built in Armenia?"

"I don't know," Chanah said. "She never wanted to return here—the memories are too painful. But she said she had a very clear impression, and she decided to face her fears and obey."

"Hmmm," I nodded. I remembered the first time I had seen the widow of Judas Iscariot. She had seemed haunted, but defiant, so I wondered what to expect.

"She admires you, Jesse. You inspire her. She sees what you have made of your life after such hard times, and she—"

My back straightened, and Chanah stepped away.

I swiveled toward her, Simon complaining at the movement with a whimper. He loved watching people through the window.

"Chanah, that was not me. Or very little of it was. It was you. You *saved* me. I am not here without you." It came out with more intensity than I'd intended. I blinked, searching her eyes for a reaction, waiting for the scolding she was bound to give me.

"I am flattered, dear husband." Her tone was calm and diplomatic. "But you give *me* strength as well. We are one. We rise and fall together, and after we covenant together with God in the Lord's house, nothing will ever be able to separate us. Not ever."

She spoke with such power, such conviction, that I felt my bones melt and my heart quiver. She had just proved again that it *was* her, and yet had shown how it was not. Somewhere, in some deep part of me, I understood, but it was difficult to articulate. I nodded, and she hugged Simon and me again before showering both of us with tender kisses.

The morning of our departure dawned overcast and cool, for which we were grateful. We would be walking two full days to arrive at the coastal city of Joppa, and the cooler weather was much preferable to scathing heat, especially for the children. We carried a minimal amount of supplies, as we intended to purchase most of what we needed along the way. We left our mules and carts behind, Chanah's parents agreeing to care for the mules. It still surprised me that they hadn't yet fully yielded to their daughter's patient Christian importunings, but she didn't seem overly worried about it.

With my burgeoning business and Levi's success as well, we were able to provide the necessary funds for several other saints who accompanied us. I worried that we might not have enough for ourselves for the entire journey, but Chanah had no such reservations.

At the last minute we learned that two of the apostles would accompany us—Andrew, whom I had met, and Philip, whom I had not. They arrived shouldering their own heavy packs, and they didn't complain that we weren't bringing any mules. They were accustomed to being weighed down, they joked, and they praised God for blessing them with strong backs and straight feet.

The journey to Joppa seemed faster than I remembered, perhaps because the apostles regaled us with so many tales of their journeys preaching the word and establishing new outposts of saints. Andrew had lately returned from Arabia, where he said seeds planted by Paul more than ten years earlier had flourished in miraculous ways all along the Red Sea. Philip had traveled to Carthage most recently, and his report was both more harrowing and less positive for the church of Christ. He prophesied, though, that not many years hence there would be more Christians in Carthage than in all of Israel and Syria combined. He also insisted that there would be a temple there. That seemed a strange claim to me. I had met a few Carthaginians, though Chanah reminded be to be careful how I judged.

The winds were favorable when we arrived at Joppa, and our appointed ship—*Diana's Daughter*—awaited us, having just taken on her cargo of cloths and silver. When the tide was turned, we set forth toward Antioch. My mother and Levi chose to remain above decks with Elhanan, a seventeen-year-old who acted like a ten-year-old on that ship, fascinated by everyone and everything. Chanah and I took Matthew and Simon below to rest, along with many of the other saints, including Jarah bat Elizur and her husband Artemis, who did indeed look the part of a former gladiator. He had an ugly scar along the left side of his neck and many more on his arms, hands, and lower legs. More than that, he looked like fluid steel in motion, or like one of the great cats with their awful, deadly grace.

It was somewhat warmer below decks, and the seas were calm, so I felt a much-needed sleep coming quickly. I think Artemis did as well, but Jarah and Chanah struck up a conversation that was hard to sleep through. At least I was lying down instead of walking.

"Things are not as difficult for the saints in Jerusalem now as when I left," Jarah said. "I am happy to see that."

Chanah nodded. "After what happened to King Agrippa the First following his execution of James…" Her voice caught. That was a hard subject, with the event little more than a year past. Her eyes filled with tears. "John took it hard, but he said the Lord had a purpose in it, and that James was already hard at work with the spirits on the other side. The son, Agrippa the Second, doesn't wish to tempt the fates, and he takes a dim view toward Jewish leaders who continue to persecute the saints. It has made things easier of late, for sure, though we are still careful. The winds can change at any time, as they have in the past, and the adversary is always looking for an advantage against us."

Jarah was somber. "We heard of Agrippa's demise in Armenia. His actions were seen by many of the people there as an injustice against all the gods and a reminder that rulers should uphold Roman law and rein in their passions. We already had good relations with the local leaders, even some of the Jewish ones, though I agree with you—we must be on our guard." She looked at Artemis, who gave her a grave nod.

There was more to that look, and Chanah caught it. "I don't believe we will be called upon to physically fight, Jarah," Chanah said. "We must battle in other ways and trust in the Lord's protection."

"Perhaps you are right." Jarah's tiny smirk proved she wasn't convinced. "But God can make his people mighty in arms, as he has in the past. King David was a great warrior, and the might of God's people shone like the sun, bringing peace across a great empire. Will he never lead us in battle again?"

Chanah was silent for a few moments, and I could see the struggle in her eyes. She was a pacifist, yes, but she was no fool. "If the Lord asks us to fight, we will fight, but I pray that day never comes, because once the battle is joined, its end is elusive. The bloodlust overcomes the strongest of men—even David, who was not allowed to build the temple as a consequence."

I remembered learning that, but I was conflicted. God had rescued his people before with fire and sword. Then again, war was so terrible, so destructive, so deadening and final that it must always be a last resort. Would we have to fight at some point? Against whom? Rome? The Sanhedrin who ruled by Rome's sanction? Even for someone like me, someone for whom fighting had so often seemed easier than diplomacy, contemplating conflict within or against the Roman Empire seemed preposterous. Then again, I was not God.

Jarah's voice rose. "Lucifer wins when he kills Christians and stalls the work."

Chanah shook her head. "Lucifer only wins when a person knowingly turns away from God. If they die in his service, as Paul has taught, there is rejoicing in heaven—sadness for the suffering but rejoicing for the victory of their eternal soul."

"And what of their families, left to agonize in destitution?" challenged Jarah. "And what of our freedom to worship, even in our homes? What if they take that away, as in the days of Daniel?"

Chanah took a deep breath and shook her head. "Those are good questions, Jarah, but we are called to have great faith in the Lord's wisdom and mercy—as much as we can—and to help any who suffer or stand in need. Until the end. That is easier said than done, of course. But if we choose to go to war, many innocents will die or be terribly maimed. Women will be widowed by the thousands, children orphaned, men forever scarred."

Artemis fingered the scar on his neck as if remembering the day he received the wound. "And what if they attack us?" he challenged. "Do we just lie down and accept death?" His jaw hardened. It was clear he was not about to take anything lying down.

I understood how he felt. I wasn't about to surrender to pagans, either, and I would fight to the death to protect my family.

"I cannot say," said Chanah. "It depends on how the Lord directs us, by his Spirit directly or through his prophets. We must trust him, which sometimes is not easy." She looked at Jarah. "You know that already."

Jarah's face froze, and her eyes grew wide. It was clear Chanah had struck a chord. For a moment I thought Jarah would explode and storm off in a colossal fury, but then she calmed considerably. It was clear she had great respect for Chanah. "We will be ready to do whatever the Lord asks, including defending our homes and families and fellow saints." Her tone implied they had reached a good compromise, and Chanah didn't challenge her.

"We will learn more in the temple, Jarah," Chanah said confidently. "We have so much to learn, and so much to share with others. I fear sometimes that I have neither the capacity nor the strength, but I will not allow my faith to fail. My lamp will not go out."

When we arrived in Antioch in less than two days' time, we were met by several of the elders in the city, who led us to accommodations near the temple. One of them told us that there were plans to construct permanent structures for housing the pilgrims who would come on a regular basis, and that Peter had already secured the funds to get the work started. As it was, my family was assigned a small rented house, recently vacated when the owner, a widowed merchant, had decided to move further up the coast and live with his son.

We were eager for our visit to the temple the next day, and so we ate little and prayed much, speaking in hushed tones as if we were about to enter the Holy of Holies—which effectively we were. It was frustrating that we couldn't enter the magnificent temple in Jerusalem, but it had become too defiled. Nor would the priests have allowed us access. The good news was that Jesus was restoring *all* of his covenants to the earth, and everyone, not just priests, was able to participate.

When we arrived at the temple the next morning, we took some time to appreciate its exterior beauty. It had been constructed on a low rise in the northeastern part of the city amid a cluster of minor estates and small vineyards. Its grounds were colorful and well-manicured, and there was a gravel walking path that wound around the building through a variety of trees, including pines and cedars. Its light-gray walls were of local stone, strengthened with famed Roman cement, and the doors, fashioned of hardwood banded in brass, were tall and stately. It wasn't as ornate as some of the great synagogues, and a far cry from the majestic Greek and Roman temples, but I was still astonished at the craftsmanship of the structure.

Our group of about twenty nearly filled the entry hall. A man and a woman greeted us.

"Welcome to the Lord's house," began the woman. "We hope you find great peace here today."

The man smiled warmly. "We were advised of several groups coming over the next few days. Can you tell us from whence you hail? We will also need to speak to the leader of your group."

Andrew and Philip both stepped forward, and each held forth a small rolled parchment. Andrew spoke for them. "I am Andrew, brother of Peter the Chief Apostle, and this is Philip. Here are our writs from Peter. We are members of this group from Jerusalem."

The couple clapped their hands for joy after seeing the parchments, and the man said breathlessly, "Paul has been here, and it was Peter who dedicated this structure to the Lord, but we have never had two apostles here at the same time. Welcome. Welcome!"

His voice had grown quite loud, and the woman put a finger to her lips, tapping him on the arm to get his attention. He looked momentarily embarrassed, but then gleefully ushered us through a set of intricate wooden double doors into a larger room. Several rows of benches with their backs to us faced an altar on the opposite side. Beyond the altar was a single door, tall and ornate like the others. According to Chanah, the room beyond represented the greatest glories of God, similar to the Holy of Holies, but I didn't remember what else she had said.

"Who gets to go through that door?" I asked her in a whisper.

She poked me lightly in the ribs, smiling. "I told you. Everyone. After the ceremony."

Andrew prayed, and then the two leaders began to instruct us, going back to the beginning with Adam and Eve, their words coming primarily from a large scroll they laid upon the altar. I cannot describe the simple grandeur of the great plan of God that was revealed to us that day. As I made additional covenants with him, I felt as if I had become part of a grand army that straddled both sides of the veil between the victorious courts of heaven and the contested battlegrounds of earth. Our little family received sublime and eternal promises that day as well, and for the first time I saw real long-term purpose in my life. I thought about the futures of our children, and their children, guided by the Holy Spirit and an ever-burning faith in their Redeemer. It was paradise as I'd never been able to imagine it, and that feeling lasted the entire trip home.

The next few years were peaceful, and we were happy. My business continued to flourish, and Elhanan became very talented, so much so that I encouraged him to strike out on his own. He wasn't ready to leave us, though. He often said he knew he was where he was supposed to be, and it was hard to argue with that. His presence was a blessing.

Chanah and I welcomed two more miraculous children into our home—both girls. Marian was born four years after Simon, and Sophia two years later. I often found Chanah crying her praises to God for our children and how they were ours forever. I joined her in the praises, though I was quieter. I still didn't feel I fully deserved such incredible blessings, but she deserved them.

God *was* good, and he had a job for me to do in protecting and providing for my family. I was grateful for that.

Shortly after Sophia was born, however, my mother fell very ill with a wasting fever that was sometimes accompanied by convulsions and vomiting. Chanah spent countless hours at her side, and she sent a request to Father Gideon to come minister to her, as Jesus had modeled for the apostles, as Peter and John had done for the lame man at the Beautiful Gate shortly following the Day of Pentecost, as the other apostles, members of the Seventy, and faithful sisters had done since on many occasions. As Mary had done for my uncle Levi.

I prayed for a miracle and tried to have faith, but after three weeks my frustration was ripe. Of course I knew my mother would eventually die, but if there was power to save her, why couldn't it be used? Where was Father Gideon? By the end of the fourth week I had resigned myself to the fact that she would pass, though Levi and Chanah continued to have hope.

The cheery way in which my mother greeted her trial and likely end only made me angrier. I complained to Chanah, but every time I did she would take my face in her hands and tell me how good God was to us, often reciting long lists of the blessings she felt we'd been given. She was right, of course. But it was hard to focus on blessings while I watched my mother shrivel and suffer.

Finally, Father Gideon arrived, and he brought Paul with him. Paul looked weary, having recently returned from a three-year missionary journey, but his eyes were bright and he greeted us like family. He reverently entered my mother's bedchamber and knelt by her side. She had been moaning softly as she tried to sleep, but her eyelids fluttered open and she smiled at Paul.

He took her hand and whispered a few words to her before calling for us to join him. I was hesitant, even knowing how things were supposed to be done in the more egalitarian way of the Lord's church. We laid our hands on her head, and Paul uttered the most amazing prayer I had ever heard, pleading with God, and then commanding—commanding!—my mother to be healed and to arise, telling her she still had work to do on the earth. I couldn't imagine myself having the same courage—let alone the faith—to proclaim such a thing.

My mother's eyes went wide. Tears streamed out and fell on her pillow. Then, to our amazement, she rose to her feet as if she were ten years younger. She embraced Paul, then Father Gideon, then Levi and Chanah and Elhanan, and finally me. I studied her closely, wondering if this was just some burst of energy fueled by hope that would soon run out, but she brushed the tears from her cheeks, straightened her robes, and marched out of her room to find Elhanan and the children. I had to rush to catch up.

"Mother, you should rest. You have been sick for many days."

She stopped and turned before ascending the stairs to the second floor. Her smile was bright, her skin showing its normal color. "And now I am healed, my son. I knew I could be if God willed it, and he did, so that was easy. The hard part will be making sure he didn't do it in vain." With that she patted me lovingly on the arm and then briskly climbed the stairs. I stared after her, dumbfounded, as she disappeared.

I turned to see Paul standing behind me, his smile as broad as the Jordan River in spring. "Your mother has strong faith, Barabbas. I do not often see the like. She trusts in God's will. She was prepared to die, knowing what glory awaited her on the other side of that passage, but she was also willing to live on here and suffer further for the glory of God. You are indeed a blessed man, Jesse Bar Abbas."

He grabbed my shoulders, squeezing hard, and I gave him a sheepish smile. Chanah was behind him, beaming, and then the truth of what I had just seen fully penetrated my heart… and my stubborn mind. I had personally witnessed God's power manifested physically, and I could never forget it.

Paul turned to Chanah, his tone apologetic. "I am grateful for the blessing of being able to be of service, but you need not have waited so long for us, dear sister. Your faith, along with that of Ruth, would have been enough. Jesse and Levi are more useful in these things than they will admit as well."

Chanah shook her head. "We obeyed the Spirit, which charged us to wait for Father Gideon. The blessing is ours, for a special witness to the divinity and power of our Savior is here today, under our roof, blessing our family. We are beyond thankful that you came. If you can tarry, we would be honored if you would sup with us."

My mother bounced around with so much energy for the next six months that I had a hard time keeping pace. She and Levi took in an orphan, an eight-year-old girl named Esther. She was a Samaritan who had fled her abusive slave master in Jericho and had somehow made it through the mountains to Jerusalem. She wouldn't talk about what she'd endured, and I was familiar enough with the haunted look in her eyes not to press. I feared, though, that she would be driven mad by her terror. I had seen it before, too many times. Fortunately, I was proven wrong, the love of her new family proving stronger than the terror.

Chanah grew more beautiful and wiser with every passing day. She spent considerable time meeting with some of the leaders of the church, and I gathered that some important decisions were being made, with her voice being heard. I also understood that there were strong differences of opinion on several matters, most notably the focus of the missionary work, which was still accelerating at breakneck speed, straining families and resources.

Paul believed that little detailed logistical planning was necessary, that all missionaries should let the Spirit guide them in the moment on where to go, whether to the next village or across the sea, whether to the Jews of a place or to the Gentiles. Peter was convinced that sound planning would be more powerfully guided by the Spirit and that the first focus should be the Jews, since they were God's covenant people. The Gentiles could seek out the church if they wished, and they were welcomed. He also argued that it was time to consolidate the gains made by the early missionary efforts, that spreading too far too fast would lead to weakness and apostasy. Paul contended that the more broadly the message could be spread in a relatively short period of time, the safer the church would ultimately be given the always unpredictable political winds of the world.

Chanah was torn but believed a compromise between the two approaches would be wise, and that the Lord was patiently guiding them toward such a compromise. It was difficult because of the long-standing dispute between Peter and Paul regarding Mark, who had abandoned an earlier mission with Paul but held great favor with Peter. But it would not be impossible. She had such great hope for the saints, as we were now publicly called—even by some of the Roman leaders. I knew she was pouring her heart and soul into the welfare of Christ's church. For my part, I was far from expert in the things of either God or mankind, and while I admired Paul more than any other man alive, I could understand Peter's argument more easily. I didn't take a strong position, though, as I was sure that whatever was decided, it would have little impact on me.

On a cold winter's night, I was awakened when Chanah shouted next to me and sat bolt upright. I hadn't even known she had come to bed. She had been out late meeting with the elders and a few of the woman leaders, including Mary, who was still spry and sharp of mind despite her advancing age.

"Barabbas, he's in danger!" She slapped my chest, and I coughed at the impact.

I sat up, trying to read her eyes in the darkness. I could see tears on her cheeks, glistening in the scant light.

"Who?" I asked, trying to shake my grogginess.

"Father Gideon," she said with a sob. "He has been betrayed!"

An adrenaline surge had me fully awake in an instant, my muscles twitching to take some action. "Who betrayed him?"

She arose and started dressing hastily.

"Come, Barabbas, we must go to him immediately. Bring…" she hesitated, but just for an instant, "…bring your sword."

I had already stood up, and despite my shock at being asked to fetch my short sword—a relic of days past—I was quickly ready to leave, grabbing the sword from behind the chest in our room. I hadn't held it in years, and I shuddered at how comfortable it felt in my hand. Would I need to do violence to protect Chanah and Father Gideon that night? Would God allow it, or perhaps even command it? I felt too willing—and that scared me.

We stopped to say a brief word to my mother and Levi before we exited the house, and then we hurried through the darkened streets of the city, Chanah aimed like an arrow at her destination, which was in the direction of the Upper City. I followed without question, my senses fully alert.

After about five minutes I heard some muffled but angry voices ahead. Chanah stopped and handed me a long black scarf. "Cover your face, Jesse. They cannot know who we are." We had entered the upper city, where the homes were much larger and farther apart, some surrounded by walls.

Before I could ask who she was talking about, she was off again, moving swiftly while she wrapped a scarf around her head. I did the same, then freed my sword from my belt.

The sounds grew louder until I could discern one of the voices as that of Father Gideon. Dim light emanated from a first-floor window a few houses beyond us. Outside the large house of polished stone stood two Roman guards gripping tall spears. Chanah slowed, lowering her head and not looking at the guards, who had heard us approaching. I tried to hide my sword behind my leg, but I knew they would recognize that. How long did we have before they readied their spears?

Chanah was a quick thinker. "We have found another!" Her voice was unafraid. She pointed at me. "They injured my husband, who wounded one of them. The rest have fled."

The guards looked at each other, and one of them nodded. The other guard went inside while the first approached us. He kept his spear upright, much to my relief. It was nearly impossible to best a well-trained Roman soldier one-on-one once his spear was lowered and aimed at your heart.

"Take me to him," ordered the guard when he had reached us. Chanah turned to me with an anguished look on her face, then closed her eyes and nodded.

I knew what that meant. Without pausing to think I lunged at the guard, my left hand reaching out to push him in the chest while my sword point took him in the hip, sinking deep. He screamed once before I pulled the blade free and cuffed him hard in the head with the flat side. He staggered backward, stumbling as his hip gave way, his spear clattering to the stones of the street. I rushed upon him to land another blow, but he was already unconscious. I had swung hard. I hadn't killed him, though, and a strange surge of pride leaped in my heart. I ran for the side of the house where Chanah stood, knowing that the other guard would be emerging after hearing the shout. Would there be others?

The other guard didn't fully exit, though. We heard him running for the door, but he stopped at the threshold to assess the scene. Upon seeing his companion on the ground, he yelled back inside, "Ignatius is down! We are under attack!"

There was a great commotion inside, followed by a stern command from someone else: "Kill him."

My heart froze in that instant, and somehow I knew what was coming. I could almost see it happening. I heard a spearhead strike flesh—not once, but three times, in the way of the Romans. It was a very distinctive sound, one I had made myself.

Chanah screamed, her senses lost. Luckily, I still had mine. Father Gideon was beyond our help, so my sole purpose became protecting Chanah. Grabbing her by the waist, I led her to the back of the house before the guard could return with others, then down a narrow alley to the next street. She quickly regained her senses and moved quietly and quickly with me. We ran hard, taking no particular course at first, then circling our way back toward our house. My heart surged with adrenaline. If someone stepped out of the shadows to harm Chanah, I would become one of those Babylonian berserkers of old, and God would have a hard time dissuading me from deadly force.

Fortunately, we made sure our escape before the passages to the Upper City were blocked. We arrived home safely, and well before dawn.

We were too distraught to work the next day. Chanah could barely leave our bedroom, and the children at first thought she was sick. I told Elhanan, my mother, and Levi what had happened, and they did their best to cheer her, but to little effect.

At noon I took her some food and found her on her knees, sobbing. She heard me enter and looked up. Her face was splotchy red, her eyes haunted. I couldn't bear seeing her like that. I set the food aside and knelt beside her, wrapping an arm around her shoulders. She leaned against me, and then a giant sob wracked her frame.

"Oh, Jesse, what have I done? How could I be so foolish and… and evil?"

I grasped her hand and squeezed, swallowing hard. I had never seen her like that, and it tore at my heart. How could I help her? What strength did I have to give her, when she had always been *my* source of strength?

"We tried. The Romans can be ruthless. What more could God have asked of us?"

She looked at me and cried, "But he didn't ask us to do it! I dreamed Father Gideon had been taken, and I knew it for a true dream, but then I assumed we were supposed to rescue him. I didn't ask God if it was right, Jesse. In my arrogance and ignorance I assumed God wanted us to go. Father Gideon was betrayed twice last night. Once by a greedy traitor who I saw in my dream…" her voice became a whisper "…and the second time by me."

I didn't know what to say. I knew her actions had been uncharacteristic, but she couldn't be to blame for what had happened.

"I'm sorry, my love," I said, my voice starting to crack. "My arm was not strong. I faltered. I should have killed that guard cleanly. Then perhaps we could have rescued Father Gideon."

She angrily shook off my arm and turned toward me. "No, Jesse. You were right not to kill him. Don't you see? We shouldn't have been there at all! God did not send us on that errand—*I* did, as if I knew better than God. And now Father Gideon is dead." She put her face in her hands, and the sobbing began anew.

"They would have killed him anyway," I offered, "if not last night then soon. At least we are safe, and they didn't see who we were."

She sobbed a while longer, and then looked up at me again. "We attacked one of their soldiers, Jesse. They will not take that lightly, and they *will* blame the Christians. They will also do an investigation, and you know how thorough they can be. If I had taken my dream straight to the apostles, we could have figured out what to do with God's help. Maybe Father Gideon would have been called upon to die for the truth anyway, but if not, God could have saved him…if only I had trusted him and been humbly patient."

I didn't have an answer to that. We were in trouble, and we had potentially put many others in trouble with us. I stayed with her the rest of the afternoon, and we prayed several times, pleading for forgiveness and direction. By the time evening came, Chanah's tears were exhausted, and we were somewhat calmer.

When we emerged from our bedroom, the first to run up to embrace Chanah was young Sophia. She was a perceptive child, and she seemed to know that what Chanah suffered was no physical ailment.

After a quiet dinner, during which Chanah tried to reassure the children that she was okay, smiling as best she could, she announced that she needed to meet with the apostles in the city and discuss something important with them.

At first I objected, but she was insistent. She also begged me to stay, just in case I was needed at home. I knew what she meant. I prevailed upon her to take Elhanan with her, though. After they departed, my mother and Levi helped me pack some things, just in case we needed to leave quickly. They didn't seem nearly as nervous as I was.

It was well into the third watch when Chanah and Elhanan finally returned. I was in a hazy half-sleep, trying to keep watch as I sat in the front room. My senses snapped to alertness when I heard them approach the door. I was on my feet in an instant, and I met her at the threshold as she opened the door.

"You are safe," I said. Relief washed over me like a giant tide, and I embraced her. Then I stepped back and looked at her face. She seemed afraid, perhaps more so than she had been earlier.

"What happened?" I asked. "What did they say?"

"My dream was indeed true." She walked inside and sat down on the floor, her back against the wall below the window. Her cheeks were streaked with dried tears she hadn't bothered to wipe away. Elhanan sat down a pace away, and I knelt in front of Chanah.

She let out an exhausted sigh. "It is horrible, my husband. I can scarcely believe it. Father Gideon was falsely accused to the Romans of stirring up sedition…by one of the followers of Peter."

That was bad.

"Peter is livid," she continued, "that any of the Saints would betray each other, and that any apostle should have *followers*—we are all supposed to be followers of the Savior, not of any man or woman. He mourns the loss of Father Gideon grievously, and… and he tried to blame himself." She breathed deeply, as if short of air. "But I didn't let him. He is a good man. He is stubborn and sometimes harsh—especially with Paul—but he is not overly proud like I am. He seeks the Lord's guidance and accepts the chastening he sometimes receives from him. I…"

She paused, closing her eyes. Several seconds passed. I looked over at Elhanan, who was staring at the floor. I was about to open my mouth when Chanah leaned forward and grasped my hands, her eyes focused there. "I had begun to wonder if I supported Peter as the Chief Apostle, Jesse. I still wonder. That is why I began to be so proud and foolish. That is why I almost got us killed. I admitted all of this to him tonight and begged forgiveness. I beg it of you as well. I am so sorry."

I swallowed, trying to absorb what she was saying. Peter, Paul, and many others had been warning the saints about apostasy for quite some time, but I had never paid much attention to that, because it could never apply to us. I had Chanah, and she was a rock, standing steadfast and secure against the storms. And there she sat before me, admitting to feelings of apostasy?

Chanah sobbed softly, and I stroked her hair and cheek, thinking about what to say. Finally, it came. "Even the best of people will make mistakes, but as long as they admit them and take responsibility for them, and truly try to change, then how can we judge them? Jesus is our judge, right? And he chose Peter, just as he chose Paul, knowing they weren't perfect and wouldn't always get along but would keep trying and would get the job done. He chose you for the same reasons. You are the best woman I have ever known, and you are proving that again."

She stifled a sob and shook her head. "No, Jesse. I have made such a mess of things. Peter already knew there were rumors of sedition reaching the Romans, and he was in contact with Antonius Felix, seeking to reassure him of the fealty of the Christians. But now that a Roman guard has been attacked and seriously wounded, the procurator is angry and doesn't want to listen. That is because of *me*, Jesse. God trusted me with that dream, and I chose to take the solution upon myself. If I had told the apostles first, Peter could have exposed the traitor to the Romans and proven our fealty."

"How?" I asked. "He didn't know who it was."

A look of profound sadness and guilt washed over her face. "No, but I did. Not at first, but after working hard to remember the face I saw in my dream, I know who it is. He has just admitted it to the apostles, but now it is too late."

CHAPTER 9

Then Peter opened his mouth, and said, Of a truth I perceive that God is no respecter of persons: but in every nation he that feareth him, and worketh righteousness, is accepted with him.

Acts 10: 34-35, KJV

The leaders of the church counseled for many days about what to do. Many argued that the saints must leave Jerusalem, at least for a time. Others argued in favor of staying and sending another embassy to the governor. They believed that leaving Jerusalem would weaken that embassy and make it appear both disingenuous and distrusting of the Romans, who seemed to get more upset when people expressed distrust in them than when they openly defied them—a god complex if I had ever seen one.

The first decision they arrived at was that my family and I would need to leave Jerusalem, immediately and permanently. It seemed part safety precaution and part punishment, though the leaders stressed to us that it was not a punishment. Of course, even if it was solely a punishment, I preferred it to being handed over to the Romans.

I was supremely grateful they hadn't opted to do *that*. They could have. Maybe they should have. Chanah and I had definitely violated Roman law, and we were taught to uphold the law except in extreme cases of injustice. Apparently the leaders had decided the killing of Father Gideon was such a case.

Still, it was hard to take in what their decision meant. I was a Jewish man from Jerusalem, the seat of ancient Israelite power. I had never realized the pride I'd come to derive from that. I knew those streets and buildings and houses as I knew the callouses on my hands. I felt safer and stronger in Jerusalem than I did anywhere else, and I was being required to leave it all behind.

Mary had interceded for us with regard to our journey. She had arranged with the famed Christian centurion Cornelius to get us onto a ship at Caesarea, though our destination was not yet known. Paul would choose it, and because it was he, Chanah and I felt somewhat better. Elhanan and our other children—and even my mother and Levi—were excited. To Simon and the girls especially, it seemed like a grand adventure.

While Levi, Elhanan and I packed up our trade supplies, Chanah and my mother organized our personal belongings with the help of the children. We had two mules and two carts, but we didn't dare purchase a third mule for fear of arousing suspicion. That meant there were things we would need to leave behind. We informed our neighbors that I had received a large commission from a visiting Roman official in Caesarea who had been sent to improve morale in the region through a series of public festivals. It was a plausible enough story.

Two days later Chanah led us in the final prayer in our home. It was a poignant yet beautiful moment, after which we turned our faces toward an unknown future. We journeyed through the Lower City toward the Jeshanah Gate on the west. My sword was hidden beneath my robes, and I could feel the cool steel of it against my thigh as we walked. I tried to appear calm and unworried, but my senses were alert. I was greatly relieved after we passed through the gate and were on the road to Emmaus, which would take us to Lydda, then Joppa. From there, we would turn north along the great coastal road called Via Maris that would carry us to Caesarea. It was the most direct route, and it was also the safest.

Mary and John met us at Cornelius's house in Caesarea, a large, sprawling two-story structure with a terraced courtyard and elegant peristyle in the middle of the many exterior rooms, which included three baths and a sizeable chamber for receiving audiences. The coolness of fall was kept at bay by thick window coverings and a host of fireplaces, which were stocked with wood that had been soaked to let off a sweet, spicy smell. The building was a castle—one of the largest and most well-appointed homes I'd ever seen, much less entered.

Cornelius was away at the Praetorium when we arrived, but Laelia, who I remembered well, greeted us warmly. She ensured that our animals were cared for and our belongings secured, and then got us settled into a pair of spacious rooms on the west side facing the sea.

Cornelius's wife and two teenage sons were visiting kin in Asia Minor, but there were three younger daughters at home, along with all their grandparents and at least two sets of aunts and uncles. There were also several servants, a few of which lived in the house. Whether the aunts and uncles were visiting or were a permanent part of the household I couldn't tell, but every person present had become a Christian.

Cornelius returned that night, and word came to us from a servant that he had arranged a feast for us and his entire household in the grand audience room. My family and I arrived in the room before he did, but it was just a few minutes until he entered.

My vision swam as he came into view. It was hard to focus, much less think. I knew his face, though I had seen it only once. He had almost killed me. Chanah asked me what was wrong, but I told her everything was fine. I knew there was nothing to fear, so I was able to recover and smile at her.

We celebrated the beginning of the Sabbath with song, scripture, and the breaking and blessing of bread and wine. Cornelius administered the Lord's supper after explaining that Paul had given him the authority to do so, and rather than having it passed around, he chose to personally bring the bread and wine to each person, as I had seen Paul do.

When he got to me, last of all, he drew back the bread when I reached for it.

"You remember me, Jesse Bar Abbas, do you not?" he asked quietly. "I was not a Christian when last we met, and neither were you."

I nodded but didn't raise my head to meet his eyes.

"You influenced me that day in Alexandrium, you know. I was captivated by your encounter with Mary, the mother of our Lord, and I could not get it out of my head. I began to pray to the God of Israel that day, and those prayers were different than any I had uttered before. I couldn't deny what was happening in my heart and mind, and while I am a proud man, I am not so proud as to think I am greater than God."

I nodded again, not knowing what to say.

"Arise, Barabbas, my brother."

I rose slowly, still not looking at his face.

He extended the plate of bread. "In the name of the Son, take the bread, brother, and remember the body he laid down for you."

I reached hesitantly to take a piece of the bread, which I could tell was of fine wheat flour, not the coarse barley to which

I was accustomed. After I swallowed the bread, he offered me the flagon of wine. "Drink, brother, in the name of the Son and in memory of the blood that he willingly shed for us."

Time suddenly seemed to stop, and it was as if my entire body hummed with energy. I took the wine, and as I drank I succinctly felt a hand rest upon my shoulder from behind. When I turned to see who'd touched me, there was no one there.

Cornelius fell to his knees, leaving me standing with the flagon of wine.

Chanah and my mother gazed at me with tears in their eyes.

What had they seen, and why couldn't I see it? Had I truly felt a hand on my shoulder? If so, whose could it have been and why had it affected everyone so? I had heard the stories of some of the righteous dead rising from their graves at the time of Christ's resurrection and visiting people. I had also heard the testimonies of many saints who said they had met with and been ministered to by Christ himself in the months following. But it hadn't felt real to me before, so I didn't know what to think about something so supernatural.

I had never felt such enlightening power in a single touch before, though I was quite certain that the Lord himself would never visit me in such a fashion. If he did, I would wish my bones to melt into the earth. So it must have been someone else.

After several moments of silence, I sat on the smooth floor and waited.

It seemed a very long time before Cornelius retrieved the flagon from me and regained his feet. He returned to his place and sat before addressing the group.

"My eyes have seen the testimony of the world's Messiah coming full circle this day." He stared into the distance a moment before focusing again on the group. "I am reminded of two things: God's perfect plan, and my own nothingness. Every day

I see the miraculous ways in which he guides events, laying bare my own foolishness. Today he has reminded me how carefully and patiently he has been preparing me to assist more effectively in his work."

He smiled at me as if he were truly grateful.

"I must tell you a story now that I have only ever told my wife. That was a long time ago, and the memories were faded. Until tonight. I hadn't thought to share it with you, but my path is being manifested by the Lord as we dine here together. I remember where it is I must go next, and I will soon discover what it is I must do there."

Chanah and my mother were spellbound, though he hadn't even begun the story. I was still reeling from what had just happened, but I listened carefully as well.

Cornelius took a deep breath, then spread his arms wide. "I was in my twenty-fifth year when I led a century of men protecting a Roman embassy to a powerful Ethiopian prince who ruled a vast amount of territory in the fertile south, west of the rift. His name was Cush, and he was said to be the most beloved of all the Ethiopian lords, a great visionary. Emperor Tiberius believed that Cush had discovered rich veins of gold, and our embassy was a pretense. The goal was to find those deposits."

It was odd to hear a Roman centurion openly impugning the motives of a Roman emperor, but nobody seemed to react to it.

"We were welcomed with great fanfare and extensive ceremony, but I knew when I first looked into the eyes of Prince Cush that we weren't dealing with an awestruck fool. He knew the power and reach of the Empire, but while he treated us with honor and respect he did not fear us as so many others did.

"Our leader was Avitus, the aggressively ambitious son of a leading senator." Cornelius smiled slightly. "After I told him about my first impressions of Prince Cush, he became convinced that the prince would lie to us and lead us on a fruitless tour among all the wrong parts of his land. He believed I should stay behind to see what other information I could pick up in their city while he was away with the prince. He left me with just an eight-man contubernium, one large command tent…and our most stubborn mule." His smile grew broader at that recollection.

"Cush's father was the oldest man I had ever seen. It was said he had passed a hundred years, yet he was healthy and energetic, his mind clear and sharp. His eyes were the most sparkling obsidian I have ever seen, and they could pierce clean through a man.

"His name was Jerem'Ai. He showed up outside our tent the morning after Avitus had left with Prince Cush. With him were a man and a woman of middle age, dressed in red and black, the colors of their royalty. The man introduced himself as Takshem, the woman as Meru. It was the strangest first conversation I have had with anyone save the apostle Peter."

Cornelius was a natural storyteller, and we were all captured.

"Jerem'Ai didn't speak, but Meru indicated that he wanted me—and only me—to accompany them to 'lands that were higher.' She didn't say what that meant, but I asked how long we would be gone, and she assured me we would return before the others. I believed her. Normally, of course, I would have been nervous—a single Roman centurion in strange and exotic lands. But strangely I wasn't, and so I agreed, leaving orders for the legionnaires to be alert and stay together while finding ways to make themselves useful to their hosts. They thought that last part an odd request, believing, of course, that it should have been the other way around."

Cornelius chuckled before continuing. "We left immediately, and my first surprise was our conveyance—twenty steeds that would have made many a Roman equite jealous. We were to have an escort of sixteen of their finest warriors, and when I saw them I could tell they were competent, though they were friendlier than I would have expected. My second surprise was that we headed south—not toward the great highlands of Ethiopia to the north and east. I admit to being disappointed, as those highlands were legendary.

"For the first two days we traveled through fertile, populated regions. Without fail all who saw us paused to give reverence to Jerem'Ai, who had a smile and a word for each one, though I could tell he was somewhat uncomfortable at receiving so much adoration. That, of course, was abnormal to me. Rulers crave adoration, even demand it—I had never seen it otherwise.

"When we reached the edge of the more populated regions our escort became more alert, though I didn't sense nervousness. They had the air of men who didn't expect to be attacked but wouldn't discount the possibility. They were expert riders as well, their mounts well-trained. They carried long spears, short swords, and stout short bows they could fire from horseback. They appeared to be as advanced as any group of horsemen I had seen or heard of anywhere.

"For three more days we traveled, seeing few people in the largely barren land. I worried aloud at one point that we wouldn't be able to return before Avitus had completed his tour of Prince Cush's lands. Takshem laughed, noting that Prince Cush's domains were vast, some of them not easily traversed, extending even to a portion of the great highlands. If Avitus was as greedy as Takshem judged him to be—he could tell, course—then their journey would indeed be very long. I heard both Meru and Jerem'Ai chuckle at that as well, and I was comforted and concerned at the same time."

Cornelius's eyes became more serious, and he paused for a moment to take a sip of his drink.

"At the end of the third day, we descended into a small valley, bounded on the south by a tall ridge that Meru said we would cross the next day. After building a fire, and after sentries were posted in the semi-darkness of a moon-filled night, Meru announced that Jerem'Ai would speak to the rest of us.

"I wish I could remember word for word what Jerem'Ai said that night, or that I could have written it down. He began with an account of how the world was created and inhabited by man and woman, and while I was not surprised by that—notions of mankind's origins are as numerous and popular as the stars in the firmament—it was curious that he referenced a single god, whom he called Father, who had created this world for his children.

"He claimed that the birthplace of mankind was far from that place, far from any known lands. I had never heard of an African who didn't claim that the origin of mankind was in a mysterious paradise hidden somewhere in the deepest parts of their continent. Of course, as Romans we claim that the origin of mankind lies somewhere near the Roman capital itself, and it had been so decreed once by Caesar Augustus.

"Jerem'Ai proceeded to describe the efforts of that one god to communicate with his children and give them knowledge. He laid out the plan by which this god would send his children to earth and give them the opportunity to choose him or not, by their own free will. That plan included how he would redeem those who had fallen and wished to return to him.

"He spoke of a champion, a savior, a high son of the one god chosen before the world was created, who would descend to the earth as a man and subject himself to weaker men. He would be the advocate for all men and women who chose the one true god, reconciling them to the Father so that they would be worthy to enter his heavenly abode. He said that in their language this savior was called 'Josuel,' and that he had already come."

A sacred silence seemed to permeate the air around us, and my heart burned as I contemplated what he had said. It seemed Jerem'Ai had spoken of Jesus of Nazareth at about the same time Jesus was preparing to begin his ministry in Israel. But how?

Cornelius's voice grew softer, more reverent, as he continued. "Jerem'Ai stared into my eyes for a long time, and I could not look away. Then he asked me if God could trust me. I was flummoxed by such a question.

"I knew my answer, though, and I knew that the question was being asked by a man of God. To the marrow of my bones and the depth of my soul I knew he was a man of God. But instead of answering his question directly, I asked him the question that burned hottest in my heart: 'How do you know God, and is there just one?'"

"Jerem'Ai studied me for several more disquieting seconds, and then said, 'In your eyes I can see the answer to my question. So, I will answer yours.' He then expounded to me the nature of God, and the gods, and the war in heaven, and that I was literally a son of God who was loved by him, and that I had a purpose on this earth, a mission to perform, a duty to save souls. I heard the same sermon from the Apostle Peter several years later, and shortly before that I had glimpsed a portion of the truth through Jesus called Barabbas, who had received it through Mary, the very mother of the Savior of the world.

"I am a very blessed man—more than I deserve to be, by far—for I have now found the true anchors of my purpose. My allegiance is to my true general, who is Jesus the Christ, he who fought and won the greatest battle ever waged anywhere. I am his servant, to the death…and to the life."

In that moment I reaffirmed my decision serve Jesus, perhaps reinforced by the guilt I felt at what Chanah and I had done. I would die for him, or for any of those who faithfully served him or sincerely sought after him. Or, as Cornelius had said, I would live for them.

Cornelius continued after another sip of his drink. "I had a dream that night that I have never shared with anyone, and I doubt I ever will, or even can. It was indescribable. By the next morning, though my body was tired, I felt more awake and alive and determined than I could ever remember being. I was eager to see where our journey would end and what Jerem'Ai wished me to see.

"We started early, and by the sun's zenith we had reached the top of the ridge. There we stopped, and as we sat our horses Jerem'Ai pointed toward the south. Far, far in the distance, I could see a great body of water, almost as if it were a small sea. He said, 'Many people have worshipped the mighty Nile river for the life that it brings to lifeless places. That, brother Cornelius, is the source of that river, which is fed by several smaller rivers.'

"I was stunned. To my knowledge, nobody had ever found the headwaters of the Nile and returned with the knowledge. It was said to be protected by the gods themselves and that to seek it brought a great curse. Yet there I was, viewing it, in the presence of a holy man. I didn't doubt it was true, though I wondered why he had shown me, and I asked him as much.

"He simply replied, 'I was to show you this place. That is all I know. The rest is for you to determine. But know this—the Son of God walks this earth as we speak, and someday you will know that.'

"He then proceeded to describe the history of that area, and the violent peoples that had more recently come to inhabit the lands surrounding the great lake they called 'Nyanza.' It had been peaceful once, but no longer. He admonished me to remember the place. Then he announced we would be returning to the lands of Prince Cush.

"You can imagine my disappointment that we would go no further. We were looking at the head of the Nile! It was said that if one reached the source of the Nile and was worthy, he could find the ambrosia and nectar of the gods and perhaps even become a god himself. I didn't believe that, of course, but returning to Rome after visiting the source of the Nile would have earned me great honor, even if it was difficult to prove."

He paused again, an air of reverence building around him. "I soon learned the true meaning of honor."

I was netted as surely as a musht in the Sea of Galilee. It wasn't just the legendary nature of the Nile or the grand pomp of Roman adventure or the teachings of Jerem'Ai regarding the nature of God and our existence. There was something more, something that foreshadowed our future. I knew it, though I couldn't adequately explain why, and it seemed like everyone else did, too. Chanah was gripping my hand and forearm with a firm, pleasant pressure.

Cornelius continued. "Shortly after we had embarked on the return journey, at least a hundred men, a quarter of them on horses, approached from the northeast. Jerem'Ai called a halt, and while he seemed calm, Meru, Takshem, and our guards were not. I could tell when an experienced soldier went to full alertness, and our guards were there in an instant, ready to act. As was I, though lightly armed and in completely alien territory.

"The threatening force slowed their pace, but they came steadily on. The clouds seemed to gather and increase, dimming the light, and the breeze became cooler. I noticed every sound and sight of man, animal, or insect, and as the minutes passed my anxiety mounted. I was sure they had slowed to increase our discomfort as they approached, which is exactly what I would have done.

"They stopped forty horse-lengths from us. After several seconds a group of thirty organized and advanced, ten of them on horseback. They were led by a giant of a man—the largest I had ever personally seen—sitting astride a mountain of a chestnut horse that was tasseled, braided and painted for war across its head and neck.

"As the man approached, I noted the intricate braided leather breastplate across his massive chest, along with pants of thick cloth and greaves of the same braided leather but with pieces of ivory interweaved. His head was adorned with an intricately-worked coronet of what appeared to be both brass and iron, impressive for the advanced skill obvious in its working. His eyes were a deep emerald, and they were perhaps the hardest eyes I had ever seen—eyes of death, eyes without mercy.

"My only hope came from the fact that they hadn't fallen upon us already and scattered our entrails for the wild beasts. They probably could have, outnumbered as we were. The man stopped his horse in front of Jerem'Ai and gave him a hard stare.

"'You are trespassing on sacred ground, Master Ai,' he said, his voice an avalanche of smooth pebbles in a mighty storm. 'You are far from home. Your peace does not extend here.'

"Jerem'Ai bowed toward the man, then lifted his head proudly and responded. 'I could not send ahead to ask your leave to pass through, noble G'haran. We have kept to the path and disturbed no spirits. My god asked me to show this Roman centurion the holy valley, and I obeyed.'

"The man looked at me briefly, and he was clearly agitated. But he also seemed to hold some respect for Jerem'Ai.

"'Bringing a Roman was a desecration, Jerem'Ai, even if you stayed on the path. I know your god is mighty, but I do not know him, and my god is also mighty. You I can forgive, but the Roman must die.'

"Well, that was it, then. My short life would come to a tragic halt at the end of an African spear. It was not what I had hoped for, obviously, but I was determined to show the man no fear. Without even looking at Jerem'Ai, I guided my horse out of our line and walked it toward G'haran, stopping just shy of his mount, which snorted and stamped briefly but held its place. It was well-trained, as were the mounts of our guards, who remained frozen in place but still ready. Then I spoke, knowing I probably shouldn't but figuring I was going to die anyway.

"'I am a proud Roman, your highness, but I am no defiler, as some are. I give honor where it is due and take none where none is deserved.'

"For a final speech, it was short but satisfying. I watched G'haran's eyes, which bored into me like poisoned darts. He didn't respond to me—perhaps he could not deign to do it—but looked back at Jerem'Ai. Before he could say anything, though, Jerem'Ai urged his own horse forward, guiding it between me and G'haran, bumping my own mount back a step. Then he looked up at G'haran.

"'You may slay me in his place, G'haran. I have given my word that he would be safe, and by my honor I will keep that promise.'

"G'haran sneered slightly. 'Your honor, as your peace, does not extend here, Jerem'Ai. I will kill you both if I have to.'

"Jerem'Ai shook his head firmly. I couldn't see his eyes, but I could guess at the authority projecting from them at that moment. 'You will kill me or you will kill none of us, G'haran. My honor is with me wherever I am, as is my god, who will strike you down if you defy him in this thing.'

"I wondered if I was imagining things, but it felt as if a strong heat was radiating from Jerem'Ai. My horse backed up another step as though it felt it, too. G'haran schooled his features, but I could tell that Jerem'Ai's pronouncement had given him serious pause. Not understanding anything of their relationship, though, I couldn't guess at what would happen next. I expected that we would all be slaughtered. The world is brutal, and sometimes man is even worse than beast. We were in G'haran's hands, to do with as he pleased.

He was pensive for a moment before he continued. "Or so I believed then. My view is different now. I am quite certain that if G'haran had attempted to slay us, he would have been slain himself, whether by us or by God's angels. G'haran finally lowered his eyes—a shocking thing to behold—and then said in a low voice thick with surprising contrition, 'I feel your god's presence, Jerem'Ai, and not mine own. Perhaps they have worked out an arrangement, I do not know. But I allow you to pass, and I beg your forgiveness for my threats. May both our gods protect you on your journey home.'

"It was utterly amazing. I had heard fables of such occurrences in ancient history, particularly among the Sumerians, but I believed that was all they were—mere fables. Here I had witnessed something so extraordinary, so completely outside the normal course of things, that I had a hard time understanding how it could be. Perhaps that was why I had resisted the whisperings of God for so long—I believed that such things couldn't be understood, at least not by common men such as me.

"Jerem'Ai and I both turned our horses and were returning to the group when a visceral cry split the sky from the direction of G'haran's band. What happened next was like a play performed on stage with perfect precision. I wheeled my horse around, and he obeyed as if expecting the command. My eyes found the source of the cry and identified a single man charging us with a wicked-looking eight-foot spear. At the same time I heard the word 'Roman' to my right. My arm reached out almost of its own accord to catch the spear that was tossed to me by Takshem.

"Of all the martial talents I might within reason claim to have, the throwing of the spear is perhaps my greatest. I had barely taken my next breath when the spear was out of my hand, lancing toward my target, who was just stopping to set his feet, his arm coming back to make his own throw.

"He saw the danger and instinctively tried to twist away, but it was too late. My spear caught him in the chest, and at an angle due to his twisting that caused the head to cleanly pierce his heart. It was the rare perfect strike. I had seen shock in men's eyes before when blade or arrow or spear struck them, but this man's eyes filled with primal fear and rage before he stumbled backward and dropped to the grass.

"All was silent for several seconds save for the last labored breaths of my would-be assassin. I dared to look at G'haran, who had almost reached his line when his man had begun his attack. He sat calmly on his horse, his face a mask. He was a hunting cat, though, graceful and calm until the second of violence. He regarded me coolly, and clearly with some respect. Then he looked at Jerem'Ai, and I was surprised to see an expression of humble appeal.

"Of course, had one of my men broken discipline so badly, I would have felt shamed to my toes, so I understood. He had made a promise to Jerem'Ai, and then someone in his ranks had defied it.

"Jerem'Ai was truly calm. He walked his horse forward to where the dead man lay, beckoning me to follow. When he stopped, he gestured for G'haran to approach as well, then dismounted and knelt near the man's head. I followed suit, though I did not kneel, perhaps because in the back of my mind I still felt there could be another threat.

"G'haran dismounted as well, then approached to stand across from me as we gazed at Jerem'Ai, who was whispering in a language I had never heard, even among Jerem'Ai's own people. For several minutes we stood there, solemnly listening. I could tell that G'haran understood what was happening, though I couldn't tell how he felt about it.

"Suddenly Jerem'Ai snapped his head back and looked up at me, his face still calm but his gaze commanding. 'Your spearhead pierced his heart, Centurion Cornelius, which means this man's blood flowed directly from his heart to his mother earth. You are now bound to this place, and to your brother who lies before you. By my authority, and with God's approval, I release you from this binding for a time, but you will return to this place, and we shall see what God has planned.'"

"Did you go back?" asked Elhanan. He was leaning forward intently, eyes wide.

Cornelius shook his head. "No, I haven't yet. But I was reminded tonight that I am called to return, and I feel it is imminent. I had, unfortunately, almost forgotten much of what happened there. I witnessed unparalleled honor, courage, faith, and leadership, such that spared my life. How can I not proclaim their source—the one true God—to others, and live my life as close to that ideal as I can? I forgot that honor once," he looked pointedly at me, "but I will not forget again. I will return to the lands of Jerem'Ai and Cush, to learn and to share, and to proclaim my own witness of the resurrection and eternal atonement of the God of the whole earth."

CHAPTER 10

And on my servants and on my handmaidens I will pour out in those days of my Spirit; and they shall prophesy.

Acts 2:18, KJV

I don't remember much of what happened the rest of that evening after Cornelius had related his amazing story. Chanah couldn't stop talking about what he had said, but her conversation involved mainly my mother and Elhanan. There was a fair bit of crying, too. I pondered everything but had a difficult time understanding it all, so I mainly kept quiet. Sleep was welcome, and it was peaceful.

The next morning, Cornelius was gone early on some business of the Praefectus Praetorio, but he had given instructions to Laelia to take us to the market and purchase whatever we needed or wished for our voyage by sea. We bought dried fruits, nuts, and hardtack breads, along with extra skins for water, and we were grateful. But Laelia insisted on buying us new clothes and sturdy sandals as well, even a white sash for Chanah—white!—along with a necklace and bracelets that made her look like a queen. I was aghast at how much it all cost, but Laelia didn't seem worried in the slightest—joyous was more accurate—though she bought nothing for herself.

Chanah was embarrassed by the attention given to her. She tried to refuse the items, but it was like trying to shout down a whirlwind. Elhanan and Matthew thought it was amusing, and of course they were elated to get some new clothes and better shoes, plus two of the finest hunting knives I had ever seen. Simon, Marian and Sophia were most excited about the fine Roman toys they received—not plain, wooden toys such as I could provide, but finely crafted figures, including dolls and a chariot made of brass. My mother was the only one able to refuse Laelia, but she used that power sparingly and ended up with nearly as much as the rest of us.

The one odd gift Laelia procured was for me, and she didn't seem to pay for it. Perhaps the sale had been arranged beforehand. The seller—owner of the finest shop in Caesarea—seemed reluctant to give it to her after looking at me and knowing for whom it was intended, but he made no formal objection before handing it to her. It was a small brass ball, about half the size of my fist and as perfectly round as the sun. Fine etchings covered its surface, mostly lines and irregular shapes that made it look like a map wrapped around a very large pearl. It wasn't heavy, so it couldn't have been solid brass, but I couldn't see any obvious seams in it that would prove it was two or more pieces and hollow.

I objected strongly. It looked costly and fit for a king. Laelia brooked none of my complaints, and ultimately I couldn't refuse her. Before I could place it in my sack and change the subject, though, Chanah snatched it out of my hand and held it up, examining it closely for a few moments before looking at Laelia.

"Where did this come from?" she asked, curiosity strong in her eyes.

"Cornelius purchased it on one of his trips north," Laelia said. "He won't say much about who sold it to him and why, but it's one of his favorite acquisitions. He has never told me why he doesn't keep it in the house, though someday he will crack and tell me." She winked.

"So why would he give it to me?" I asked, incredulous.

Laelia shrugged again. "He knows something, Master Barabbas. He was very clear that I should approach this antiquities dealer and give it to you. He thinks you will need it someday—not to sell, mind you"—her voice became very firm—"but to guide you, and not because it's a map."

"A map?" asked Chanah.

"Yes. This is a rough map of the world, even more than what we Romans know of it. That is another mystery I would like to solve. Our world is round, you know. Any mariner worth his britches' weight in salt knows that, though some fancy it otherwise. But this isn't really a useful map, just decorative. Inside, however, there is something called a 'mooring stone,' and Cornelius thinks it will someday be important…to you."

I was thoroughly confused. "I've never heard of such a thing."

Laelia smiled. "Cornelius pursued a few stories, far to the north, perhaps even to the isles of the Britanni. They disagree on many points, but they all hint at a key to great power and prosperity. Cornelius used to believe that key was military in nature, but I don't think he believes that now."

"What does he believe?" Chanah asked.

Laelia shook her head. "I don't know, but I know he has changed considerably since he came to know Jesus of Nazareth. He is calmer, more certain, and more determined than I've ever seen him." Her voice dropped to a whisper, though there wasn't anyone close enough to hear, as we were on an isolated side street. "He serves his Eternal Lord first, his emperor second, and he senses a clash between the two coming. He has told me plainly that he is ready to give his life for the cause of the Christians, even if he has to defy the Empire or leave it altogether."

Those were dangerous words, especially for a centurion of such great rank. But it still didn't explain the gift. Chanah gave the ball back to me, and I rolled it around in my hands for a few moments, feeling the fine etchings on my skin. Who could have created something so impossibly fine and detailed? I knew some of the ancients possessed abilities that had been lost, but I had no context for comparing such things.

"Did he show it to any of the apostles?" I asked.

Laelia nodded. "He showed it to both Peter and Paul. Neither could discern its origin or purpose, and both gave cryptic answers about how there are many things in this world and its connections to the heavens that we do not yet understand. It was Paul, though, who told Cornelius that he needed to transfer this artifact to the right person, and that if he sought that knowledge diligently and sincerely, it would be revealed to him. He chose you, Master Barabbas."

I didn't know what to say. My mind was nearly numb, and my world had been turned upside down and shaken so much over the last few days that I wasn't sure I could even have a cogent conversation about tentmaking at that point. Chanah was smart and steady, though. Together, we would figure it out. If I ever lost Chanah, however,...no, that was too dark to think about.

I had thought the surprises were at an end, but that evening I was proven wrong. We had barely begun to eat when there was a minor commotion at the front of the house. Shouts of elation followed, and moments later both Peter and Paul walked into the dining hall wearing wide smiles and looking like they had never had an argument with each other in their lives. They embraced everyone and joined us for dinner. They talked, laughed, and related events from their most recent trip, which had taken them to Joppa, then Capernaum, then all the way to Hebron, then Bethlehem and finally Caesarea. Two others traveled with them, men I had not met. They were quiet, though they smiled and laughed and said the occasional word or two.

Peter and Paul also gave us updates on the wonderful things the new saints in various places were doing—the miracles of faith and healing, the many conversions and baptisms, the new meeting places and temples being built, the many missionaries departing for distant lands. It still seemed odd to me that so many would be sent away as missionaries when they were needed to strengthen the young church at home and care for their families. What great purpose would it serve if small branches developed far from each other and from the roots of the church, and both roots and branches then withered and died?

On the other hand, the church was growing rapidly, and most of the saints I had met seemed to exult in the sacrifices being asked of them. Paul was especially that way, always rejoicing that the Lord had given him another chance after his previous persecutions of the Christians. The new temples, too, which seemed such a burden, especially with so many able-bodied men being called to travel the world to spread the message of the gospel, caused continuous rejoicing among the faithful. I, too, knew what that felt like.

In the end, it seemed that both Peter and Paul had been both right and wrong, odd as that sounded to me. The Lord was bringing them together to find the right path, achieve the correct balance, and exercise faith to stay the true course. I still had much to learn about all of that, and I was grateful that I had Chanah to guide me.

After filling our bellies with the most delicious fowl I had ever tasted, plus date tarts and perfectly ripe melons, we sat back to listen to the sermons. My lids were heavy, but I knew Chanah would make sure I stayed awake. Elhanan acted as if he were fresh off a good night's sleep, and I could see that Matthew was trying hard to impress his mother by listening intently. The younger children played as quietly as they could with their new toys, though I could see Simon paying a lot more attention than he probably intended.

Peter and Paul said very little to the group by way of pure preaching, choosing instead to elicit questions and converse about them, which lasted about two hours. Before they bid us farewell to take to their beds, they greeted each member of our family, offering their blessings and giving each of us a kiss.

I had never been a heavy dreamer, and rare were the occasions I could remember the details of my dreams. However, that night I dreamed as I had never dreamed before. It was almost as if I were awake, because when I actually did wake I remembered everything with vivid clarity. When I told Chanah of my dream a few days later, on the ship, she scolded me for not telling her sooner. She called for a wax tablet and stylus so that she could write it down, claiming she knew it was important.

In my dream I tried to climb a mountain far taller than any I had ever seen, much of its height white with snow. Climbing was maddeningly laborious and sluggish, and it seemed like I couldn't make any progress. Before I gave up, I reached up to the tall golden bird I was suddenly aware of perched on my shoulder, and I offered it the curious brass ball with the mooring stone inside. The bird, which seemed distantly familiar, squawked, snatched up the ball, and flew into the sky, its great wings churning the air as it arced upward.

Satisfied, I looked around, expecting to see my family, but I was alone, exhausted, and strangely at peace with my decision to give up. I laid on my back, looking up into the snow flurries that danced above me. I imagined I could see my mother in that dance, and I smiled. She loved to dance, an inclination not strong with her son.

I lay there a long time, though the hazy daylight continued to persist. I wondered how long it would take to die from the cold, and I was curious to know what it was like to pass to the other side. I didn't seem to feel the cold, though, and that concerned me. I wanted my journey to end, my attempt to make the climb having failed. And yet somewhere in my jumble of feelings was a harmony I couldn't describe because of its vastness. I closed my eyes, thinking perhaps I could will myself to where I wanted to go…

…and found myself walking down a dim hallway with walls of damp, dark stone. It reminded me of that hallway in Herod's dungeon, when I'd believed I was marching to my death. That day seemed an eternity in the past. I was alone in the dream, however, and my body was free and strong. I walked with a purpose I could feel deep in my chest, but I didn't know what it was. The hallway was long, and it ended in a wall of fire that I should have seen coming but didn't. I walked right through it, not knowing why or how I could. I could hear screams in the distance, and suddenly I was climbing up the sides of a deep, waterless well, the fire and the hallway now a distant memory. I wasn't surprised, because it was my well, even though I had never owned my own well.

I don't know how I climbed, but somehow my hands and feet found purchase as I progressed upward. When I came out of the hole, I could hear the screams clearly. The fire had returned and was all around me, burning houses and shops in the black night, many of them built purely of wood. This was not Jerusalem, but I knew where to go. I ran, barely noticing the others who joined me as I sought to increase my pace. We ran a long distance with the screams surrounding us. More people joined us, and I wondered where we could be going and why we kept passing people who were screaming for help.

For hours we ran, until dawn broke over the horizon. There were hundreds of us now. The fires were burning out. We left the city, running across beautiful fields wet with the morning's dew. We didn't tire, and it almost felt as if I had wings, my feet barely touching the ground, our pace becoming impossibly fast, until I tripped and crashed headfirst into the water of a broad lake, my breath leaving me in a rush, my arms and legs flailing as I tried to find the surface.

I stopped breathing, but it didn't affect me, and so I swam under the surface, angling downward toward a light in the distance, not heeding the curious fish that measured my progress. Where was I going, and where were the others? If I didn't need to breathe under the water, was I dead? It was thrilling to slice through the water without worrying about air, and so I enjoyed the feeling as I swam. Was Chanah waiting for me at that light? What about my children?

Yes, it was definitely my children. Somehow I knew. I swam faster, sensing danger.

As I neared the light I noticed a frenzy of sharks guarding the way, and a long, bright spear appeared in my right hand. I thrust it ahead of me, kicking harder to close the distance, glad the sharks hadn't yet noticed me.

But then they did. There were dozens of them, and of one accord they charged, black eyes glittering with lust, teeth already dripping with my blood. There was one in particular that took the lead, and I aimed for it, desperately hoping for a way to get through. When my spear impacted, there was a tremendous explosion of power. The air filled with bubbles, and my senses momentarily blackened. When I could see and think again, my spear was gone, and so were the sharks.

Unfortunately, so was the light.

CHAPTER 11

Stand fast therefore in the liberty wherewith Christ hath made us free, and be not entangled again with the yoke of bondage.

Galatians 5:1, KJV

When I awoke, the first thought that struck me was that Peter and Paul were in the house and could interpret my dream. I knew they wanted to see us before we boarded the ship, and that Paul would be telling us our destination. I slipped away without waking the others and headed for the room where Peter and Paul were sleeping. Laelia met me along the way carrying a travel sack with some of our new clothes.

"Good morning, Master Barabbas," she said cheerily. "You seem very intent. Are you looking for something?"

I shook my head and smiled. "No, just Masters Peter and Paul. I wish to speak to them."

"Oh." I knew by her expression what she would say next. "I'm sorry, they aren't here. They had to leave very early on some urgent business in Bethany. I know they wanted to bid farewell to you and your family, but they didn't want to wake you. Paul revealed your destination to Cornelius, though. Do you want to know?"

The news of their leaving left me disappointed and anxious, but of course I wanted to know. "Yes, please."

"It is the island of Melita. I've been there. It's small and there aren't a lot of people, but it is peaceful and prosperous. You will all enjoy it there. Paul has left some instructions—"

"He left them with me." I spun to see Cornelius, who was smiling broadly. "I will accompany you to the docks today, and I have a note for you as well. An official writ, actually. It will help you with the centurion of the garrison there. I don't know him, but my writ carries my seal."

I bowed my head toward him. "Thank you, Master Cornelius. We are most grateful for everything you have done for us."

He laughed. "We are bound to each other, Jesse. I am grateful to you as well, and I have a feeling our paths will cross again, though I don't know how."

I thanked them and returned to our rooms. Chanah was up, tending to the children and organizing our belongings. My mother wasn't feeling well, but she helped as much as she could. Levi, Elhanan, and Matthew had just left to assist some of Cornelius's household staff in preparing the mules and carts.

Chanah looked at me expectantly. "When are they coming, Jesse? Since we made most of our preparations yesterday, we are almost ready to leave."

I frowned. "They were called away during the night. They are not coming." I turned to my mother, avoiding Chanah's disappointed look. "Are you well enough to travel, mother?"

She scowled. "I am right as rain and ready to go. You two should let me help more. I'm not disabled." To emphasize her point, she hefted a large bag of clothes Chanah had just tied and carried it out to the hallway.

After a quick breakfast and warm good-byes to Laelia and the rest of the household, we journeyed with Cornelius to the docks with our lives loaded onto our mules and carts. I was nervous, and I could tell Chanah felt the same. We were about to leave our homeland, probably for good.

We arrived at the appointed ship, a broad-beamed, low-masted vessel that her Cretian captain called the *Silver Osprey*, a name wholly unbefitting the old, gray barge. She seemed in good repair, which was reassuring. Cornelius took the captain aside and spoke to him for several minutes, and then he returned to us, apparently satisfied. He pulled two small scrolls from his satchel and held them out to me.

"Paul's instructions and my writ. The captain knows you travel under Roman protection. He expects favorable winds and has promised a smooth, swift journey."

I wasn't sure how a true captain of the sea could make such a promise, but I nodded in appreciation. "Thank you."

Cornelius laid both hands on my shoulders. "Godspeed, Jesse Bar Abbas." He looked at Chanah. "And you as well, Mistress Chanah. May God bless you and your family on your journey, and in your new life."

We bid him farewell and boarded the ship, our mules and carts having already been taken for loading. Within minutes the oarsmen were pulling us away from the dock and into the open waters of the Mediterranean—the sea in the middle of the lands, the many-fingered sea of the gods. My anxiety rose. The trip to Antioch had been brief, and we had stayed near the coast. This time we were embarking into the vastness of the Great Sea, on a craft made of tiny splinters.

The water was calm and the sun bright, so my fears were easily controlled. By that evening, however, the 'favorable' wind picked up and the waves became swells. We had passed beyond sight of land, too, and both my belly and my head protested vigorously that fey voyage fraught with unknown perils.

Chanah was fine, and our children bounced around with their normal playfulness as if we were still on land. I couldn't tell if my mother or Levi were bothered, because my mother looked more determined than ever to show us she was well, and Levi stayed calmly by her side.

After two weeks, with three overnight ports of call, I had acquired sea legs, though I was growing more eager by the day to abandon the confined spaces of the ship and the dry, monotonous diet of salted fish, hard biscuits, nuts, and dried fruits which left me constantly thirsty. It was useful that Chanah called us together each morning and evening for prayer and reflection. Her continued calmness and courage shamed me into taking more responsibility in those gatherings.

After nearly another week we arrived at Melita, our new home, docking at the secondary port on the island. I was happy we hadn't docked at the main port, because I had hoped for a quieter, less conspicuous place for my family to start out. But then I showed my writ from Cornelius to the man in charge at the dock, and we were treated with the deference normally shown to Roman passengers of high birth. We were also directed to the mayor of the small town nearby, called Taragh.

A fast courier ship had arrived from Caesarea ahead of us, so the woman who was mayor had known for more than a week that we were coming, and a home had already been prepared. It was stunning and welcome news. I had expected us to live in tents while I constructed our home myself, but Cornelius and Paul had surprised us again. We marveled for days at our good fortune.

―――

It didn't take me long to establish myself again as a tentmaker, though I had to travel often from our home in Taragh to the main port of Sendre and to the inland Roman capital of Medina to transact my business. The trips weren't long, as the island was less than a day's journey from tip to tip, and the roads were good. It was advantageous that Melita was considered by Rome a free municipium, which meant there was little Roman interference in the business and social affairs of the island. The Roman governor from Sicily would only occasionally visit, though whenever he did my heart felt darker. We stayed away from him and his entourage, and I wasn't tempted by any potential business with him. The rumors of his capricious cruelty made that easier.

Matthew helped me in my work sometimes, though he was more interested in trade and transport and spent more of his time with local merchants, learning their business while he promoted mine. Elhanan continued to refuse to branch out on his own as a journeyman tentmaker. He did show some serious interest in marriage, however, which was a good sign. Simon spent considerable time at the shop, and sometimes we would take him with us on our treks, especially when we went to Medina, which was more ordered and therefore safer than the port towns that were often filled with lonely sailors.

Chanah and I had read Paul's instructions, but it was more than a month before we took the time to review them carefully together. There was much there, though some of it was cryptic. One Sabbath morning we sat alone on our rooftop terrace and discussed it.

"Paul clearly wants us to start a branch of the church here," Chanah began after we had re-read Paul's scroll.

I shrugged. "But he didn't give us any formal authority to preside, so we can't."

Chanah nodded pensively, looking out toward the sea, which was only a quarter mile off. "We are to be missionaries, though, and you have authority to baptize."

"But there is no one here to approve the baptisms."

Chanah looked at me. "He tells us to bring people to the Savior and gather them. Is he not giving us authority to preside in some capacity?"

I was hesitant. The reason for our hasty departure from Jerusalem still stung, and she must have seen that remembrance in my eyes, for her head dropped and her voice was penitent.

"I do not wish to assume more than is my right, more than what is God's will." She began to tear and turned her head away. "Perhaps I am reading more into Paul's instructions than I should, especially after our actions—*my* actions—brought so much danger to the saints in Jerusalem."

I knew she suffered deeply, and it pained me to see it. "Paul tells us to counsel with the Spirit in all we do. That is the same as counseling with God, isn't it?"

She nodded.

"Then we can seek his will. If he tells us by his Spirit that Paul's instructions give us authority to preside and baptize, then we can do that."

I had rarely been so forward in discussions regarding the church, and part of me resisted my own words, but Chanah's face brightened a bit and my unease faded.

"Yes. Yes, Jesse, that is what we must do. We need to figure out how the Lord wants us to act and then proceed accordingly. Nothing more, nothing less. My pride and ignorance cannot be allowed to interfere, and neither can my fear."

Her pride and ignorance? And *fear*? I almost laughed, but she was gravely serious.

She continued. "Paul also says he will send someone, but he doesn't say who or when. At first, part of me thought we had to wait for that person, but I don't believe that is so, do you?"

I shrugged. "I think he would have told us specifically to wait."

She nodded. "Yes, I agree. We need to seek the Lord's guidance. I don't think it will come easily, especially after...well, we will have to work for it. We need to get to know the people on the island. We need to be good examples. We need to teach any who will listen, and then...and then the Lord will direct us. In his own time."

It was the kind of thing Chanah would say, but she was still not herself. I could see it in her eyes and hear it in her voice. She doubted herself greatly. And she was being too self-critical.

I reached over to take her hand, my mind scrambling for what to say. I was more accustomed to receiving counsel than giving it, though I was trying to do better, especially for our children.

"It will be okay. We'll figure it out together. Remember what Paul said at the end of his letter?"

Chanah nodded, squeezing back. "He told us we would be safe. But he also warned us to stay strong. He worries about us falling away, and I cringe at how he thinks we might."

"And yet he trusted us to come here and bring God's word with us. How determined are you to verify his trust in us?"

"Very." The resolute look in her eyes was comforting. At least for the moment, she looked like Chanah again.

Within a year the island felt like home. We spoke Greek all the time, except for the Sabbath, when we spoke in our native Aramaic. I conducted almost all my business in Greek, though the eastern traders often used Aramaic, and I encountered a Roman from time to time who insisted on Latin. That was good, as I wanted to keep my Latin fresh.

Chanah and my mother faithfully taught the children the words of Jesus and his apostles, and occasionally they would write a letter to Peter or to Paul and send it on one of the courier ships. The children enjoyed that. They also found a few teachers around the island who could instruct them in math, language, and science. Since we were considered Roman for all practical purposes and my wife could have charmed the stars to descend from the sky to assist her, this was relatively easy to do.

We invited others to learn about Christ, too. His name was spreading throughout the empire, and people were curious. For most, their interest didn't progress beyond curiosity, especially when they learned the narrowness of the path he called them to follow. They couldn't understand how obedience to all of God's commandments could make them freer, and so they politely—and sometimes not so politely—declined to progress. We didn't judge them for it. Instead, we continued to befriend them and be of service, so we enjoyed a considerable amount of goodwill.

In our second year on Melita, Elhanan was married to a Roman woman named Junia, whom he taught and baptized, and whom Chanah adored. Junia was olive-skinned, brown-haired, and green-eyed, like many young women on the island, and she loved the sea. Her father was a well-known merchant of considerable repute, which turned out to be a boon to our business even though he wasn't thrilled with his daughter's conversion to our mysterious new religion.

Soon we were selling tents as far away as Carthage, Tarentum, and even Cyrene, and with Elhanan having become so skilled we could take on the largest and most complex jobs.

It was in the third year that our Christian faith attracted the ire of the chief rabbi of the several dozen Jewish families on the island. He was a sniveling, spindly, hawk-nosed man named Jonas who had somehow discovered that we were of Jewish blood and not natively Romans.

At first, he just proclaimed us blasphemers among the congregants of the three synagogues on the island, and we endured spiteful looks and a few harsh words when our paths crossed. That didn't bother us much, since we didn't attend synagogue anyway. When he realized that most of the people on the island didn't care—and that some even laughed at him—he spread petty, baseless rumors about us. He claimed that we were fugitives from Jewish justice, which hit close to home. He claimed I was a spy for the governor, gathering information on Jew and Roman alike, and that I never traveled to see the governor when he visited because I wanted to reduce suspicion that I was a spy. He claimed that we practiced strange rituals and talked with evil spirits, and that we had caused at least three major storms.

It was all preposterous, of course, but he kept it up, and his children made sure other children heard some of the rumors as well. Every time he saw me, he publicly denounced me for blasphemy. He'd even sprinkle dust on his head and moan in anguish. The one time I laughed, it just made him more determined.

Chanah vigorously deflected every one of his attempts to discredit and minimize us, but rumors, over time, have an insidious way of entering the mind and nesting. Eventually, some of the kids' teachers made excuses to stop coming to our home, and I lost some of my best local customers, who didn't want to get caught up in any sort of conflict among the strange and temperamental Jews.

The biggest blow was when the chief mayor of the island, along with several of the town mayors, told us to stop spreading our fantastical Christian religion. They forbade us to baptize anyone—even our own children—in this new religion that caused so much anxiety and strife within the small Jewish population of the island. They wanted peace, and they threatened strong measures if we didn't abide by their wishes.

They had little power to enforce such threats given my writ from Cornelius to the island's centurion. But it still broke Chanah's heart and troubled mine, especially since my greatest hope in all the world was that my children would turn out to be better than I. It bothered my mother so deeply that she worked herself too hard as a distraction, despite Chanah's faithful assurances and kind encouragements. It wasn't long before Mother became sick, and during one of the storms Rabbi Jonas blamed us for she passed from this life.

We mourned her loss for weeks, Levi more deeply than I had ever seen a man mourn. He was glad she was in a better place, but if it weren't for the joy their daughter Esther brought him, he probably would have followed her soon after.

Jonas proclaimed that we had sacrificed my mother to our heathen god, and I wanted so very badly to kill him. The return of that lust frightened me, but I didn't share those feelings with Chanah. She had enough to worry about without wondering if her husband would go on a rampage.

Less than a month after my mother's passing another trauma enveloped us. I should have seen it coming. Simon had always been more sensitive to the opinions of others than his older brother and his sisters. He was also very private, tending to keep his emotions locked up inside for too long. Chanah had recognized that early on, and she had tried to help him open up more, but he was stubborn—very much like his father in that way.

I had sensed for some time during that third year that the taunts from the Jewish youth were bothering him deeply, but he was already becoming a man, and I didn't want to coddle him with condescending parental reassurances. At least that's what I told myself, though what was closer to the truth was that I didn't really know what to do besides take matters into my own hands physically.

After a time the taunts seemed to die down, or at least that's what Simon indicated, and Matthew as well. We were busy, and that helped, too. Matthew had officially apprenticed himself to a merchant, and Simon, who still worked with me at tentmaking some of the time, had chosen to apprentice himself to a nearby Greek carpenter as well.

But the taunts increased again after Jonas's fabulous story of the dark rituals we had allegedly used to sacrifice my mother to the demons of the underworld, and I even overheard some of them. They were incredibly vile. One evening I forcefully told Simon to ignore them, that those kids and their parents were stupid and foolish. He seemed to accept that.

A few days later I was returning from two days of business on the smaller island of Goaz just to the north of Melita. Levi and Esther had accompanied me but had stayed behind for an extra day. I had stopped to purchase a set of brass armbands for Simon, of a style which I had seen some of the Roman legionnaires wearing. It would be Simon's birthday soon, and I wanted him to know I was proud of him. I looked forward to his reaction.

As I turned onto our street and approached our house, Sophia burst through the doorway and rushed toward me, her eight-year-old legs pumping as fast as she could make them go. At first I thought she was just overly excited to see me. I worried that I hadn't brought her anything, not even one of the Roman-style sweets she loved. But the distress in her voice jolted me to a halt, and I knew something big was wrong.

"Papa, papa!" she yelled, reaching me and grabbing my arm to tug me faster toward our house. "Simon is gone, and Mama and Matthew are out looking for him. You have to find him!"

I stopped and turned her around to face me, kneeling as I did. "How long ago?" I asked. "Where are they searching? Did someone take him?" My heart panicked at that thought. It was not common on Melita, but elsewhere I had heard of Roman merchants, mariners, and even soldiers conscripting young men into their service when they thought they could get away with it, which they all too often could, Roman laws notwithstanding.

"No, he ran away!" She was hopping up and down, tears streaming down her cheeks. "You have to find him, Papa, you have to."

I stood and walked briskly toward the house, taking her hand as she trotted beside me, my emotions in turmoil. Inside, near the back of the house, I found Marian, looking smaller than her ten years. She was trying to start meal preparations, but her eyes were rimmed with red and her hands were shaking. She obviously hadn't noticed Sophia leave the house, because she nearly jumped when I appeared. Then she ran to me and threw her arms around my waist, squeezing tightly as small sobs escaped despite her best efforts to stop them. She didn't say anything, so I let her sob until it was just sniffles, then pushed her gently away and looked down at her.

"Do you know where your mother and Matthew went to look for Simon? Do you know where he might have gone?"

Marian looked up at me with her big, dark-green eyes, and then nodded as more tears began to form. "I tried to tell Mama before she rushed out, but I wasn't able to. I think he went to the caves."

"The caves?" I asked, perplexed. "Do you mean the prison caves?"

She nodded, and I could see the fear in her eyes reflecting my own. That was a dangerous place. Some of the caves were used to hold prisoners, and some were not. Some went very deep and were dangerous. The Romans who guarded the prison caves were known for their ruthlessness, too. What if they found a youth of Jewish descent wandering around their domain?

"Do you know if anyone else was with him?" I asked.

She shook her head as Sophia came over to hug her.

"Who did your mother send to check in on you?"

"Julia," said Marian. I blinked at that. It was an odd choice. Julia's husband was one of our most vocal hecklers, a nuisance in a dirty robe who thought himself the manna of the neighborhood. I admittedly didn't know that much about his wife, though.

"Has she been here?" I asked.

Marian nodded. "Yes. She said she would be back soon to help with supper. I—" a huge sob suddenly wracked her small frame, "—I can't do it myself."

I stepped forward and hugged her, then told the girls I would head immediately for the caves. I had done business with one of the local legionnaires, so I would be recognized.

"Papa, let's pray," said Sophia as she grasped my hand. Her eyes were full of the faith of her mother. I was still not the best of praying men. Sometimes I prayed, and sometimes it helped, but I relied upon Chanah to be the primary beacon of faith in our family. I no longer considered myself a terrible man, but I didn't consider myself a true and faithful saint, either, especially with the feelings toward violence that were resurfacing.

I couldn't say no to Sophia, of course, even in my haste, and so we three knelt on the floor and grasped hands as I made a simple but earnest plea to our great Heavenly Father to help me find my son safe and bring him home.

When I was done, Sophia squeezed my hand and said, "That was a wonderful prayer, Papa. I know you'll find Simon." Her smile was bright and confident, and it was hard not to believe her. Of course, I still had doubts, but at least my resolve was strengthened.

It would be a three-hour walk at a fast pace, and the day was nearly spent already, so I kissed my daughters goodbye, grabbed a small amount of provisions and some water, and headed on my way.

It was the quickest and yet longest walk of my life, and I spent most of it berating myself. Had I really thought I could be a good father? Why had I been allowed to father children anyway? What if something bad had happened to Simon? What if he were dead? How could I face my wife again? And why did everyone dislike the Christians so much? Was it worth it, standing apart, proclaiming a better way? Such rebellious, traitorous thoughts.

And then I would remember my little prayer with my young daughters, and Sophia's beaming countenance, and I would push those thoughts away for a time, only to have them return to be pushed away again.

It was a relief to finally reach my destination. The entrance to the caves was nearly half a mile from the cliffs overlooking the southwestern shore. While many referred to the caves as simply the 'prison caves,' some called that place the 'shipyard,' believing that Odysseus had hidden in the large network of passages and grottos as he gathered materials to build his raft after being freed from Calypso, fearing she might change her mind. The Greeks on the island believed the stories. The Romans, generally, did not.

A small stone building had been constructed over the entrance, and it housed eight guards. I knew they didn't patrol very far into the caves. Primarily, they supervised the slaves that were made to shore up passages, clear out cave-ins, and wall up sections that the prison master wanted sealed. New passages were occasionally discovered, and once every few years a prisoner would find a way out to the cliffs and thence to the sea if he didn't fall to his death while trying to climb down.

It was a treacherous maze, and only the basest of prisoners were kept there. Why had Simon come? Why run to the caves?

As I approached a pair of guards patrolling lazily outside the building, they nearly jumped in shock, then fumbled to bring their spears into defensive position. One of them challenged me with a croak in his voice.

"Who goes there?"

"I am Jesse the tentmaker of Taragh. I am looking for my son Simon, who is but fourteen. He may have come this way."

Both guards straightened, relaxing their spears.

"I recognize you," said the second guard. "You are Christians, yes?"

I paused, thinking. I couldn't tell from his tone if he was opposed to Christians or not. If my son was there, I needed their help. How would he react if I said yes?

But in the next instant I knew I couldn't lie. "Yes. We escaped from Jerusalem and came here with the help of Cornelius the Christian." I had added that last on a strong whim.

The first guard nodded. "I've heard of him. He's reputed to be among the finest centurions in the empire. But Emperor Nero is suspicious of the Christians."

"Ha!" said the second guard. "It's Seneca who's suspicious. Nero lets Seneca lead him by a string, with his mother holding up his robes so he doesn't trip."

They both laughed. It seemed odd they would openly talk about the emperor that way, though Nero's ascension had supposedly nearly torn the empire in two. Prison duty must have been affecting them.

"I, um…did you see a curly-haired boy of fourteen around here today?" I asked.

"Yeah, we did," said the first guard. "He wanted to get into the caves. We thought he was crazy and sent him away. Nobody is allowed in unless they're *in*vited."

They looked at each other and laughed again, then stopped and shuffled uncomfortably, perhaps remembering that I was his father.

"He walked off toward the cliffs," offered the second guard. "But that was hours ago. We can give you an extra torch if you need it."

"Yes, thank you," I said gratefully. I hadn't even thought to bring a torch, so it wouldn't be 'extra.'

Within another minute I was walking toward the cliffs, making my way by moonlight to preserve the torch. I waited until I was a good distance from the guardhouse before I started calling out Simon's name every few seconds. I ventured back and forth across the rocky terrain, straining my eyes against the dimness.

When I reached the edge of the cliffs I turned south, looking for a path down. I imagined that Simon might have wanted to find another way into the caves, even though the Romans would have closed them all off. At last I found a steep path that led downward with several tight switchbacks. The cliffs were not as sheer, and the path looked manageable—or at least it probably was in the daytime.

I was about to descend when I heard it, a rustling of stiff, dry branches to my left. I whirled toward the sound and called out Simon's name again. There was no answer, but the rustling continued.

I started walking, and as I drew closer the rustling grew more frantic. After a few more paces I stopped, staring. How had a fox gotten itself caught in a spiny frecklebush? It struggled more frantically for a few seconds as I watched, but then it calmed. It looked nearly spent.

I thought about leaving it there. It would either escape or it would die. That was nature, as it always had been. But as I was about to turn away it looked at me, and I had the strong urge to free it from the bush. I resisted, of course. It was a wild fox. It had sharp teeth, and it might have been diseased.

But the urge came again, and I looked up toward the stars, wondering. Was I supposed to do this? Chanah would have known the answer instantly, but I was alone and had to muddle through the best I could. I decided to try, aiming to get one hand on its neck while the other went under its belly to lift. As I bent over and readied my hands, the fox thrashed again in a frenzy. I waited patiently until there was a pause, and then I struck, both hands finding firm purchase in the right places.

The instant it was free of the bush I swung it toward the ground and let it go, pushing away with my feet to get clear. The fox darted away as my right foot plunged into a shallow hole and I fell backward, shouting out more in surprise than pain. When I regained my feet, I examined the hole, which my fall had made wider. It seemed to be part of a narrow crevice in the soil, and my eyes followed it up a small embankment covered in the same bushes.

The crevice seemed to disappear into a larger mass of blackness that could only be seen from a certain angle. Curious, I moved closer. When I was almost upon it, I could tell that it was at least a small cave. I wasn't sure, but it looked like there were footprints near the entrance, and so I finally lit my torch.

The light indeed illuminated footprints, and footprints didn't last long in that sandy soil. My heart skipped a beat. Could it be? The entrance was just large enough for me to crawl through holding my torch, and so I entered, anxious but determined.

It wasn't just a cave but a passage, angling sharply downward. I found a place where I could turn and go feet first, and the going became easier. After two sharp turns the passage became wider, and I could stand while stooping only slightly. Then it forked, and I paused. I looked for footprints, but the floor was all rock.

I know you'll find Simon. Sweet little Sophia's words came back to me, and I said a quick prayer. I didn't feel anything, so I chose left, hoping. That passage rose slightly for a time, but then plunged more steeply than before. I stumbled often, trying to measure the remaining life of my torch, fear growing as I descended deeper into the earth. I had never liked caves.

I came to another fork, and this time I chose to go right. Before I had gone very far, I saw a dim light up ahead. Someone was there!

My heart rejoiced for an instant, but then I thought it through. Robbers often used caves as hideouts, and while there weren't many robbers on Melita, there were some. I extinguished my torch, then made my way forward, feeling carefully with hands and feet. It was a slow process, but the light ahead remained to guide me, and I made steady, quiet progress.

At last I heard a voice, and it wasn't Simon's. Crestfallen, I tried to hear what was being said, but I was still too far away. I distinguished another voice as well, and I started to back away. This was a dangerous place, and if Simon wasn't there, I needed to be on my way to continue my search.

"No, please!" My knees nearly buckled. The voice was a shout, and it had been clear as a bell. It was Simon's.

I moved forward again, trying to move faster, and I started to pick up pieces of the conversation, the different voices tumbling over each other.

"...not your place...won't know...you can't...just a boy...I found him..."

I knew I needed surprise, so I moved slower as I got close. Then, as I rounded a short bend, the scene came into view. I crouched low, trying to stay in the shadows cast by two weak torches. There was Simon, holding a torch out in front of him and kneeling protectively over an old man who lay gasping against the side of the passage. The man had been wounded in the leg by something sharp.

An emaciated man with a wild look in his eyes stood over them, a rock in one hand, a torch in the other. He didn't seem like much of a threat, so I stood and walked into the torchlight. When he noticed me, it was as if he had seen a ghost. He cowered back against the wall, and it seemed he would run until suddenly he collapsed to his knees, letting his head fall to his chest.

I breathed a sigh of relief. I didn't wish for violence, especially in front of my son. I looked at Simon. He appeared somewhat relieved, but his face was otherwise inscrutable. I tried to picture myself in his place. I wouldn't have wanted to be found by my father. I would probably have been angry.

But he was not me. He was better. He jumped to his feet and lunged forward to embrace me, his torch discarded on the stone floor.

"Father, you found me." He was smaller than his brother Matthew at the same age, but he was no small boy. His head was nearly to my shoulders, and his arms were strong. I had never felt such joy in my life, except when Chanah had chosen me. My mind immediately went to her.

"Your mother will be so happy, Simon, just as I am. We must get home."

He nodded against my chest, but then tilted his head back to look up at me. "We can't leave Master Aurelius. I found him here. He was stabbed by a robber.

At the sound of the word 'robber' my nervousness returned. This was no place to hang around.

"Okay," I said. We can help him out of here. "But what of the other?"

"He's a prisoner," said Simon, releasing me from his embrace and looking at the pitiful man kneeling in his rags. "He found us as I was trying to help Master Aurelius back to the surface. He followed us, and then Master Aurelius fainted. He wanted to leave him behind, but I said no. Then he wanted to kill him. But then I told him the Romans had sent me into the cave to explore it, and that they were waiting for me at the entrance."

"You lied," I said. The prisoner looked up at that, shock on his face along with a flash of anger, but then despair.

Simon looked at me and nodded. I tousled his hair like I used to do when he was younger. "That was smart, son. Quick thinking, and brave."

He beamed up at me, then hugged me again.

"What of you?" I said to the prisoner sternly. "You threatened to kill this man. And I suspect you would have murdered my boy, too, so that he couldn't tell the Romans."

The man didn't reply, just stared pathetically at me. His stare became uncomfortable after a few seconds.

"Well?" I finally asked again.

A pleading look entered his eyes. "Will you please kill me?"

I was stunned. "What? Why?"

"I can't go back." His shoulders slumped as he looked at the floor. "After being so close to escape, I can't bear it. I would rather die here. Your son says we will be treated fairly on the other side, in the next life. That is more than I can say about how I've been treated here. And at least now I won't be guilty of murder."

I looked down at Simon. "You said that?" He nodded. It was true, or rather, I strongly believed it was true.

My gaze returned to the prisoner. "Why are you a prisoner here?"

He looked up and gave a coughing laugh. "For a murder I didn't commit. I've been here a long time. I don't have any idea how long."

Suddenly Aurelius propped himself up, leaning forward. His breathing was no longer labored, and his eyes shone with a fiery light. He raised a hand and pointed at the prisoner.

"You shall walk free of this prison. A man will come and find you and will offer proof of your innocence. Wait until he comes. It will be soon." With that he collapsed back against the wall, and I heard his last breath rattle from his chest.

Simon had never seen a man die, but he took it in calmly, a few tears running down his cheeks. The prisoner stared at Aurelius's lifeless form for a long time, but I doubted he had any tears left to give.

I finally addressed him. "You will be tempted to follow us. Don't."

The man looked up at me, confused. "You heard his prophecy. It was right before his last breath, so it must be true. I will not follow you."

I nodded. "Good. Let's go, Simon."

The return through the passages was easier than expected, probably because I was so elated to have found Simon. My body brimmed with energy, my mind and heart with hope. Simon didn't talk about why he'd run away, and I didn't ask. There would be time for that later.

My anger grew as we trekked home. This was Jonas's fault, all of it. He incited people against us, including the youth. He knew I had favor with the Roman centurion on the island, so he attacked my family indirectly, through the endless taunts, the rumors of impropriety, the accusations of devil worshipping and worse.

By the time we arrived home, I was primed to finally take some action. I was ready to confront him, provoke him, find a way to hurt him. I told myself I didn't want to kill him, but that wasn't entirely true. He was a threat—to me, to my family, and to all the Christians on the island.

Chanah could sense it, of course, and after dinner she led me up to our rooftop terrace to talk.

"I know you're angry, Jesse," she began. "I am, too. Especially after what happened to Simon. What Jonas is doing is horrible, an affront to human decency and to God. But we cannot physically threaten him."

I knew she was right, but I was trying hard to convince myself otherwise. "If I can get him alone, I can make him promise to stop. And if he won't promise…well, the centurion will believe my story."

The look of horror on Chanah's face froze my heart. I, too, could hardly believe the words had crossed my lips, but my anger at the man was still boiling, thoughts of Simon so close to dying in those caves fresh and festering.

She recovered enough to speak. "That will only make it worse, and you will violate your covenants. Those are too precious, Jesse. Those covenants protect our family eternally, and it is our eternal souls that ultimately matter. We need each other. We need to be together, not just now but in the next life."

"And what if the actions of this one man drive many away from the truth and cause them to violate their covenants with God? Aren't we taught that sometimes it is better for one man to perish than for an entire people to be dragged down to hell?"

Chanah nodded. "Yes, but only God knows when that is necessary. Do you know that is what God wants in this circumstance? Do you remember the mistake *I* made? And that was after I had argued with Jarah about choosing peace!"

I turned away, my chest burning. I didn't know. I just wanted to make Jonas pay.

She placed herself back in front of me and reached up to touch my face. "I'm sorry, Jesse. I know you're trying to protect us. You're trying so hard to make a good life for us. And you did something extraordinary yesterday that you won't even give yourself credit for."

She paused, thinking. "You often say I saved you. But we are all in need of saving, my love. Sometimes we need more help than at other times, but none of us can do this alone, including me, as I've definitely proven. You saved Simon. Your son. If you hadn't, I couldn't have. The Lord guided *you* there, not me. His father. God trusted you to do this, and you did, my faithful and brave husband. If you travel the path of vengeance now, no matter how strong your arm or how true you strike, God will not be with you. Jonas may have the sharks swarming around us, but he cannot destroy our testimony of the gospel unless we let him, and he is not more powerful than God. There are other ways we can remind him of that, without spear or sword or arrow. Or perhaps God can remind him."

It was supremely difficult, but I followed my wife's advice.

CHAPTER 12

*For I will shew him how great things
he must suffer for my name's sake.*

Acts 9:16, KJV

The next few weeks passed in relative peace. The news that Simon had run away traveled fast on our small island home, and the fact that he had found a new outlet from the notorious prison caves caused quite a stir. The Roman centurion came to thank Simon personally, which raised his stature among the other youth of the island—Jew, Roman, and Greek alike. The entrance was quickly sealed up, of course.

Winter was fast approaching, which meant I was busy finishing up projects that needed to find a ship before the weather became perilous and all the ships harbored until spring. I was also building a stock of tents that I could sell the next year, including a few of a new design that would fill a contract with a Roman legion. That business had been steered toward me with Cornelius's help, but it had been difficult to procure nonetheless.

One night I went to bed very late. Even though I could see and feel a storm coming, my body was so exhausted that I fell into a deep sleep within minutes of lying down. But it seemed only a few minutes had passed before my eyes popped open as if there had been an earthquake. I'd been dreaming of a ship being tossed in the storm, of people panicking and the crew throwing cargoes overboard to lighten the load. It wasn't uncommon anymore for me to dream of the sea, though, so I closed my eyes again.

A few seconds later I heard and felt an impact that pulsed through the ground from the coast nearby. Was it really an earthquake? No, I reasoned, but I knew something was wrong and that I needed to help. It could have been a ship, though I dismissed the thought that it could be the ship from my dream. I threw off the blanket and started dressing to go out in the storm. Chanah stirred and then awakened.

"Jesse, what is it?" she asked in concern.

"Something about the storm," I replied. "I need to check it out. I won't be long."

I hastened to my sons' bedroom, thinking to take Matthew with me, but as I approached their doorway he stepped out of the room, fully-clothed.

"I'm ready as you asked, father. Where are we going?"

Perhaps my mind was still muddled from the long day of work and little sleep. I tried to remember having called to him, but there was nothing. Could I have called him in my sleep?

"When did I call you?"

He cocked his head slightly. "Just a minute ago. You said to get ready to go outside. Something about the storm."

I hadn't. I was sure I hadn't. "Okay, well—" I stopped as an impression came that was stronger than any I'd ever felt. There were people in danger, out in that storm. A lot of them. I grabbed Matthew by the shoulders. "I need you to gather the young men of the village. Bring them here and get all the tents organized for use. And tell them to gather firewood. The rain will soon pass."

"Why, father? What has happened?"

I shook my head gravely. "I don't know, but we're needed."

He ran for the stairs as if his task were the most important thing I'd ever asked him to do. I followed at a brisk walk, and before I had descended halfway, I heard more footsteps behind me. I turned and looked up to see Simon, also dressed for the weather.

Apparently, I'd called for him, too. Or someone had.

I didn't know what was going on. And then it hit me. I would need a runner who could carry messages swiftly.

"Simon, good. We must get to the beach. I need you to carry messages." We descended the stairs and burst out the front door in a rush, running hard for the beach, which was more than half a mile away. The rain pelted us with fury, the winds whipping like a thousand chariot drivers, the trees threatening to snap. But our breath came easily into our lungs and gave our legs strength, and we nearly sprinted the entire way.

I wondered just before we broke through the trees and onto the beach if we would actually see anything. My sons would think I'd gone crazy if there was nothing there, if a mere storm could cause me to have fevered dreams.

But there it was.

My mind wanted to stop and stare for a moment in stunned silence, but my body carried me forward even faster. The ship was enormous, probably a grain ship. She was broken near the stern, the pieces of her clinging doggedly to the sand, clay, and rocks near the shore amidst crashing waves and raging winds. Several of her crew had already washed up on the beach, some struggling further up the sand to escape the waves, some trying desperately to help others. There were many more further out in the maelstrom clinging to flotsam that had kept them from being swallowed by the angry sea.

I angled toward the closest person, who looked to be one of the ship's crew. He was lying on his back, exhausted by his escape. Though he was safe from the waves, he was wet and cold and probably in shock.

"Good man!" I shouted as Simon and I reached him, "how many of you are there?"

The man opened his eyes and looked at me as if I were an apparition. "We are nearly three hundred on board, including soldiers and prisoners. Bound for Rome," he added, probably hoping to elevate their importance.

I put my hand on Simon's shoulder. "Run back to the village. Tell the mayor to send word to Mayor Publius in Medina by fast horse that we have three hundred people shipwrecked and in need of immediate aid. Then go to Matthew and tell him to bring the tents and the firewood with the young men. Go quickly!"

Simon bounded away, running faster than I had ever seen a fourteen-year-old run, and I spared a second of pride as I watched him.

I turned back to the man lying at my feet. "Are you injured? Can you walk?"

"I…yes…I mean no, I don't think I'm injured. I can walk."

"Good. You must be on your feet and moving in this cold. And I will need your help to gather others. I am Jesse." I reached down, and he grasped my hand, groaning as I pulled him to his feet.

"I am Gaius," he offered gratefully, "a member of her crew. Her name is…or was, *Daughter of Troy*. She got us to this beach before she died, all praises to her and Diana."

I scanned the roiling surf in the patchy starlight. The storm was breaking apart, though it still threatened more violence. I saw a man clinging to some wood and jogged toward him, Gaius's heavy footsteps right behind me. When I saw his face I thought he had died with his hands still locked onto the wood. But he stirred as we splashed through the froth toward him, then lifted his head in amazement.

He sputtered something unintelligible, and then we got our hands under his arms and dragged him up the shore to a safe spot. We left him lying on the beach coughing up water as we returned to look for more survivors. Five more times we dragged people up the beach—one of them a woman who kept screaming about her boy—and then men from the town and surrounding villages began arriving, first a handful, and then a rush that grew to at least sixty. I didn't see Simon among them. He must have stayed to help Matthew organize and transport the tents.

We spent more than two hours rescuing crewmembers, soldiers, passengers, and prisoners from the sea. It was Gaius who spotted the woman's son as the sea was carrying him away from the shore. Gaius was a strong swimmer, and the activities of the night had fired his flesh so that he was able to reach the boy, who was tenaciously clinging to a barrel, and bring him safely to shore.

We paused, then, and spotters from up and down the shoreline reported that there was nobody else alive in the water. Men had boarded the wreckage as well and reported it empty. The winds had subsided from a ferocious harangue to a scowling huff, and the starlight was stronger.

Gaius and I sat heavily on the sand with some of those we had helped, trying to catch our breath. I turned to Gaius and thanked him.

His eyes widened. "You thank me, a stranger who would have lain on that beach and done nothing but for you?"

"You barely escaped with your life, and you would have been up and helping soon anyway. And your swim to save that boy…"

"Gah!" He waved his hand. "I couldn't stand his mother screaming about him any longer, that's all."

I would have smiled, but I was too tired. Then I realized something. "I haven't seen any bodies."

"Oh," he said gravely, "you'll see them soon enough. The sea is right gloating when she wants to be, and she'll toss them up to mock us soon enough."

I looked up and down the beach as far as I could see. A few fires had been lit, and by heaven's grace tents were going up all along the shore—big and small, most of them mine, all of them beautiful on this cold, wet night. Matthew and the young men must have arrived some time ago with tents and firewood, and their work was proceeding rapidly. A small fire had been started near us, and I spotted one of Matthew's friends tending it.

Gaius hadn't turned around to see the tents and the fires. He was still talking, staring at the wrecked vessel.

"A right crazy man he was. I could've predicted the storm, too, was I not below deck. But then he promised we'd all survive—every last one of us! And that was after he'd convinced the captain and the centurion to toss over most of our supplies and all of the cargo! I'm guessing he was the first to die, and it makes not a whit of difference to me. We should have killed the prisoners, including him, when the storm hit. The sea wouldn't have cared if he was Roman or not."

I was surprised the soldiers hadn't thrown the prisoners overboard early on. It was a common practice, especially in stronger storms, a generally plausible excuse that saved the hassle and expense of Roman trials. But then I thought about the implications of what he'd said.

"How many prisoners were there? And what was the nature of their crimes?" I felt a knot in my gut forming at the thought of prisoners let loose in the village while most of the men were here at the beach. Chanah and the other children would be in danger.

I rose to my feet, new energy flowing into my legs.

"They weren't the vilest sort, if that's what you're asking," Gaius said. "Mainly petty thieves, plus the crazy man who was arrested for blaspheming some god or another. I'd nail everything in your village down, though, if you know what I mean. In the morning, that is—they'll all be exhausted for tonight. We were thirteen days in that Poseidon-cursed storm."

I took some solace in his words, but I was still anxious. "I need to go find Publius, the chief man of this island, if he's here yet—and your captain if I can—and see where things stand."

"Right good. I'll come with you." Gaius was on his feet quickly, and we were off down the beach toward the largest group of survivors, closest to the fractured ship. Gaius spotted several other crewmembers along the way, their glad, surprised greetings echoing with hope and relief.

I saw Publius at the same time Gaius spotted his captain. The two were talking with each other intently as we hailed them. "Gaius!" the captain called back. "You are safe, the gods be praised."

Publius nodded to me in his usually guarded way. "Your boys did good, Jesse, though I still don't know how you were here so quickly."

I shrugged, not sure how much I should say. "I heard the blow of the ship on the sandbar and the rocks near the shore, and I just knew there was trouble. I had tents, in case there were people who needed them, and Matthew and Simon wanted to help." I looked away sheepishly; it was always embarrassing for me to talk to Publius. He was an intimidating man.

"Well, all the same, we—"

"Captain!" A man came running up to stop before the captain, panting for breath. "Captain, we've checked every group all along the beach. It's...it's a miracle, sir. He was right."

The captain cocked his head. "Right about...?"

"We're all here, Captain. Everyone survived, not a head was lost. I've never seen or heard the like."

"Did you double-check that, son?" asked the captain, somewhat uneasily. His eyes were wide, and he looked more frightened than amazed or grateful.

"Yes, Captain, I did, and one of the soldiers was with me to make sure. Two hundred and seventy-four survivors, none hurt seriously, and none lost."

There was a long pause, and I noted a look of intense puzzlement on Publius's face. He wouldn't easily believe such a report, but the crewman didn't look delirious from his ordeal and didn't have any reason to lie.

"Where is Paul of Tarsus?" asked the captain.

Paul? Surely not...

"He's just to the west of the ship, with the centurion and some of his men. The other soldiers are making sure the prisoners stay where they are, and most of the soldiers are still armed."

It registered as another miracle that soldiers made it out of the water with their weapons, but my mind was still locked onto the improbability that a man like Paul—if it was indeed the same Paul of Tarsus, and somehow I knew it was—could land, shipwrecked, on our tiny island, deposited here as if by the hand of God. But for what purpose? To chastise me and Chanah for not building the strength of the church faster on this island? For myself, I knew I truly hadn't done what I could have.

I excused myself quietly as Publius and the captain began arguing. Publius was still dubious, and the captain seemed more fearful of approaching Paul than the centurion. I was walking back the way I'd come, looking for Matthew and Simon, when a hand pressed upon my shoulder from behind and I heard a clear, fearless voice.

"Barabbas."

I stopped dead in my tracks. I knew that voice. I was elated. I was nervous. My heart leapt with joy. A knot formed in my stomach. I turned slowly, joy overcoming my hesitation. I couldn't help but smile. "Master Paul. This is a miracle."

No sooner had I spoken than I was engulfed in a powerful embrace. After a few seconds he let go and took half a step back.

"I did not think to find you here, Brother Barabbas. But I had no idea where we were until a few minutes ago." He laughed. "I knew there was a purpose in this storm and that I was not to arrive in Rome just yet, but I never imagined I would get to see you and Chanah on my journey. What a tender mercy for me."

"Chanah will be overjoyed, as will the children." I paused. "My mother, however, passed away recently."

Paul's expression turned sad. "I'm sorry, Brother Barabbas. She was a faithful woman, though, and a hard worker. I'm sure the Lord is keeping her busy. Do good, and you will certainly see her again." He clapped me on the arms, and then shivered. "Come, Jesse, we must get warm. I see women bringing food as well. I haven't eaten in several days."

Sure enough, scores of women, boys, and girls were walking toward the groups of survivors, arms laden with trays of food, jugs of water, blankets, linens, and small clay jars of healing salves and ointments.

Paul led, and he guided us straight for the largest group, where Publius and the captain had been joined by the centurion.

Gaius was with them, too, mumbling about how it was impossible that everyone could have survived.

The centurion treated Paul with a deference he might have shown the emperor himself.

It wasn't much later that I found myself sitting with Levi, Elhanan, Matthew, and Simon around a blazing fire with Paul and a few of the soldiers and sailors. The captain, the centurion, and several of the prominent men from the island, including Publius, were also gathered with us. Most of the women and many of the men had returned to Taragh and the villages, including Chanah, Junia, Esther, and our daughters, who had all helped provide the food. Some of the survivors along the beach had already fallen asleep in the tents, while others sat tending their own fires, some exhilarated by their survival, others somber about their near death.

Paul was seated between the captain and the centurion, relating their storm-wracked story to Publius and the other Melitans. We were already in the fourth watch, as the Romans reckon it, but I could not be tired in Paul's presence. There would be time for sleep when Paul slept, and between bits of the harrowing tale, he was teaching another of his powerful sermons, maintaining the attention of even the coarsest of the soldiers, who were clearly grateful and amazed to be alive and on dry land. They would remember that night.

I looked at my natural sons, Matthew on my right and Simon on my left, to see if they were listening. They didn't notice me watching, so enraptured were they by the apostle, and a great peace settled upon me. Oh, how I wanted my sons to be more than I was! And here was Paul, providing them with truth and power and a brilliant example of a man to follow. I praised God for the help he was providing for my sons and my daughters.

I barely noticed Paul reach toward the base of the fire to push one of the bundles of branches further into the flames. But I saw the snake. It emerged from the sticks and struck so fast Paul couldn't react. When he pulled his arm back, it was latched onto his hand. The entire group gasped, but nobody moved.

I identified the snake by its deadly markings, and my heart sank. It was the death adder, marbled black-and-red and half again the length of a man's arm. Its venom guaranteed a painful demise. How could it have gotten there, hiding so close to the flames?

Paul calmly grasped the viper's head with his other hand and removed it, then threw it into the roaring flames, where it sizzled and popped.

The crowd was hushed for a few moments, dumbfounded by the strange event, and then one of the men from the village spoke to Paul, pointing a damning finger. "You have been condemned by the gods, for who else would have sent the death adder?"

It was no surprise to me that it was Jerahmeel who spoke. He was the island's most devout worshiper of the goddess Diana. He wasn't a bad man, but he was usually too quick to judge and often unthinking in his actions.

I didn't know what to believe, for the snake's appearance did seem truly supernatural. Was this God's appointed end for the greatest man, save Jesus only, that I had ever seen? I glanced at my sons, who seemed remarkably calm.

Paul stood, his stricken hand resting casually at his side, and looked at Jerahmeel with the calm of the River Jordan at the winter solstice.

"Do you believe this creature was sent by God or by the devil?"

"I have heard some speak of God and a devil," Jerahmeel began uncertainly, "but there are many gods, and some of them are capricious and vengeful." He kept glancing at Paul's hand as he spoke, obviously waiting for the venom to begin its deadly attack. His voice grew in confidence. "Perhaps one of them saved you from drowning, and another is angry at the interference. Perhaps you have offended one of them in some way. I cannot say for certain. Whichever god sent the viper, you will certainly die."

Paul nodded and smiled. He still wasn't showing any adverse effects. "So, I am subject to the whims of the gods?"

Jerahmeel paused, looking again at Paul's hand. He glanced at me, having seen me arrive at that fire with Paul, and also having heard Chanah and me teach on occasion.

He cleared his throat. "I am but a man. Who am I to predict what the gods might do?"

Paul smiled, his eyes full of understanding, not challenge. "I am but a man as well, but I have met the very son of the true God, and I can promise you he is not a capricious being. If he had chosen to call me home from this mortal existence tonight, he would have had a sound purpose for it…and he would not have sent a snake."

Jerahmeel didn't respond, just kept staring at Paul's hand.

"Either way," said the captain, "it has wrought its work in you, and you are lost." Murmurs arose among most of those present, soft arguments about what the meaning of it could be, after all that had happened. Many appeared sad, since they believed Paul had saved them from the storm.

Paul turned his attention to the captain. There was mild surprise and disappointment in his voice. "How have you forgotten so soon, captain? Who is more powerful, the God I serve, or the devil, or some other god?"

The captain squirmed. I tried to focus, but I couldn't help imagining the venom that would take hold of Paul at any moment. He would fall thrashing to the sand and die an excruciating death. My sons were there. I didn't want them to see that.

"God is more powerful," supplied Publius, seeming to understand something still lost on Jerahmeel and the captain.

"Indeed," said Paul, turning toward the portly mayor. "How, then, can he not protect me if I am his servant and I am doing the task he has assigned me. I have work yet to do, here and in Rome and elsewhere, so I am not afraid of this viper's bite."

The crowd remained hushed, staring, waiting.

Paul turned himself and silently stared out at the sea, which was now calm compared to its recent tempest. Dawn was approaching.

Minutes passed. The hand that should already have swollen and turned purple continued to look normal.

Finally, Paul turned to the captain and extended both hands.

"Behold, captain, the power of God, your God and my God, the Father of us all."

His stricken hand was completely unblemished. Even the puncture wounds were gone. The flesh was healthy and whole, as if the death adder had never existed.

I blinked rapidly, my hope rising.

Paul turned to me. "Jesse, God has worked through you this night as well. I would stay with you and your family, if you are willing."

I scrambled quickly to my feet, my boys doing the same, and then gave him a quick bow. "Of course. It would be our honor."

I glanced at Publius, who was staring at me strangely. I was not concerned, though. He might be curious, but he wasn't the type to get offended easily.

"I will arrange lodging for the others," Publius announced. "Master Paul, you and the centurion may appoint those who shall stay in my house."

I suddenly noticed Jerahmeel. He was on his knees. It seemed as if he were about to prostrate himself before Paul when the apostle held up his hands. "Do not worship me. I am a man, as I said, just like you. God has done this. Give thanks to him and be ready to give him the honor."

CHAPTER 13

Howbeit they looked when he should have swollen, or fallen down dead suddenly: but after they had looked a great while, and saw no harm come to him, they changed their minds, and said that he was a god.

Acts 28:6, KJV

As the morning broke our group on the beach disbanded. The centurion ordered some of his men to sleep and took others with him as he headed down the beach to set up regular patrols and arrange more care for the wounded. The captain and a few of his men went with Publius, and they had a significant walk ahead of them. Paul accompanied me and my boys to our home. He still looked overjoyed to be alive and with us, but the growing light also revealed how weary he was. We passed a few women from the town carrying additional food and supplies to the beach, and all of them bowed to Paul, news of the multiple miracles spreading.

Paul still had not asked me about the mission Chanah and I had been given on the island, but I was sure that would come later. That he was there was incredible, and even if he chastised me for not doing enough, I would be happy for his company. He would have to stay on the island for at least the winter, until ships could sail the sea again. Our home and our children would be blessed by his presence.

Chanah held the door wide as she welcomed the famous teacher and prophet into our home. She bowed slightly. "Master Paul, we are overjoyed that you have been preserved this night. Our home is yours."

Paul brightened as he accepted her greeting. She blushed, and I could tell she was nervous. While I knew she was as happy as I that it was Paul and that he had escaped such calamitous circumstances, she too would feel ashamed to explain how little we had done in establishing the church on Melita.

After crossing the threshold, he turned to both of us, grabbing us each by a hand.

"The Lord bless you, Jesse and Chanah. You have done wonderful things here. I know what you are thinking, but I was not sent here to criticize or judge your efforts. I was sent to minister *with* you, and I am grateful for the opportunity."

Our heads had drooped, our eyes lowered. He gave a tiny laugh. "You have nothing to fear from me. Please, let me see your faces. Let me look upon you as your brother, not your lord. You have but one lord, and that is not me."

The peace emanating from that travel-worn, undernourished servant of God was impossible to deny. Chanah was first to react. She burst into tears and embraced him. "I thank the Lord he has sent you." She broke away quickly, smiling widely and wiping tears from her cheeks. "I'm sorry, you must be exhausted. We have a bed prepared, and more food if you'd like."

He laughed. "I am well enough for the moment. May we sit for a few minutes?"

I tasked the boys to get some sleep, and then we sat on the cushions in our front room. Paul no longer seemed as tired. Instead, he seemed content.

"You have been through some trials here." It wasn't a question. Chanah and I looked at each other. My first thought was that compared to being chased by a storm for nearly two weeks, surviving a shipwreck and being bitten by a death adder—in addition to being a prisoner bound for Rome to be judged by the emperor!—we had it relatively easy.

"Nothing that isn't common to mankind," said Chanah smoothly. "We have been blessed beyond measure. Jesse's business thrives, our children are healthy, and we have been safe, as you promised."

Paul nodded. "You have remained faithful as well. I can see it in your countenances."

His gaze switched to me, and I blinked, swallowing hard. Had I *truly* remained faithful? I still harbored violent thoughts toward Jonas and others. I still shirked some of my responsibilities as a husband, father, and teacher of the word of Christ. I was still Barabbas.

Paul gave me a puzzled look, frowning slightly. "Are you all right, Jesse?" He leaned forward and placed a hand on my shoulder. "Have you not let the Lord fully heal you? Have you not let him show you who you really are?"

I felt a wave of power in his voice and in his touch. Tears sprang to my eyes, my hands trembled, and before I knew it I was sobbing. I wasn't even sure why.

Paul let me cry for a minute, then removed his hand and leaned back. "Don't worry, Jesse, it will come. Trust him, be faithful, and it will come. Don't hold yourself back. His power is limitless. It is impossible for us to fully comprehend that, but we can still have faith in it, and it is just as real. Believe me, I had a hard time acknowledging that and forgiving myself, even after I knew he had forgiven me. I can still see Stephen's face as he was being stoned. I *facilitated* that. But I know that God worked his purposes through Stephen that day, and he still does. Stephen's martyrdom is a shining example of faithfulness for those who might doubt or falter."

I looked up, blinking the tears from my eyes. I knew Paul's story well. I knew the story of Stephen the Martyr, too. But it was hard. Very hard.

"How many have been baptized here since you and Chanah came?"

I thought for a moment. "Twelve, including Elhanan's wife. Her name is Junia. They live just up the street."

Paul smiled. "That is wonderful. And you and Chanah administer the sacrament to them every Sabbath?"

I nodded, looking at Chanah, who also smiled. She reached out a hand and grasped mine.

"And there are some who persecute you for your faith, including, I presume, the local rabbi?" Paul asked.

I nodded again, and Chanah chimed in. "He is relatively harmless, though we did have a scare with Simon, who was upset by things the youth were saying—things Rabbi Jonas encouraged them to say."

Paul nodded knowingly. "The pattern of opposition doesn't vary much, but it can be intense. Will you tell me about what happened to Simon?"

I briefly related the story, and I admitted to some of the hard feelings I harbored.

When I had finished, he again grasped each of us by the hand. "Thank you, Jesse and Chanah. You are an example of the believers, and that example has prepared a fruitful field. Now we must harvest it."

Paul barely had time to rest and recover his strength over the next two days before all the people of the island were clamoring to hear from him. Many had gathered to the beach where the great ship still lay grounded and broken, a tilted mass of timbers and tarred rope. It was a festive atmosphere in and around Taragh. Publius had declared a public holiday across the island, and since the crops had already been harvested and the sailing season was at an end, most people wanted to come and see.

When I commented to Chanah that the gathering must be the harvest Paul had mentioned, she was doubtful. "No," she said, "I think some seeds will be planted today, but most people came for the festivities and to satisfy their curiosity. Accepting the gospel of Christ requires real sacrifice, and it is easy to find rationalizations to avoid it."

We had seen that before, but after such powerful miracles I was hopeful. Paul seemed to agree more with Chanah, though he was still optimistic and prepared himself diligently. We owned a few scrolls of the ancient scripture, but none of the newly published words of the apostles. The synagogue, of course, had a much larger library, and so Paul went to Rabbi Jonas and asked if he could study there for a few hours—as if it were just a friendly professional courtesy! What surprised me even more is that Jonas allowed it.

Paul wasn't as skilled of a storyteller as Cornelius, but he was a powerful preacher, and he was well-schooled in history, the arts, and science. His voice naturally carried further than would be expected from the frame of a smaller man, and his tone could be mesmerizing. Publius had ordered a platform built for him as well, so that more could hear. By the time he was about to speak, nearly five thousand people had gathered along the beach and the grassy incline beyond. The survivors of the shipwreck, including the prisoners with their watchful guards, sat nearest to Paul, and he greeted all of them individually before he ascended the platform and began.

He was masterful. Most wept. Only a handful decided they didn't want to hear and left. By the time he finished more than two hours later a hush seemed to have fallen over the entire island. I could feel the Spirit of the Lord strongly, and I was glad. Chanah was enthralled, as were the girls, including Esther. Elhanan and Junia were ready to do whatever Paul asked, as was Levi. Matthew and Simon were more muted in their reactions, but I could tell they took it seriously.

After the sermon and the subsequent feast; after the following day of games and theatrical performances; and after the crowds had broken up and returned to their homes, Paul went to work with an energy that embarrassed me. He was five years my senior, but he acted ten years my junior. He insisted on helping with the tentmaking, and since much of our winter activity was mending, he traveled around the island nearly non-stop, preaching and working on tents. Elhanan almost always accompanied him, and I went along occasionally as well. His zeal was contagious.

He performed many healings across the island. He counseled those being healed to give the glory to God and to focus on how they might help others in turn. Still, many people proclaimed that *he* was a god, and most returned to their old ways, some of which were sinful. I learned, with some counseling from Paul, not to get so angry at those people.

Soon we had visitors showing up on our doorstep—sometimes entire extended families—saying that Paul had sent them to me to be baptized. At first I was stunned and a bit uncomfortable, but we made many trips to the nearby estuaries and did the work Paul asked us to do. Chanah kept meticulous records of who had been baptized. She also started writing an account of everything that was happening on the island and in the church.

On one of the rare days he stayed in Taragh with us, Paul sat with Chanah and me and organized the new converts into three branches of the church that could meet in their separate localized groups on the Sabbath. He asked who should be ordained to be priests for the administering of the sacrament, and who would make good teachers. The whole exercise stretched me considerably. I felt like I was making decisions too momentous for my place, a fish out of water, but every time I tried to express that Paul just smiled and continued on. He knew I had Chanah, of course.

I finally expressed my feelings of inadequacy one too many times for the patient Paul, though. I had never seen him annoyed before.

"Jesse," he chided. "you are a smart and capable man. How many languages do you speak? Four?"

"Just three," I replied humbly. "Aramaic, Greek, and Latin. My Hebrew is very basic."

He raised an eyebrow. "Well, I was required to study Hebrew, but my Aramaic is awful, so we're even. How many new tent designs have you come up with in the last ten years? I'm not talking about custom tents, but new features that can be applied to any tent."

I thought back. "Three, I think."

"And how many times has your family gone hungry because you couldn't find a market for your work?"

"Well, none." I looked at Chanah, who seemed to be enjoying the interrogation.

"How many times have you left your wife and children to chase strong drink and women?"

"None, but I—"

"But nothing. Who found Simon when he ran away?" He loved that story, and he had spoken several times with Simon himself about it.

"Um, I did. But Marian told me he probably went to the caves."

"I see. And who was the first person on the beach the night of the shipwreck?"

I didn't answer, just lowered my eyes and studied the lines in my hands.

"Jesse, the past is behind you. Barabbas is dead. Christ can make all things new, including a thief and a murderer, and he has done so with you. He needs your help now, Jesse. He needs your talent, your dedication, your focus…and your confidence. He trusts you more than you think, else I would not be here."

Chanah nodded, looking supremely satisfied. Paul went back to studying the various papers she had prepared, and our meeting continued with renewed purpose.

Members of the Roman garrison and the ship's soldiers always saluted Paul, and the centurion who was escorting him to Rome rarely checked in on him. My fears regarding the prisoners from the ship evaporated like the dew. They stayed obediently quarantined in a camp built for them, volunteering for work parties under guard by a mere handful of soldiers. Some of them were baptized as well, which caused a small fuss among some of the mayors.

And then there were the children. Dozens of them surrounded Paul when he was outside, swirling around him like happy butterflies as they played their games, and asking endless questions. Paul seemed most happy around the children, and he would often stop to address one or more of them with a few words and a smile.

Matthew and I were with him one morning in Medina when one of the young boys mentioned the cave opening Simon had found. He and another boy had gone in search of it, even though the Romans had sealed it up. Paul smiled and laughed as they described their adventure and told him how they had found a safer way down the cliffs. When they had left, though, Paul's look grew serious, and he turned to me.

"Tell me again about the man who died in the cave that night. Aurelius was his name?"

"Yes. There isn't much to tell. He was wounded and we couldn't have saved him."

"Yes, I know. But he seemed to prophesy at the end, yes?"

I nodded, and then Paul slapped me on the back. "If I can, I will go there soon and find the prisoner who he prophesied about. Can I take Simon with me?" Of course I said yes. Simon would be elated.

We were just about to return home from Medina when a young boy arrived bearing an urgent request for Paul's assistance. Mayor Publius's wife was gravely ill, and the doctor feared she would pass within hours. Publius himself had commissioned the runner to find Paul and bring him if he could.

Paul, Matthew, and I hurried to Publius's house, which fortunately wasn't a long distance.

When we entered, Mayor Publius immediately ushered us into the bedchamber, where his wife lay on an elevated bed, glistening with sweat and in obvious pain. Several other women attended her, including two I knew to be their grown daughters.

She looked from Paul to Publius. "What did you do, my husband?" she asked. "I don't want him here. I don't believe he is who he says he is, and he has already made himself the practical mayor of this island. He is an opportunist and a conjurer, leading our people astray."

I looked at Paul to see his reaction. His expression was kind, and his eyes locked onto hers before he spoke, one hand raised to forestall Publius's response.

"I am but a man, Mistress Lucia, and I will leave here with the spring sailing season. But there is one who would never leave your heart if you would let him in, one who would bring you indescribable gladness. He is Christ Jesus, the Messiah, the Son of God, the Maker and Ruler of heaven and earth, the Redeemer of the whole world."

He endowed each of those titles with such glory that I caught myself gaping, my eyes watering.

Paul continued. "He loves you and every other person on this island with a perfect love. I could not pretend to be him, though in his name and by his will I do many mighty things for the benefit of others. *He* can heal you through me if you'll let him and if he has a purpose for you in it. But neither he nor I will force you to be healed, as that is never his way. It is your choice, and it is your faith and desire that matter most. I am sorry, dear sister, if I have offended you in any way."

With that he withdrew, and poor Publius was left spluttering in exasperation. When we exited the house, he caught up with us, hustling to put himself in Paul's path.

"Please, Master Paul, there must be something you can do. It is the fever. That's what is making her speak irrationally. She doesn't realize what she's saying."

Paul smiled weakly, placing a hand on Publius's shoulder. "I will pray for her, good Publius, but you and I both know that she resents me. God forces no one to be healed through the grace and mercies of his Everlasting Son, though he calls to us all the day long, his gracious arms open wide."

Publius blinked rapidly, eyes darting back and forth between Paul and his house. "I can convince her. Wait a few minutes, will you? Please?"

Paul paused, seeming unsure for a moment, but then nodded. And so, after Publius had re-entered his home, we sat on a bench in the garden portico outside the doors. Paul asked Matthew and me to join with him in prayer, and while I can't remember anything he said, I felt at peace, like a lamb nestled against its mother for the night.

It wasn't long before Publius returned, and while I had never seen a volcano—much less the erupting of a volcano—I witnessed it in Publius. He cried and cursed, wagging an accusatory finger at Paul as he loomed over him. Then he turned away, grabbed his head in both hands, and cursed some more.

"She is dead!" he said several times, along with several variations of, "You didn't come soon enough!" and "You must be a false prophet…or a demon sent to torment us!"

I stood up, shocked. I was prepared to defend Paul, even from the Chief Mayor. After all Publius had seen with his own eyes, how could he believe Paul was an agent of Lucifer? I had thought him a good man who kept his ego in check, but maybe I'd been wrong. Maybe he was like so many others in powerful positions, who could turn treacherous at the shifting of the wind. I began to look for a way to get us out of there. Matthew seemed calm, though, all things considered. How was he handling it so well?

Paul continued to sit and listen, impervious to the tirade of angry curses and flying spittle. When the anger subsided, he rose, clapped Publius on the shoulders, stared at him intently for several seconds, and walked past him...into the house.

He motioned for Matthew and me to follow. After a careful look at Publius, who appeared confused—we hurried after him. When we entered the room where Lucia lay, the other women in the room cast angry eyes upon Paul, the hopelessness there revealing sharper accusations than all of Publius's railings.

Paul didn't hesitate but approached the bed and stood beside the still woman. He took one of her delicate hands in his, placed his other hand on her forehead, bowed his head, and began whispering. I couldn't tell what he was saying, but apparently some of the women could hear him clearly, and their reactions varied from shock and disdain to outright disbelief. Suddenly Paul stood straight, still grasping the dead woman's hand.

At that moment time froze...at least for me. I couldn't move, didn't blink, and hardly even breathed. It seemed that a window into the heavens opened. A bright, swirling oval of light appeared, nearly overwhelming my senses. I couldn't see through it, but I could feel it, like a thousand suns warming every particle of my being, bringing a rush of knowledge and understanding that no number of famous Greek philosophers could have put into words.

In the next instant the window was gone. I blinked, focusing on the body of the woman as she rose at the gentle pull of Paul's hand.

The other women in the room gasped, and the two daughters lowered themselves to the floor with fluttering eyelids and then fainted in each other's arms. The others swooned as they grasped for something to steady themselves.

All eyes were on Publius's wife, whose smile was as broad as the Nile Delta and whose eyes sparkled as she looked at Paul.

After a moment he let go of her hand, and she grabbed the arm of the woman nearest her, who shook her head and mumbled, joy and fear on her pale features.

"Sister, I have returned. And I have wonderful news!" She clapped her hands and embraced the startled woman, who finally decided to accept what she was seeing and return the embrace. Both cried with joy.

The others joined them, and the daughters began to stir.

I looked at Paul, who stepped back to let the women enjoy their reunion. He returned my gaze with a weary look of satisfaction. "You saw?"

I nodded, the warmth fading, my mind trying to question if I had really seen what I thought I had seen.

"God has granted us all a great gift this day, Jesse," Paul said. "I almost doubted, but I trusted him and heeded his command." He breathed heavily, looking at Publius's wife again before adding, "She will do great things…and you and your children will witness it." With that his knees buckled.

I caught his arm, feeling my own weakness. Fortunately, Matthew was with us, and he helped us find seats on some thin cushions near one wall, where we leaned back and rested our heads.

It was another full minute before Publius returned. Perhaps he thought the sounds from inside were mourning, because he had scarcely set one foot inside the room before he fell to his knees, eyes locked on his wife, who beamed at him before rushing to him and grasping his face in her hands. She knelt with him, then kissed him on the lips. It was an incredibly forward thing for a woman to do in front of company—but it seemed right all the same.

The news spread like a raging wildfire, of course, and within an hour hundreds of people crowded around the mayor's house, chattering and cheering and questioning, all hoping to get a view of the woman who had been miraculously raised from the dead by Paul.

I wondered how many times that had happened while Jesus ministered in Israel. And I marveled that all of Israel hadn't followed the Messiah in everything he asked of them. What great evil or determined ignorance could continually deny such miracles? A new confidence and hope surged within me, and though I worried about what would happen when Paul left, I knew I could trust in the Lord.

CHAPTER 14

But God hath chosen the foolish things of the world to confound the wise; and God hath chosen the weak things of the world to confound the things which are mighty.

1 Corinthians 1:27, KJV

Winter was coming to an end. The centurion who was Paul's lenient jailor had secured passage for Paul and a few of the prisoners on a merchant ship from Syria that had wintered in the main port on the island. It would be difficult to bid farewell to Paul. Chanah and I were near to mourning. But oh, how he had blessed our family! We counted ourselves more fortunate than any family on earth, and we understood it was time for others to receive his tender but bold ministering.

Chanah wanted to throw a great feast in his honor with dozens of guests, but Paul prevailed upon her to prepare a simple meal in an intimate setting with our family. He had a stiffer argument with Publius, who wanted another island-wide spectacle to celebrate Paul's miracle-filled stay on Melita, but Paul finally convinced him to forbear.

Marian had just turned eleven, and Sophia was almost nine. They took great pride in helping their mother and their sister-in-law Junia prepare and serve the meal. They also got to sit on either side of Paul when all was ready. Paul himself offered a prayer, after asking permission of Chanah and me. That still felt odd sometimes—him asking permission for such things in our home—but he had oft explained the primary significance of home and family to the community, to the church, and to the kingdom of God. No apostle presided over a man or woman in their home.

I expected the meal to be a somber event, but Paul entertained us with numerous stories of his travels, including his meetings with saints, elders and apostles in many places. Some of his stories were serious, but many were light-hearted—including some embarrassing episodes about himself. On one occasion he had fallen into a pig pen while trying to stand on a fence and preach in Galatia. On another he had mistaken a Greek merchant for the mayor of a Thracian town and had nearly caused a riot. We all enjoyed good laughs as we ate.

After we had finished, Paul sat up straight, a wistful look on his face. "Thank you Chanah, Junia, Marian, and Sophia, for the wonderful meal you prepared." He gave individual looks to Marian and Sophia, who blushed. "I am well-fed" he patted his belly, "and happy. But the day after tomorrow my journey must continue, for the Lord has called me to Rome."

He paused, looking both contemplative and emotional. "I have written the saints at Rome several times over the years and received correspondence back from them. There were hard times and much confusion when Claudius temporarily banned Jews from Rome nine years ago. The saints who were Jewish descendants weren't excluded from the ban, and congregations—even families—were torn asunder for a while. There are many patient, faithful saints in Rome and throughout Italy who I long to see, and that desire grows daily." He chuckled. "I had thought my appeal to Festus for Roman judgment was merely a legal stratagem to preserve my life, but now I am certain that the real reason was to convey me to Rome so that I could fulfill some purpose in the Lord."

He smiled. "The Lord has wonderful things in store for the people of Rome. And—" his face became troubled "—more trying times as well. Perhaps Rome will become a great crucible from which some of the finest steel will be produced, at least for a time. But I cannot see it clearly yet."

His face brightened again. "Every soul is a great treasure unto God, so I will rejoice in every person who I can help bring into his embrace. At the end of this mortal existence, at the end of all things on the earth, we will gather before his throne and weep for joy, singing praises to the Father and his Only Begotten Son."

His eyes were focused near the ceiling, and he had raised his hands in supplication to the heavens. All was quiet for several seconds, and then he dropped his hands and smiled, looking at each of us in turn.

"I have word from Cornelius." The change of subject surprised me, but I was eager to hear the news. "A courier ship captain sailed early from Cyrene and just arrived here. He had a letter from Cornelius addressed to me." He paused to let that sink in. How could Cornelius have known Paul was on Melita? Only God could have told him.

"He is, as he expected to be, in Africa, in lands to the south of Ethiopia. His entire family, his former servants and their families, and several legionnaires and their families are with him. Philip has accompanied them, too, and a miraculous work is taking place among the people there. He is happy, and he sends greetings and blessings to all of you. He also mentions that if any of you wish to visit, you are most welcome, and he can find you safe passage."

I couldn't imagine taking such a long trip for just 'a visit,' though it would be fascinating to experience those lands, just as it would be captivating to see many others. Melita was our permanent home, and we were happy there. Perhaps one of our children could someday undertake the journey. God only knew.

Paul continued, changing the subject again. "I have been pondering deeply and praying much regarding my assignment in Rome…and I have asked Levi and Esther to accompany me." Chanah's eyes snapped immediately to Levi, who looked somewhat sheepish for having kept the secret. Then she looked at Esther. I knew her departure would be hard for Chanah, Marian and Sophia. She was a divinely bright young woman and a joy to be around. Her testimony of the Savior burned brightly, and she was not shy.

Paul smiled. "I know this is a surprise, but I feel strongly about it, and they have agreed. They will, I'm sure, send you a letter once they are settled." He looked at Levi, who nodded.

"Now," Paul said, "I wish to leave my apostolic blessing with all of you, including the babe in Junia's womb." Chanah's eyes went wide as saucers, and she looked at Junia. Yes, Junia had already known and hadn't yet told Chanah. She smiled sheepishly, too. I thought Chanah might explode with excitement, but she held herself together, looking again at Paul.

"May the Lord continue to bless and prosper this household, and may he bless all who come in contact with you. Remain faithful, and he will guide you to places you cannot imagine. He loves you, and I love you. Remember that, and all will come out well."

The rest of the evening was spent in remembrances of happy moments, and in Chanah's rejoicings over Elhanan and Junia's child, which she announced proudly would make her a grandmother in every way that truly mattered.

The next morning, Paul came to my shop and asked to speak with me alone. Levi, Elhanan and Simon went into the house. Paul sat on the stool next to mine. He looked at me with penetrating eyes and nodded sagely.

He could usually tell what I was thinking at any given moment. It was uncanny and disconcerting, but little about him surprised me any longer. Of course, it would have been easy for anyone to tell what I was thinking and feeling that day. I was deeply sad that Paul would be leaving. I was also nervous because of the responsibilities he had left me to continue his work of traveling and teaching on Melita, though I was less fearful than when he had first arrived. During his stay, he'd ministered to me and my family as much as to everyone else, and he had instructed Chanah and me in a great many things having to do with ministering and administration.

Chanah was providing strong leadership to the large and growing group of faithful Christian women on the island in their efforts to provide relief, comfort, and teaching among the diverse group of people on Melita. She seemed to have completely forgotten her shame from that fateful night in Jerusalem, and I was glad. It felt like we were growing together in ways I hadn't thought possible. We had Paul—and the Savior, of course—to thank for it.

Our children loved Paul like a grandfather, and he felt the same about them. They were stronger than I was at their ages, and they were determined to resist temptation. I was in awe of them. Again, Paul was a big part of their strength, as was Chanah. I knew they would face many trials, but I had finally learned to pray for them with real faith and earnestness, and my trust in the Lord's help for them was increasing.

Paul finally spoke. "You have made a good life here for your family, Jesse. You and Chanah have become influential people. Did you ever envision that happening?"

I shook my head vigorously. "No. I just wanted to make tents, take care of my family, and be a good person."

"Yes, and that is exactly what you needed to do. The little things are often the most important, especially when it comes to family."

It struck me that I had never asked Paul about his family, and I didn't remember him mentioning them. He read my thoughts as I was about to ask.

"My family left me when I converted. My wife's father moved them, and I have not been able to find where they went. Perhaps someday, if the Lord wills it." He began to tear up as he stared out the window, and a lump grew in my throat.

"My greatest hope is that someday, somehow, they will come to know their Savior. I pray for it every day, Jesse, without fail. And when I see them, in this life or the next, I will shower them with tears and tell them how much I love them, and how hard I have tried to be faithful—for the Lord and for them."

Tears ran down his cheeks. It was a sacred, personal moment. I couldn't imagine how he always acted with so much hope and enthusiasm and faith. If Chanah left me, I knew I wouldn't survive long.

I tried to express that. "Chanah is my rock, and our children priceless jewels. I don't know what I would do without them. Chanah has more faith than any ten Jews I've ever met…except you, of course. And our children are following her example."

He smiled at that, then nodded. "Indeed she does, but don't sell yourself short. I have often thought about what you have gone through. Not only have you survived it—and I know you've been in some dark places—but you have never surrendered to the darkness. You've kept going, and you recognized the great good in Chanah without running away from it. Many in your place would have—or they would have tried to bring her down to their level."

He studied me intently for several seconds. "You are a remarkable man, Jesse, and yet you still stubbornly refuse to fully forgive yourself, even though the Lord has forgiven you."

He waited patiently while I processed his words. Finally, I found the ability to respond, my voice low. "I want desperately to be redeemed, but how can he fully forgive me? I understand now that my release by Pilate wasn't my fault, and was even necessary to God's plan, but I still see the faces of the men I killed, especially the ones who were innocent of any crime. I can't make those images go away. I'll settle for partial forgiveness, and I will give my life for Jesus's name when the time comes."

Paul nodded solemnly. "You will indeed give your life for him, Barabbas. But perhaps not in the way you think. You will live a long life, and if you give your remaining time on this earth to him, he will help you do amazing things with it. He will also help you reconcile your memories and feelings.

"There are images that haunt me, too. Men and women I delivered to the jailors. Children I separated from their parents, and unjustly so. Oh, at the time I felt a deep, burning fire of righteous indignation at the blasphemous Christians who were rotting Jewish society, and so I felt justified. Or did I? I have wondered about that. I had to work too hard to convince myself that my actions were worthy, and that should have been a sign.

"But I was too proud. The accolades and rewards from the Sanhedrin kept coming, and I reveled in my power." He had raised a fist high, and he slowly lowered it. "It took the Lord himself appearing to me to shake me awake to the truth. I believe I had fallen further than you, Jesse. Thankfully, I chose to follow him rather than run from him, and it is the best choice I have ever made, even though it cost me my family." He paused just a moment as he raised a finger. "The second-best choice—and it was a difficult one—was to fully accept his atonement and forgive myself after he forgave me."

We were both silent for several seconds. I knew he was right, and I knew he had felt what I felt. And yet part of me wouldn't let go. That part of me said I deserved to be punished, continuously, at least by myself.

He laid a hand on my shoulder. "He knows you, Jesse, just as he knows me. He knows more about us than we know about ourselves, and his love is without bounds and beyond comprehension. Do you believe me when I say that I saw him in person and felt his powerful presence?"

Tears welled in my eyes. "Yes."

"Do you believe that he has forgiven *me* of my sins?"

"Yes." I knew that was true.

"My baptism was the greatest day of my life to that point. My old life was buried that day, my old sins extinct as though they had never existed. My garments became white as snow—just as Isaiah so beautifully and magnificently taught. A new path of discipleship had opened up to me, with a promise that if I did my best and endured to the end I would become a joint heir in the heavens with our Savior.

"After this life, when we stand before him to be judged, he will not torment our minds with memories of sins he has already blotted away. He will not remember them, and neither will we. All of that is real, Jesse, and I will proclaim it and live it until my dying breath. We have so many witnesses! And so much help is available to us through the Holy Spirit."

His brows furrowed at that point, and the look in his eyes that I already thought was intense became even more so. His stare captivated me, and my heart was fully opened to his words.

"Why does God ask his sons and daughters to make priesthood covenants with him?" he asked.

"It is to bind us to him, and him to us, so that he may bless us as we live up to our covenants," I answered.

"Exactly. It is also to endow us with power to do his work. None of us is perfect in keeping our covenants with God, but he is perfect in keeping his. He knows when we are trying, and he blesses, strengthens, and empowers us to do better. I see that promise manifested in both you and Chanah, and in your children. You cannot deny it."

He was right. I couldn't.

"Jesse Bar Abbas, I will say it again…the Lord *has* forgiven you your sins, and he will give you opportunities to preserve the true faith when the apostasy comes, as I now know it will, at least for most. You will go forth from this place as a shield and protector, and your seed will follow your example. In some future day, when the fullness of the truth is restored again, many of your seed will embrace it and will stand as protectors to the faithful once again. So does the Spirit bid me to tell you."

I felt like I was in a trance, and yet it seemed I was more aware and clear-minded than I had ever been. His words of promise and prophecy were crisp and full of meaning in my mind and in my heart, seared there as if with a hot iron. I knew he spoke truth to me. I knew he would not lie. And I felt the witness of the Holy Spirit. I felt it!

Paul removed his hand from my shoulder. "Now, I'm sorry it took so long for me to get to my main purpose."

My eyebrows rose. It had felt like he had finished.

"This island needs good teachers, but it also needs a good bishop and his strong wife to guide the branches and help them grow. I had thought Publius and Lucia might be the ones chosen for that, given their growing faith and their long experience in leadership, but the Lord has let me know that isn't the case. It is you and Chanah. You are the leaders of the saints on Melita, and they will need your strength in the days to come."

My puzzled look made him chuckle. "Yes, Jesse, you heard me correctly. The Lord has called *you* to be the bishop of his church here on Melita, and I have the authority from Peter and the other apostles—and through them from the Lord himself—to do so. I have already spoken with Chanah about this, and she consents. Do you?"

My throat was locked momentarily. Why would Paul call me to serve in a role with such broad responsibility? People would look to me for counsel on difficult problems. I would be required to discipline those who went astray. With Chanah, I would serve as a mouthpiece for the church with community leaders, and perhaps—I gulped hard, which at least meant my throat was working again—with Roman leaders. I had never felt so unqualified for anything in my life.

But how could I decline? Paul, whom I trusted completely, was asking me to do this, and I had Chanah to help me, and many others I could rely upon as well. The church was growing rapidly, and there were many on the island who already showed great faith and steadiness. Paul had talked much with me about the sharing of duties and how the body of Christ—his church—worked with every member doing their part and assisting each other.

Suddenly a calmness settled over me, and I *wanted* to do it. That was a shock. Tears came to my eyes, and I finally nodded. "Yes."

Paul grinned in deep satisfaction. "Thank you, Jesse. Thank you for your service. The Lord will help you and Chanah—I promise you that. Send me letters while I am in Rome if you need counsel, but seek it first from our Father through his Son and the Holy Spirit, and also from others of the elders and sisters on the island that you choose to assist you. Perhaps Publius and Lucia could be among those you ordain to that capacity."

"I will," I said, my voice quivering slightly.

"And even if you don't need counsel from me, send me letters anyway. I love you, Jesse, you and your family. You are a joy to me beyond expression."

"I…am glad," I replied, daring a small smile. "You know that we love you as well. We scarcely know what we will do without you. But of course you will have much work to do without us bothering you."

Paul laughed at that, then clapped me hard on the shoulders, his eyes sparkling.

"Oh, beloved Jesse who was once called Barabbas. I will always have time for you, for you are truly my Friend."

END OF BOOK 1

EPILOGUE

For God hath not given us the spirit of fear;
but of power, and of love, and of a sound mind.

2 Timothy 1:7, KJV

A week had passed since Paul departed for Rome. His letter to the saints on Melita describing my calling and duties as bishop was read in our three congregations the following Sabbath. By Publius, not by me. I was grateful Publius agreed to do it, glad too that he was willing to provide continuing counsel and assistance in my new duties.

I took a break at mid-day to ponder and plan. I thought about writing Paul a letter as well, but it was too soon for that. I could write to Cornelius, though. I had many questions I wanted to ask about his new life and how he and Philip were building up the church near Ethiopia. I remembered the mooring stone, too. Perhaps he could shed some more light on its function and purpose.

I wandered upstairs to our bedroom, where I kept the mooring stone in a locked trunk. After retrieving it, I sat on our bed to examine it closely. I hadn't done that for many months. The brass ball looked the same as always—no discernible seams, no flaws, no clues. I held it closer to my face to study the 'map.' As I did, it seemed to change. The lines became sharper—some raised, some etched. And there were fewer of them. The ball also seemed slightly larger, though that seemed even more impossible than the rest.

It was trying to tell me something. Or rather, someone, perhaps God himself, was trying to tell me something through it. I knew that if I studied it enough and asked Chanah for her help, we could figure it out. Laelia had said it was supposed to guide us somehow, and we surely needed guidance.

"What is that, Father?" I jerked in surprise, but it was just Simon.

I smiled at him. "Something Cornelius the centurion gave us, but he didn't explain what it was."

"It looks amazing." Simon was fifteen. He was a good student, and he took his apprenticeships with me and the Greek carpenter Ambrosio seriously. He was becoming more confident and assertive. I was proud of him.

"It is. I just can't tell *how* amazing. Here, have a look."

He took it, his eyes wide, following the various patterns with his eyes and fingers. It hadn't changed back to its original design. After a few moments he asked, "Can I show it to some of my friends?"

I shook my head sternly. "No. This is a secret we must keep for our family. It looks valuable, and some may become jealous, though we will never sell it."

He nodded. "I understand, Father." He handed the ball back to me. "Can I work in Master Ambrosio's shop this afternoon? He said he needed me, and I'll just switch it with tomorrow afternoon."

"Yes, that's fine, son. He likes your work, doesn't he."

Simon nodded self-consciously.

"Good. You have a talent for carpentry. We may want to talk about you giving up tentmaking so you can focus on carpentry."

Simon's eyes lit up, a little more than I had expected. I smiled. "Go on. We can talk about it later."

He bounced from the room and out of the house, and I chuckled. I wished he'd told me earlier that he liked carpentry a lot more than tentmaking. Elhanan and I could handle what needed to be done, even if I had to scale back slightly.

I stared at the ball a few more seconds, thinking of Paul and the joy it had been to make tents and travel with him. I said a silent prayer for his safety, secured the mooring stone back in the trunk, and returned to my shop.

I didn't unlock the trunk again for three months. It had been a busy spring. When I did, the mooring stone was gone.

ABOUT THE AUTHOR

M.D. HOUSE enjoys a successful career in the mysterious world of Corporate Finance, but he has long had a fondness for creating and telling stores...and for watching and playing sports, which is good, because it means he isn't sitting all the time... and for politics, which is probably bad. *I Was Called Barabbas* is his second full-length novel and first work of historical fiction, but more are coming (including more from Barabbas).

CPSIA information can be obtained
at www.ICGtesting.com
Printed in the USA
BVHW031350260822
645602BV00015B/898